ANYTHING
BUT
STEADY

ISBN 978-1-80227-386-1 (pbk)

ISBN 978-1-80227-517-9 (hbk)

ISBN 978-1-80227-387-8 (ebk)

Published by Ink Whale, Lexington, Massachusetts.

This is a work of fiction but set in real political times and in real places. All characters in this book are products of the author's imagination.

First Edition

Editing: Siobhan Dignan

Cover and Interior Design: Jason Anscomb

ANYTHING BUT STEADY

OFRIT LIVIATAN

For Y.O.U. my O.A.K. & R.I.L.Y.
And in memory of Abba – our first author

PROLOGUE

IT'S TIME FOR *MY* SIDE OF the story. Many voiced my tale, but no one heard it from me, Northern Ireland. Not until now. Please don't misinterpret my intentions. I am humbled, indeed quite flattered that my trials and tribulations gripped and mattered. But the way things panned out, the risk of self-polishing my image is no longer an excuse to keep silent.

I want secrets to be my yesterday. My action plan for rebuilding my reputation involves the literary medium. Best that you recognise my project's ambition at its outset. It's understandable if you find this upfront disclosure slightly smug. Critical historians will raise eyebrows as well. They'd never accept that recording history could be another form of written art. Nonetheless, these days I find myself energised by the power of prose, and by W. Somerset Maugham's famous quip: 'There are three rules to writing a novel – unfortunately, no one knows what they are.'

My innermost malignancies require careful addressing. It's wrong to confuse our inertia and qualified street tranquillity with social metamorphosis. We need more, loads more, which we miss, because frost coats my people's appetite for change.

You won't hear me denying that glory clouded my foresight. It did. Not too long ago, my charm transfixed countless dignitaries. Real movers and shakers were part of my every day. But my allure sprang not from natural magnificence (which I invite you to enjoy), but solely from my troubles. And my troubles – where did they come from? Because humans are involved, perspectives fluctuate, and complications endure. Yes, I also contributed my share of toying with admirers. I bewitched them to believe they would be the ones to sort out my demons.

"What's changed, then?" you might justifiably inquire. Well, anxiety happened. Losing the forefront is never easy, but it's far harder when you still have history to make.

This was my dilemma: chronicling experiences long told and chewed would fall flat on my target audience. You'll recall that some of the world's iconic storytellers sprang from my paved womb. Similarly, summoning one of them to reimagine circumstances is a lost task, too, given that our built-in biases are as ancient as the Greeks. More recently, but before the Irish Famine, before my birth and before all the 20th-century mayhem, the always incisive Thackeray called it: 'There are two truths,' he scribbled of Ireland. 'The Catholic truth and the Protestant truth.'

My 'It's Time for Experts' chapter elapsed as well. Trust me: we all mastered the optics of intentions, honeycombing earnest tutors into sounding recommendations without following through upon advice. Nowadays, we have a Silicon Valley size industry supporting mirror truths and post-conflict, yet we are in reconciliation limbo.

But, while crying over my death by a thousand cuts, a virgin – no, a junior to our multiple versions' story – surprised me: Ella R. Goldin, a young, idealistic, non-Christian American who read about us. Perhaps saw some footage too, for she recognises my denizens' diction when she hears it. Ella is resourceful on peacebuilding, and despite her cultural background, she is enthusiastic about me.

Is Ella the wisest choice to re-envision my horizon? Is your rationality sensing that urgency sedated my judgement? Perhaps. But my bones believe in Ella's potential, and, you'll see, it's endearing to be inside her racing head. She could help our social paralysis by the mere fact that every one of my people, community aside, is a carrier of the hospitality gene. If she wants to prevent my obsoletism, why not let her be my go-getter? If she won't solve the problems, she can't hurt them either.

My past saturates the here and now. So, if clarity demands, you may see some injections of my own in the subsequent pages. But economically: only as far as accuracy demands. In return, I humbly ask for your gracious patience. Kindly bestow Ella an appropriate window to connect the dots, and give the two of us a sincere chance, please, dear reader. I think, I hope that Ella will validate my educated guess. Our finish line is in sight.

BOOK ONE

CHAPTER 1

SPOTLIGHTS AND DIRECTIONS

"REMARKABLE. MY ESOTERIC HOMELAND? NAH. REALLY? It can't still captivate the world."

He critiqued you, plain and simple. But a little sting won't get in the way of a real Northern Irish accent. Never is the number of times you have met a real Irishman in your Harvard Square pub. It's a Saturday night, big deal. Tonight's bars' carousel only just dawned. Eye on the ball, Ella; this chance-meeting might be the best thing that leaped into your PhD.

"I am sorry. That was pretentious. Your Guinness was my poorly judged signal for an interest in Northern Ireland."

How funny: when he threads the place through his razor-sharp jawline, it sounds like Norn Iron.

"Hhhh. Excuse me. The black stuff always gets me into trouble."

At twenty-eight, you should be able to cook up a better reason for mishandling frothy alcoholic drinks.

"Promise not to laugh?" I'll take fingers combing through an almond prairie head-top to be his solemn pledge. "Your charm should thank an old movie."

"Hmm. Intriguing."

Brits are known to say things ironically. Maybe the Irish are the same?

"Cinema – always our sexiest marketing strategy. Which film was it?"

Shit. If he isn't from the Irish side of things, I may have blown it.

"*In the Name of the Father.*"

"Of course. Our claim to fame right up there with *Game of Thrones.*"

He keeps smiling, so the film's Irish agenda wasn't a spoiler after all. "My mom made us watch it over and over. She wanted politically active offspring."

"And – was she victorious?"

God, he's milk-white, but the blue eyes are beaming.

"That all depends on your definition of success. My sister heads a non-profit, and I research peacebuilding."

But his attractive baritone won't lure you into sharing the unintended outcomes. Nope, it's safe. He's clueless about the powers of his accent – pixie dust for turning an ordinary looking dude into an irresistible young Daniel Day-Lewis.

Okay, woman. Even for your romantic hopelessness, that's a push too far. Remember: you are here to ensure Emily's 'accidental' encounter. A minute ago, you were worried that your favorite pub was still mimicking the Old Burial Ground nearby. But the pool table hasn't kick-started the evening yet, so what's your rush with this guy you've just met? Descartes himself would intuitively renounce your rationality.

"That's a sad-looking pint. Shall we fix it?"

"I'm Ella."

"Daniel."

No. Fucking. Way.

"A pleasure to make your acquaintance, Ella."

Warm palm, a bit on the dry side, but his smile recognized the opportunity.

"So, opting for an Irish pub in America's imitation of the *real* Cambridge ... deep Irish roots then?"

Huh. It makes perfect sense. You never thought of your regular bar in that way. But why wouldn't he be here to capitalize on his Irishness? The know-it-all hands-clasping behind his bony neck is communicating loud and clear the score in this ping-pong of flirtation. No, you must not be unwitty with the banal 'Protestant or Catholic?' inquiry he's bound to get day and night.

"Shocking as it may sound in hyper-Irish Massachusetts, not a single drop of Irish blood runs through my veins."

That Body Language TEDx could have helped decipher his much-too-frequent self-grooming gestures. Unfortunately, you passed on it as another chance to perfect procrastination.

"I am the product of Westchester County, New York, colloquially known as America's Jewish breeding ground."

Is it peculiar – or just academically unwise – that you never looked into the number of Jews in Northern Ireland? Ah, well. There are probably enough of them there too. A dispensable question when you are in the company of live research material.

"So, is your dissertation some sort of comparison between Northern Ireland and Palestine-slash-Israel?"

Phew, you are out of the uncomfortable woods. Culture-based inferences are a shared sin, then.

"Very much in the figuring out phase of my degree."

There was no reason to turn around, so why is he looking away?

"Our bartender is a bit dozy. Unwilling to facilitate my promise to refresh your drink."

He has a point. The guy forgot about this side of the counter in a bar perfectly suited for a single bartender.

"Are you game for an alternative, Ella?"

The place is turning stuffy. "Do you see the girl over in the corner with the white blouse? That's my roommate, Emily."

A bee could sign up for productivity lessons from that woman. Not a hill climbed, and she's already being cradled by the captain of the Mountaineering Club.

"She looks quite safe in that fella's hands, eh?"

Why wouldn't he fidget staring at these two? Any straight guy would feel threatened by the muscles on those arms, and 'jealous' could be the common denominator for straight women. When would you start listening to Emily's tips about open houses? A year of shared address is above and beyond to internalize that the girl is the frontier of extracurricular efficiency.

"No real risk in suspending your wing mission, now, is there?"

His choice of wing over the spare wheel metaphor is charitable.

"True. The mission was for them to reconnect."

"Job done. You're more local than me. Lead us to excitement."

Could he be a go-with-the-flow guy in addition to noticing your favorite jacket sliding to the floor while picking up the check?

Unrealistic expectation is your refuge, but he was the one pushing the pub's exit. It was foreseeable that a town jointly housing MIT and Harvard won't be the natural habitat for the laid-back type you hope to meet. And yes, his red and blue plaid clashing with the black T is duly noted, even if the untucking error was missed. All that could have been acceptable on your single night out of the week. However, this walk down Massachusetts Avenue leads to Davis Square, a favorite among your wannabe-detective friends.

So now what? Well, they do know you. They all spotted the pile of books about the Troubles – his conflict – on the floor of your room. It's their half-gone semester too. Yes, in Longfellow's hometown, they'll quickly decipher this is the 'ships that pass in the night' instead of a 'meet-cute' escort.

"Aye, confessing is embarrassing, but my choice of architecture was another countless casualty of *The Fountainhead*. Though she was wrong about MIT."

"Who?"

"Ayn Rand. Oh sorry, you didn't know? She rubbished MIT in that book."

Ayn Rand? That's his term of reference? Whatever charm his phony sublimation of superiority may have carried, you are safe from any 'crush' endings here. Embrace this worry-free intellectual experience of a night.

Wait. You can do more than that. This is a novel occasion to put therapy advice into practice: treating people like it's the last time you ever see them. Let's see, question marks over his cuteness don't negate a well-crafted pair of hands. Ayn Rand would concur they fit Daniel's vocation choice. And over the years, his 6ft build must have reaped a constant stream of romantic benefits. If it wasn't midnight on the weekend, I'd text my therapist right now with this mental maturity. Could have made her night too.

"But to be fair, Belfast, where I'm from, deserves most of the professional credit. It's a mash-up of Victorian splendour cheek by jowl with dereliction."

Is this guy's three-to-one speech-to-walk ratio confidence or insecurity?

"Thanking her streets individually in my Pritzker Prize acceptance speech would only be fair."

"Let me make sure I understand. Isn't your description of Belfast typical of any busy metropolis?"

"Ah, so we haven't yet had the pleasure of your company?"

Nuh-uh. His smile may be as mysterious as a curveball, but at least you know that Belfast is Northern Ireland's largest city. Really, utter foolishness hasn't leaked out ... yet.

"So, are you planning to transform your hometown, then?"

"Not as my launching career move."

Introvert, he ain't. More like taking a little too far the 'fiery ambition impresses women' routine. Looks pretty safe to ask outright.

"May I ask why?"

"Belfast is small."

Should size count against Belfast?

"Actually, it's more than size and non-existent skyscrapers. It's hard to be visionary when everyone is in your business."

Could Belfast be full of architects?

"Everyone knows everyone."

That should help with patronage, would be my guess.

"Teaches you to play it safe. Anyway, whatever was a career choice back home sort of evaporated since I arrived here for my masters."

"When was that?"

"Summer."

Newbie – few months top. For all you know, the guy might still be underestimating distances on US roads. Don't forget how condensed Europe felt to you on Goldin family trips, not only due to Natasha's sweaty hip in the backseats of mini cars. As an aspiring architect with an aesthetic viewpoint, he's probably still awe-struck by the American over-confidence scale. Or maybe not.

"My passion now is for grand-scale projects."

"It sounds like Belfast needs something grand."

He laughed with a big smile instead of voicing a 'That's so funny!' A cultural pat on the back whether he's British or Irish.

"One hundred percent! As a football – sorry, I know you have a different football – I mean, as a soccer fan, well, seeing your stadiums made ours look like community stadia."

That's a unique way to open up, but can one be sure this is what he is doing?

"Olympic arenas, too, have been uninspiring of late."

I really wouldn't know.

"You'd think an Olympic Committee should know a thing or two about competition, no?"

"One more example of a camel being a horse made by a committee."

Wow, you are scoring comedy points with this Anglo/Celtic, or whatever he may be.

"And you, Ella, toiling away in the vaulted Harvard corridors?"

"Tufts. The Fletcher School."

"Is that the Uni in Medford?"

"Yes. We are almost in Medford now; any of the streets around here take you there in ten, twenty minutes tops."

The unavoidable social ambush at Davis Square is no longer scary. Because every one of these friends successfully passed Fletcher's Admission to pursue a degree in Diplomacy and International Relations. They'll be faster than a Lamborghini catching onto Daniel's dissertation business. A worry-free night over anyone not getting along.

MY BELFAST, NEARLY 30 YEARS EARLIER

THAT'S ONE MISERABLE NIGHT to be out. Traffic wild, but at least we escaped the worst of it, was Oliver's inner observation as his foot pressed the accelerator. Should be at the Women's Centre before long. He may have felt relief, but a rapid glance towards Maeve, passengering on his left, revealed a halo of anguish mighty enough to pierce any darkness.

It touched Oliver. Though less than the shoot-to-kill prospects on his life should Maeve's brothers, or his own mother for that matter, ever discover their destination. Thankfully, meeting unexpected traffic congestion beheaded that morbid line of thought.

"That's odd. A checkpoint here? Was there a bomb alert?"

Maeve's response disclosed to Oliver that his guard had slipped, for he'd spoken aloud. "It's a sign. A direct message from your employers, the Crown."

Oliver shook his head three times, now motivated to ensure his thoughts would be his alone. *No. Just a textbook example of active security.*

"Turn around, Oliver." Steel entered Maeve's voice. "What's the point of getting abortion advice when we want to be together?"

Stunned by her mental U-turn, Oliver kept his eyes on the road. He reckoned Maeve would read his tightening lips, so best just to speak up.

"No worries. The lads will clock my warrant card and we're away."

He knew his colleagues in the RUC, as it was officially known, or 'the filth' as it was unofficially known by many, would wave him through the checkpoint. Yet, Maeve's growing impatience outpaced the officers' vehicle searches.

"It's not a long queue and they're getting through it fast." Oliver's attempt only fortified her stony expression. "We don't want to keep her waiting too long. She's keeping the Women's Centre open as a favour."

"I'm serious. We'll find a phone; tell her I changed my mind. It happens all the time. Then she's away home for her tea. We can get out of this traffic unnoticed by security if you turn left here. Now."

Over-riding her uterus was counterproductive. So Oliver made the turn with the goal of finding a parking spot in which to advocate meaningfully on their prudent choice. Alas, overt and covert security seemed tighter than the marked activity Oliver remembered from the tasking sheet back at Musgrave Street's RUC Station. Nowhere to pull over, he wondered what was going on.

"Why won't you head to Grosvenor Road and drop me at the Royal?"

As Maeve added her navigational input, Oliver couldn't help but smile grimly at the irony of her destination choice – a hospital of all places. No hospital in Northern Ireland carried out any terminations, which is why they needed the Women's Centre to find their way to a clinic in England.

"Can dander over to a mate from there."

"A mate of whose?"

"What's the difference when it saves you driving around in circles like a melter wasting petrol?"

Galled, Oliver recognised she was right. Meeting Maeve's family in the normal way was never on the cards. A family home located on Colinward Street in the western enclave of my capital was like walking into the Chernobyl reactor for someone like himself. The 'IRA OK' and 'sniper at work' graffiti all around her area were permanent reminders of why he travelled inside an armoured car. The rare occasions he did collect her from her terraced house required Oliver's unerring concealment of all vocational evidence. These included his bulletproof vest, personal radio (volume off), and the cherished weapons that felt like integral body parts on any other occasion. The words of Seamus Heaney, who had the audacity (in Oliver's view, the insolence) to refuse the United Kingdom's poet laureateship, on saying nothing were singing in his ears.

Such local markers also resurrected in Oliver his most suppressed thoughts. A conscientious RUC inspector and a lad of his specific Antrim background needed to do more to get to the bottom of his lover's family. Scraps of information Oliver incrementally accumulated fixed his curiosity on Ciaran, Maeve's second-oldest sibling. Heavily grilled, as windows were in that part of town, they were powerless to conceal Ciaran's reign of pubs frequented by Provisionals. Therefore, his year-long romance with Maeve marked for Oliver nearly twelve months of sleepless nights crammed with visions of daytime encounters with her brother: Ciaran masked in a balaclava and dark sunglasses, and Oliver cocooned inside thick police gear.

Go right ahead and say it: "C'mon, they'll never last. A cop and a woman from an IRA family? Too soon for your early 1990s."

Well, nowadays, the only thing I stay convinced of is Niels Bohr's famous observation that 'predictions are hard, particularly about the future.'

Anyway, at that point, Oliver nurtured his own logic. *It's impossible for a single set of parents to have bred both my Maeve and a poster boy for terrorism.*

In hindsight, attributing Oliver's wide-shut judgement to the defence mechanism known as repression is effortless. But one ought to remember that psychological questions around self-deception are vast and, in some cases, denial can be a welcome protective response. Similarly, Oliver's rationalisations found support in the reality that the choices of few could impact many.

During my Troubles, a large number of my Catholic inhabitants found themselves in schizophrenic torment. You see, IRA empathy could exist in tandem with depression over that organisation's violent campaign and triumphant recruitment. Post-ceasefires, haunting issues and mysteries about victims, injustices or atrocities persisted. So, faced with a harsh lover's dilemma, classifying Oliver as delusional shouldn't be automatic. And whatever he inferred about Maeve's family, Oliver's zeal to face Ciaran in Castlereagh or any other interrogation centre remained inexhaustible.

But one rapidly escalating verbal exchange had finally led to his reserved demeanour exploding: "Your brother is a bloody Provo! I do have eyes in my head."

"Wind your neck in," countered Maeve, irate, "before you go

around accusing folk. Just because people living on these streets support the IRA doesn't make them active volunteers. Jesus, I thought a smart copper like you would have more of a clue." His otherwise self-monitoring girl was on a roaring verge.

He tried to defend his suspicions, but she wasn't finished with him yet.

"So wise up! Insinuating, when you know none of my family, is beneath you."

Sensing Oliver thought her indignation a cover-up, Maeve added, in a louder, firmer tone, "And, by the way, whatever came of our agreement that your career won't get in the way of our relationship?"

"The bastard's personality profile is vivid from the Hubble Space Telescope." An untypical incapacity to withhold crept into Oliver.

"Aye right. Yet, your *Darth Vaders* pinned nothing on him. Is it any wonder why folk around here only call the Peelers when they're looking to work as a tout?"

Maeve saying such a hurtful thing to his face shocked Oliver. He almost replied, *and what if you were mistaken for a tout thanks to your relationship with me*, but he caught himself.

"Irish humour? I suppose you think that's just banter."

Receptive to his dismay, I disagreed with Oliver on this point. Comedy consists of jokes precisely deviating from the expected, and in that, Maeve brilliantly followed black humour to its letter. But I share this to illustrate my heartache: within a population particularly fond of good craic, jokes were never universal. And within these lovers' personal universe, such remarks forever delineated the limits of information-sharing.

In those dark days of my history, one erroneous turn of the steering wheel amounted to a death kiss. Upon entering the RUC's combat zone of West Belfast in his non-work car that night, Oliver's internal compass assumed the Bikini Amber alert

level. Reaching the Grosvenor Road's red lights, he took his left
hand off the gear stick and threaded it between Maeve's dress
and thigh. To his crimsoning astonishment, Maeve hadn't re-
sponded with any reciprocating gesture but simply continued
to gaze out the passenger window, occupied with thought. The
green light was the starting signal for a short, silent, menacing
drive towards Maeve's two-up two-down house on Colinward
Street. Oliver parked as close to her street, without being on it,
as was safely possible, switching off the engine and headlights.
Only then Maeve turned to him. As they embraced silently, her
trembles vibrated through his body, and the saltiness of her tears
aggravated the shaving cut cradled inside his thick cotton indigo
polo neck.

"We need to do *something*, love." Trying his best to be gracious, Oliver tenderly stroked Maeve's auburn ponytail, pausing
only three times to gently lick her teary cheeks. Maeve laid her
head on his left shoulder wetting his upper arm (the concealed
bulletproof vest kept his shoulder dry), but suddenly broke away
from the embrace.

"No, there is an alternative! Oliver MacIntyre ... will you be
my husband?"

Oliver was unable to identify whether the blast he experienced came from a nearby bomb detonating or his own brain
exploding. His body reacted to the marriage proposal with an
outburst of vomit shot with accuracy into the middle section of
Maeve's pink floral dress. Instantly, the stench of one-week-too-
old sausages with two eggs and black pudding filled the Vaux-
hall Cavalier.

"For fuck's sake. If anyone gets to boke, it's me, the one up the
spout, remember?" Maeve struggled furiously to open the door,
but Oliver had all the safety locks on. "My favourite dress, and
now it's bogging. What have you been eating? It smells rank."

Exhausted, he sighed, regrouped, and wound down the driver's window. Then he helped Maeve wipe herself off, ripping out pages from the vehicle manual she'd found in the glove compartment.

"Are you okay?" she finally asked.

He nodded, thanking his good instincts for placing the Ruger Speed Six in the back today. *The Poetry of Robert Frost should be thrilled to have escaped too.*

Then silence as they both processed what had just happened. Astute Oliver conjointly discerning that eloping would be a fruitless suggestion. He heard himself saying, "But you must wish for the real white wedding … in a church. With *your* priest and your family."

"They'll attend."

Oh your lot wouldn't miss it for the world. To carry out my bloody execution, he thought, but a group of rowdy pedestrians passing at that moment barricaded his tongue. Better that way.

Maeve remained oblivious to Oliver's inner predictions – her father's reaction to his proposal, and his mother's: 'I'll die six times before entering a Popish chapel!'

Once the street was clear again, Oliver shot the bottom line, "Well, at least none of your five brothers will expect a best man request."

Releasing a sincere smile, Maeve leaned across to kiss Oliver's cheek, catching his grateful gaze at the gesture. *Thankful he should be*, she thought. *An anosmic won't confuse him for a jasmine blossom.*

Maeve exited the car, rushing the short walk to her home, hunched and self-conscious of the melanoma-like mark of Cain vomit stain on her dress.

A dark sitting room welcomed her swift entrance, misty with her father's cigar smoke and roaring with the telly. Five empty beer bottles stood in a perfect football defensive wall on the glass-topped oak side-table. Bordering the table's width was the three-seater beige wool tartan settee, overtaken by her father's spread-out drunken body.

Here we go again, Maeve sighed.

"Back from servicing the oppressor, are you now?"

Recognising the thickening alcohol in her father's tenor voice, Maeve held off any response and searched for the whiskey's location.

"Repulsive, that's what you are, Maeve Catherine Donnelly." Her father's grousing was now elevated to shouting, leading Maeve to wonder whether the remark was literal. "If it weren't for your mother, you'd be out on the street tonight."

He missed landing a sixth bottle on the table. It toppled over, clattered and spilt the contents, but he continued to let the accusations fly. "With that savage, Cromwell's name, no less." He spat as if the name itself were toxic.

Maeve stared at the wet carpet as Lorcan ranted on.

"That new 'RIP Tout' graffiti two doors down can't have escaped your notice. A bright uni type like you should be able to put two and two together."

So, he knows Oliver's name. And possibly his job? Cold fear crept inside her. *Mum would never.* Her brain went spinning into a turmoil of speculation. *Who told? If it came from Ciaran, surely he'd find a way to inform me directly. In many more ways than one. Who was it, then? What came to light? And how much does Da know? Hard to tell when he's legless.*

Maeve tried to remain composed despite Lorcan's shower of threats to renounce her.

No, it's impossible. It can't be. Oliver's line of work isn't exposed. We've been so careful. Her slow inhale provided sufficient space to calculate: exposure jeopardised her family and Oliver in equal measures. No one in her close circle should be rushing to inform on this public shame. *As much as he has his own interests and faults, Ciaran knows to look after his own family.*

Reading – to the point of memorising – every printed word in the liberal *Fortnight* magazine was another source of confidence-building. *The past and present are immaterial. The future will surely look the other way.*

Maeve was always counting on the promising prospect of the long haul. *They'll come to terms with my choice of a husband the same way people learn to accept cureless diagnoses.*

Now, re-energised by the potential mortality of contempt, Maeve turned to organisation.

"Get your claws away from me, hoor."

She obeyed for appearance's sake, all the while pondering the best path to maintain the number of Lorcan's empty bottles at a half-dozen. *I'll just hide the other bottles in the house and clear the spilt beer. That's my best shot for some cooperation. Not from him, from Mum.*

Maeve was thinking towards that conversation the next morning but also hoping with regard to the tumultuous road ahead.

The house door shutting behind Maeve signalled the heavens to unlock once more. Dwarf balloons dribbled down Oliver's windshield. *This must be how Madison Square Garden's floor feels over in New York,* he thought. Silvery, opaque and numerous, they were as incapable as the dark night when it came to concealing the fastened steel gates of the Lanark Way interface ahead. Lighting a feg momentarily blinded Oliver's eyesight. It didn't disguise the irony that his favourite poet's famous line 'good fences make good neighbors' could have been conceived only in an across-the-Atlantic Derry.

Good neighbours? Perhaps in New Hampshire, America, light years away from here, his bitterness chuckled. *On this side of the pond, we can't even agree on the name of that terrorist-manufacturing factory.*

My objective is to make our contradictions plain and clear. Unionists opt for Londonderry over the Nationalists' Derry. 'Stroke City' has become a compromise choice. Not for the medical condition it too often nearly brought on myself, rather for the punctuation we place between these disputed names in a bid to keep everyone, and no one happy.

Still parked, by then fully adapted to his vomit's odour, Oliver's thoughts returned to the summer before last. *Another day to meet terrorists moving about.* He smiled, remembering his queasy feeling on leaving the fortified RUC station with his mobile support unit that day. Crammed inside the Land Rover manoeuvred by a colleague, he gripped his rifle, feeling ready for whatever the standard patrol may bring: detonating grenade, gunfire, offensive chants, street chaos at the road stop they were to set up. But as soon as the gates of Lanark Way opened admitting them onto the Springfield Road, he saw Maeve.

That was the only time Oliver hadn't turned to check that the gates closed behind the army vehicle escorting his unit as additional cover. The ever-present clicking in the armoured vehicle disappeared, as slow-motion displayed Maeve's seven graceful strides from the Springfield Road into Colinward Street. She wore a puffed-sleeve golden dress, giving her an aura of glamour miles away from the setting, but I am uncertain Oliver even noticed her attire.

He knew Maeve had speared his heart long before he made any mark on her life. That is, of course, if one disregarded two decades of security-related damage inflicted on the streets where she spent her childhood. The mystery she carried for him that day would kindle his immediate recognition of her three weeks later. *Love at first sight is real*, my romantic Oliver discovered, spotting Maeve on the doorsteps of Elmwood Hall at Queen's University. Stopped in his tracks on his way into an evening of poetry.

I should like to think that an RUC officer's appetite for poetry doesn't come as a complete surprise. Indeed, it's a truism that poetry's popularity spikes in celebrations as much as tragic commemorations but is otherwise regarded as the poor relation of expressive media. All the same, terrible periods such as my late 20th century proved a significant audience driver. And it was my own Seamus Heaney who, during his 1995 Nobel Prize address, hammered home the value and power of poetry.

"The ship and the anchor," Mr Heaney called it. "Satisfying contradictory needs" of truth-telling without hardening the mind.

Cruising my rumbling surface in those darker days, Oliver frequently mused over poetic inspiration. His friends found it unusual. Some colleagues may have pointed out that poetry was more associated with the Irish Catholic Nationalist tradition.

I am not here to play judge but to tell you that, on that night, Maeve owned Oliver's focus. And he realised an unforeseen benefit to his literary interests: reading Frost in place of playing darts and snooker *certainly* made all the difference to his life.

As Maeve's kind green eyes found his own sapphires, he approached her, composed and calm, while his soul was an emotional maelstrom. Her elongated-stem body indulged in a tight lavender dress made him forget a breath or two, and right there, entrenched his imperishable attraction. Any lines Oliver recited to Maeve's desiring ears – standing on a multitude of poetic shoulders – could have been, and perhaps were said by others elsewhere and frequently. But when Oliver said them to Maeve, they felt singular.

True, that's the standard explanation offered by people who are in love. But there was one significant and positive difference: reciting his favourite poetic lines to Maeve blocked for Oliver the noisy reality that their erotic magnetism would forever twin with censorship. It was helpful that, by then, he had already completed the 'need-to-know-basis' police training.

Oh, the rain has worn itself out, and I'm knackered too. Restarting the engine, Oliver took one last drag from his dying Silk Cut and drove eastward.

CHAPTER 2

REVELATIONS

WE FOUND GAS IN the middle-of-nowhere Western Massachusetts. It's unfair to now demand that the station dispense coffee any less revolting than this brew. And you better dispose of this gigantic lidless paper cup before the car welcomes Daniel back, or a spill is going to be inevitable. Another thing to dispose of is the urge to fall for him before the slightest peek at his uncensored anatomy. Oh, he's back in side-mirror view. No, far too risky to rely on an unplanned coffee spill to get him to shed his large black sweatshirt. I am not detecting a belly. Hmm, for a fashionably challenged guy, a semi-toned torso should have erased the need to choose a bland top.

True, his sweatshirt's *The Dark Side of the Moon* artwork constrained the color's wiggle room.

"A Pink Floyd fan, I see."

You hadn't needed his smile to figure out it was his way to check out your musical preferences. Meanwhile, that black sack drives a sharp blade into the inflated 'not-this-time' mountain of clothes warming up your floor back in Medford. Well, maybe Northern Irish men dress down. This Berkshire day trip is young enough for a fashion-conscious passerby to notice why you chose this semi-hugging foliage-hued crimson dress.

His blue denim reveals no visible sag. In fact, the curves might signal fine-squatted quads; the stretched back-pockets sit well too. Long legs – the way you like it. Okay, is this erotic hunger wise? With all due respect to promising signs and original foreign-born testosterone, your last three fiascos call for greater vigilance. Your sister Natasha, along with your loving parents, would agree. Don't forget that you are identifying as a female. How would social psychology react to a woman who thinks solely in terms of the hip-to-waist ratio? That field suffers enough problems replicating results. Spare them your issues.

Adjust the mirror, and he'll notice your hand. The gas attendant's mesmerized gaze tells you all you need to know anyway. He was ecstatic with the driving offer, and now his Northern Irish accent will redefine what joy means to anyone we meet. *Cyrano de Bergerac*, on top of endless books and movies, illustrates the hard work of making someone fall in love. Yet, all that's required of Daniel MacIntyre is a few soundbites to bring humanity to its knees.

With that cryptic sweatshirt, I can't tell if he's hairy. Oh, the gas transaction is completed. Lusting must return to 'hold' mode. Just stare at the phone as though you are heading Massachusetts' Meteorological Agency during foliage season.

Insecurities are unfitting. Remind yourself that Daniel was engaged in some mental undressing of his own at pick-up. The descent from your apartment's door to the car was a magnetic field. He minimized his strides for his thigh to meet your hip all the way down the seven wooden stairs and over a hundred feet of sidewalk to the car.

Will you ever learn to pace yourself? Didn't Dad's fave Barry White song warn of the waste in haste? Barry directed his restraint advocacy for night-time, so it must hold at noon too. Wise to first learn something about Daniel when 'zilch' sums up your current knowledge level. Although, Saturday night back at the pub revealed an impressive ability to maintain stoic tendencies despite substantial alcohol consumption. Yep. It won't require Euclid of Alexandria to know that the next sensible step should be better clues, particularly as you misexpected his surprise transformation into the image of attractiveness.

"Well, I heard, but now believe that America continues to keep some dry towns."

His description of your alcohol-infused friends began to reveal that you'd appreciate his humor. Your friends liked him as soon as he bought two consecutive rounds. Still, just because you cannot yet pinpoint the end of his cultural mannerisms and the start of his personality, that isn't the most probable reason to be falling in love.

Honesty begs the question: would you invite Daniel on this day trip were you not threatened by Emily's escapades with Climber? That guy has been camping on the other side of our shared wall since the night you met the socially skilled Daniel. But should Emily's unending sexual rewards carry any weight over your choices? Outside classes, they only leave the bed for grocery shopping. Well, if they ever end up moving in together, remember to list 'weed dependency' as a pre-requisite in the new roommate search. There's no going back from the constantly stocked-up fridge Emily and Climber have been diligently smoking through.

But if you are already craving Daniel, yes, don't pretend. Instead, seize the opportunity to grasp the real reasons. Whatever transpires, it'll help in authoring the always entertained, never scribbled op-ed on 'Why *I never saw it coming* is utter bullshit to explain finding love.' Thinking through your decisions should supply a safety net against another doomed relationship.

"The lad in the petrol station suggested we head to Mount Greylock for the best autumn colour. Oh, so sorry, Ella. Did I give you a fright?"

Keep cool. "It's gas in this country, you know."

"Duly noted. Though, I am quite sure I paid for gallons, not thermal units."

Yes! Our opening act is coming with a pocket of hickories and red maples.

"That's just brilliant. I have never seen such colours on trees. Is it this good every year?"

Okay. Call it like it is. The Berkshires was FDIC insured to blow Daniel's mind. "Yep, but you're right; it never gets old."

Was this destination chosen for Daniel to fall in love with you, or for you to fall in love with him? Pretty ridiculous to assume control over emotions – or is it? It could be, if your therapist's eternal mantra, 'anxiety restraint *can* be trained' is correct. Mom's frequent 'envy sees only the sea, not the rocks in it' to tackle every sibling's jealousy also lends support. If it's possible to actively seek emotions, love shouldn't be any different, should it?

Today's plan had been to explore if the chemistry outlasts Saturday's pub exit. With that clarified, not only are you enlisting the chemistry of leaves, but you're also unable to pretend that a night at your parents' cabin hasn't already blipped on your radar. No overnight bag in the trunk beyond your walking sneakers. You have stuff there, and Mom's disposable toothbrush stock offers more color options than the foliage. Ending up there will have a few downsides. For one, the curtains – forgetting they were once green – could detox the toughest form of sex addiction, even if Daniel wasn't training as an architect. And if there was ever a way to certify buyer's remorse, the groaning cherry furniture in the living room owns that trophy. Sexual energy is the last thing that castle in the Berkshires serenades.

Don't forget that the shack is the home of your best debates with your one and only sister. And Natasha wouldn't need more than a gentle prod to customize her beloved theories to explain how to make someone fall in love. No, she is too sophisticated for fate. Natasha's initial 'love reason' will be luck. Yet, there isn't a more obedient slave to the sociological imagination than Natasha. So she'll have to concur that love is socially embedded.

"We, as human agents in that structure," as Natasha loves to frame it, should therefore be able to make someone fall in love with us. If sociology – the Bible for your family – is correct, then creating the production line feeding into Daniel's heart ought to be a realizable quest.

Well, well, never the definition of a thrill-seeker, but this is basically the sexiest I have ever felt driving through the flaming Berkshires.

"Yes, New England's falls are pretty special."

"Special? It's bonkers! Nature's Disneyland."

Many grown-ups are Disney-obsessed. He's genuinely amazed. Perfect timing to surprise him with the adult section of this theme park.

"Over there, on the left. Slow down a bit and you'll catch one specific sugar maple. It's okay, no one is behind us – you can slow down. Yes, right by that green house. Yes, that's the one. Its secret twin found a permanent home right across from my Berkshire childhood room."

"Ah, now I get it. Inspiration for your frock?"

Not a moment wasted; he is observant after all, and taking in far more than the low-cut design.

"Wait. Didn't you say you're a New Yorker?"

"Through and through. But my parents have a small place up here in Lenox. It's nearby, actually."

Mission accomplished. His popping neck vein hasn't missed the bedroom's proximity.

"May I ask—"

"No, no. Stumbling over a trust-fund American is rom-com stuff."

And in that case, he would have been at the Hamptons rights now, not Western Mass.

"A second home here is the Odyssean way for less-than-rich New Yorkers to knot themselves to the mast of urban exits."

I should have done more advanced research on whether the second date sex rule is acceptable by either community in Northern Ireland.

"I am happy to assuage your worries by stopping there on our way back. After last week's storm, my mom would appreciate it."

"A cottage is a big Irish thing too. Donegal, mostly. What do your parents work at? Or you can tell me to keep my nose out."

"My dad is a newspaper editor. Mom, a clinical psychologist. But in her case, it's a lifestyle – a condition really – far beyond a career."

"An eventful childhood, so."

If Daniel only knew half of it.

Why shouldn't he be so focused on driving? He's been sitting at the wheel all day. These pitch-black two-lanes aren't even a walk in the park in the daytime. Safety first. The last two road signs concurred with him. You need to stop acting like a junkie when the day offered adequate buzzes of flickering romance inside the car and during the hike. He gazed at you more than at the scenery. He didn't miss a chance, real or imagined, to rake leaves off your 119lbs of body mass. Remember your breasts tingling when he brushed your hair? Affection proclamations weren't absent either.

"These purple leaves must be so surprised to find the ground five and a half feet sooner than expected."

Kissing opportunities will come back, that is if my over-availability doesn't terrify him first.

"Your Berkshires suggestion was spot on."

His calmness should be your example.

"Thank you for showing me why New England autumn is so famous."

Shit, you are an open book. Worse – a never-locked digital library, coercing the poor guy for reassurance.

Reveling in the unpredictability? That would be a big ask from the Magellan of insecurity. One moment you are immersed in infatuation, the next, digging for all his weaknesses. Not only did you examine his paleness in every possible light throughout the day, now you are leveraging the rose-white moon for the task. Constant processing cries for a break. His brain can share the burden. He seems ready to invest even if he isn't electrified by love just yet. What Daniel certainly is, should architecture prove a failure, is a candidate for any glow-in-the-dark modeling job. Skin cancer has to be an epidemic in Northern Ireland.

Enough. This adolescent infatuation with 'finding your soul mate' is the root of continually focusing on the negatives. Grandma at least had the 'First-Generation' excuse to live in a soap opera. She'd endorse Daniel at first sight. Her dementia won't stand a chance against her lifelong obsession with plump lips for her descendants. Daniel is safer than a buckled-up infant in a car seat from her 'men with tight lips are misers' adage. That is if the two of them ever reach the 'bring him to meet me' mountaintop.

I should take him there regardless of relationship prospects. Daniel would get a kick from her Roman-style senior housing in the heart of New Jersey. Grandma would feed him right away. As soon as they laid eyes on him, my family all would. Yes, you can talk with them about anything, but if you want to avoid the family ophthalmologist, don't share your morning BMI doubts about Daniel. Scarsdale Bagels would be extra welcoming – a way to make up for some of their loss since Mom and Dad went keto.

Does he know the Palazzo that Isabella Stewart Gardner gifted Boston? He's slated to visit that museum if my sister and Mark are coming up to see me any time soon. Positive framing, especially for Mom, is a precondition for the family meeting. Otherwise, the poor guy would face her entire background quiz before the appetizer. Well, that's one way to engineer slowness into my Daniel hysteria. Yes, there's only one way to read this sudden Route 7 traffic jam: the universe is signaling you to dial down manic enthusiasm over a guy you met only a few days ago.

"I meant to tell you, Daniel. I had a question about Northern Ireland on my midterm. I hope it's okay to ask; you never told me if you were a Catholic or a Protestant."

"Why, would it turn the tide?"

"Of course not!" Yay, there's a tide – a pull! "Though it seemed to matter for the exam."

"Cheers, Ella. That's a solid B right there!"

Too early to delight yourself with his rolling laugh. Just because humor tops your sexiness trait scale doesn't translate to his having an identical list. He may be Irish, but he's unmistakably a He/Him/Masculine Male first.

"Congratulations. You are one of the privileged few to enjoy the good fortune of going out with that rare species, a Northern Irish mixed breed. Dad's a Protestant, Mum's Catholic. So that makes me a Jaffa."

Bingo. A dating confirmation. Don't scare him now, but he does need to ditch the 'mixed-breed' description ASAP. Strange that news of such political incorrectness hasn't made it to Belfast by now.

"Was it difficult growing up with a hyphenated identity?"

"Hmm ... an excellent question. I never thought of it that way."

How could he not?

"You know how it is: it's your life, and you just live it. And Northern Ireland today is nothing like those films about the Troubles that you like."

It would be nice if one day he were able to show me.

"But I suppose my mixed identity offered a combination of a blessing and a curse even post-ceasefire."

"How so?"

"The mechanics of the curse are rather straightforward, aren't they?"

His gaze registers my nod.

"The blessing – at least for me – was to grow up without having to choose to be one or the other."

You may have just hit the jackpot. The entirety of Northern Ireland embodied in one cute guy.

"So, can I lend a hand revising for any other midterms?"

Seems that communication won't be one of our problems if this relationship is going to last. "I only have a couple more left – on unrelated topics, unfortunately."

"Perhaps for your research then?"

Sexy and research sorted all in one guy. Could this be the most fun PhD ever?

"Tempting." Take your elated voice down a notch. "Our driveway is coming up on the right-hand side." He should start signaling; the turn is abrupt.

"An intentionally unrepaired lane, I see."

How did he know?

"Unlit driveway too."

"Are you sure you haven't met my folks before?"

Daniel will hijack Dad's heart if he ever repeats his description of the porch as "unkind to burglars but user-friendly." I guess loose and squeaky boards are useful for the upcoming Halloween. It was worthwhile bringing him here just to change your perspective on this architectural horror.

"It's all in the fence, Ella. Northern Ireland, where *everything* in the place is fenced off, is the best teacher – better than architecture school – on territoriality. A fence symbolises that you are the type to protect your property."

Is that why we always had dogs?

"So, will we need to pick the lock?"

"There should be a key above the doorpost." Whether it is un-corroded enough to do the job is a totally different ball game. "I need to give you a fair warning: my parents' cherish the concept of do not discard."

"I am not the type to be easily intimidated by clutter."

"That'll come in handy, Daniel."

Good, the key is managing to turn after all. "Welcome. Let me just get this hill of mail out of our way ... Oops, sorry, didn't mean to push you back like that."

"Ella, I ..."

"No, no. Carry on; I want you to kiss me." Wow, the car's air freshener cannot take any credit. This fresh aroma is his and his alone. How can he still radiate freshness after all that sun? Oh, a very poor outlook for my panties against these Niagara Falls.

"Daniel, you're shivering. Are you cold?"

"Quite the opposite. You're delicious, did you know that?"

Be my guest, knows-its-craft tongue.

So that's what male softness tastes like. Ah, there's the Her-shey Bar we shared earlier.

Erections don't lie. He is patient; take your time too. I can take my time when my breath is slowing down ... I can control it. Yes. I. Can. There is no way his palm had missed that south-ern drench. Yes ... please don't stop maneuvering.

"Ella ... you are so sexy ..."

"So are you. Yes, there too ... but slower ... yes, you can press a little harder. Kiss me. Ouch, no, it's okay. I *really* like it. I. Really. Like it."

"May I liberate them from your bra?"

"Go right to it, my Simon Bolivar." Ew! How could I say that aloud? Well, fuck it, he wants to fuck you; that's what counts.

"Jesus, Mary and Joseph. So much more than I dared to imag-ine."

He *had* imagined.

"So tender."

Impatient nipples, let him taste you. Get to know him; he might be a keeper.

"Let's enter first. There's a bed behind this doorway." It's only appropriate to step away from the *mezuzah* when both of us could be posing for *Playboy*.

Hey, something is mega strange around here. "Hang on. Do you see that blue sofa? It always stood against the wall." Mom re-decorating? New red and yellow throw pillows, indoor plant, really? Looks like the rest of the old furniture only got moved around.

"*Feng shui*, perhaps? Many empty-nesters seem to go through this phase."

"Impulsiveness isn't my parents' strongest suit, but WOW, WOW—"

"Why the surprise? You can't be astonished that your sexiness is ... motivating. And that's understating it."

"No, no. The feeling is definitely mutual ... but promise not to ... please don't take it the wrong way—"

"What is it? Should I get worried?"

"No, no. It's really, really awkward to admit ... sorry, this is my first—"

"No way! Oh, shite!"

"No, no. No. Not that. I meant to say, this is my first ... my first encounter with manliness in its unaltered form."

"Seriously?"

"Daniel MacIntyre, you have officially claimed my Greek God status. But with a huge, dream penis."

"I'm honoured ... and touched. As you can tell, I couldn't feel more empowered right at this moment."

Good. At least Mom kept the bedroom in the same place.

"So, where were we?"

"You were kissing my tummy."

"Aye, and you were running your fingers across my chest while I was about to remove your knickers."

You must reward him in some massive way for not freaking out about your reactions. With so little chest hair, I guess he needed that sweatshirt. He may not have survived in an Ice Age, but my! The little body hair he owns is beautifully symmetrical.

"You are spectacularly sexy when fascinated. Work away; he's all yours. Just gentler ..."

"Sorry." It's different than I thought.

"A fast learner."

It must have something to do with the desire to be taught – Kant during sex? If ever there was proof you need to urgently schedule additional therapy sessions. Wow, but it's different. Velvety. Slicker than the Jewish ones?

Ready already?

"Condom? May I?"

"Sure. But let me guide you just a bit. It's quite sensitive ... yes, perfect."

He is so nice. Just like his penis. It feels the same. Oh, it doesn't. Oh, God. Is that the foreskin rubbing against my Jewish clitoris? Did I just cross the uncut Rubicon? Don't even think about it. Verbalizing a Red Sea Crossing metaphor would amount to calling God's name in ... oops ... oy, vey—

"Apologies. I came too fast ... I—"

"No. No. It's fine, Daniel. Really. Firsts define the unplanned." Not every one of your weird thoughts needs uttering. Surely, you have scared him enough for one day.

"Soon, I promise, we'll try again. Like half an hour from now?"

Shit, it's blazing. Daniel isn't bothered by this solar insurgency one bit. Forget about reaching the blind's pull cord when his head has expropriated your entire arm. Did Mom put up new curtains? The greyish blue isn't a disaster, but the silver rod isn't spectacular. Noisy sleeper, but an adorable dreamer; hopefully, you are part of his—

Oh, shit. Forgot to silence the phone too.

"Mom, hey. Hold on, making my way to the kitchen." That woman's intuition could sharpen Cutco knives.

Daniel isn't bothered by the phone. I'll reciprocate his 'How to Sleep' lessons with 'How to Extend Orgasms.'

"Lenox … You're welcome … Yes, no, it was dark when we … I got here. Nothing leaks indoors … Yes, I'll keep Peter posted if there are … Kudos on the new design … Yes, I do like it … I'm whispering because my friend is still asleep … Kind of a new friend … C'mon, Mom … Daniel … Yes, I'm sure we'll find something in the cabinets. Yes, I'll check the expiration date … I won't forget to lock up. Love you too, hugs to Dad and Pushkin … Yes, in that order. Why is he barking?"

Never again underestimate the power of a situation. Thank goodness his name sounded normal enough to spare further inquiries.

"Holy shit, you scared me."

He and his are awake again!

REVELATIONS ARE ALSO A
THING OF THE PAST

"I'LL HAVE TO LEAVE the first lecture for today." Maeve was more than halfway to Queen's when she noticed that her library card was back home at Colinward Street. Exiting her second black taxi that late November morning to make the quick trip to her desk at home, Maeve stopped in her tracks. For there was Mum, Eileen, dolled up in a navy frock at the house door, welcoming the neighbourhood's nosy parkers.

A summit? Now? With them? What for?

It's no secret that West Belfast in the early 1990s wasn't the domain of openness and trust. Because the lines between security and protection were as navigable as the Amazon jungle, warnings found furtive ways to slip out. Similarly, support, as well as menacing disapproval from family and friends, was served in whispers, certainly not by way of formal social occasions.

Clocking her mum greeting the biggest gossips on the street, Maeve instinctively understood that the Donnelly matriarch's mid-life crisis arrived in the shape of breaking traditional codes. Her God-fearing Catholic mother was conducting the first-of-its-kind Falls Road gathering: assembling her neighbours to pre-emptively offset the standard methods' reveal of a family calamity.

That's why she scrubbed the entrance, polished the windows, and cleaned the front room like a madwoman.

Anyone familiar with the Donnellys could tell you that upon deciphering her mother's intentions, Maeve's fury would soar.

Why can't they get their heads round the fact that our engagement is not going to end, with or without their blessing? And Mum, of all people! So much for all her big talk about not letting her simple life become a modern-day Romeo and Juliet. Why couldn't Mum keep her neb out of our business?

Astutely aware of the toll and peril placed on the family, Maeve also appreciated that hers *was* the secret of a lifetime. 'Marking the family card' as some might say around here, should be done right then, including a personal appearance.

So she hurried away, down past the Royal, over the Westlink and towards Great Victoria Street, only her thoughts raced faster.

What did Mum tell them was the reason for having all those biddies round? 'It's sensitive' *must have slipped out.*

Her perfectionist mum would ensure a faultless occasion. *When did she bake?* It would be a breeze for Eileen to conceal a dozen freshly baked scones, perhaps one of her oft-praised apple tarts too. With her five sons hardly around, Eileen didn't worry about anyone barging into the empty house. Da at work changing lightbulbs over at the Royal, and Mum knows Monday was her busiest day at Queen's.

Everyone Mum invited is already aware that Patrick is heading for America. So I am her focus. Presenting herself in the worst plight, it's all out pity Mum is after. No better way to fend off scorn.

Maeve's flowering imagination was accurate as a calculator. The decision about her eldest son's move to Chicago broke Eileen's heart, especially since she wasn't entirely sure of the precise reason. After graduating as a mature student with first class honours from Jordanstown, her first cub was venturing to America like a restless night fox. The plum community-development job with his name on it was now going to the neighbours' boy, a vessel empty of qualifications.

Did Mum already set the stage with wet cheekbones? She won't just utter the scandalous news without foreplay.

If you are entertaining Eileen and Maeve's relationship as mother-daughter symbiosis, you are right. It was mesmerising to watch Maeve's mind charting the pointed event to near perfection, almost word for word, reaction for reaction.

By a West Belfast coincidence, all invitees shared two Christian names: Collette or Dolores. As a result, the entire area had got into the habit of addressing them by last names only.

Mrs Duffy titled Eileen's news 'a death sentence' and Mrs Mullaly sneered that there'd be no mercy for a turncoat like Maeve. Mrs Tolan kept on repeating 'unforgivable' while clasping her hands for added drama. Mrs O'Kane contemplated the Donnellys' tarnished reputation as six heads nodded and six pairs of lips tutted in agreement. The sensitive Mrs McCann gripped onto Eileen's right palm and pressed it hard against her own left. The hope of the family, with her uni grant and all – why is she marrying now, *him*, and throwing it all away?

As Maeve predicted, Eileen's despair performance was epic, complete with smeared mascara.

"What plans I had for my selfish daughter since she was a restless wean in my arms! A picture in her white dress. My only girl, the perfect church wedding at St. Paul's. All of yous there. Photies under the cherry blossoms. Now everything's scattered like broken crystal."

Well-versed in her mother's strategies, Maeve guessed Eileen waited for Mrs Magee's confirmation before inviting any of the rest.

None of them would appear without Mrs Magee. She's probably sitting in the middle of the settee, for she'd be the lone one to vouch for me. Only then would Mrs Devaney make one of her welcome 'we all lose our way sometimes' platitudes.

Mother-daughter bonds, even the symbiotic, come in numerous forms, and in no way were Eileen and Maeve carbon copies of each other. But one trait did characterise the Donnelly women: they dealt with stress points head-on.

Thus, Oliver was mildly surprised by the enquiry office's call for him to identify a visitor; but the image of his fiancée on the CCTV monitor left him in shock. Chilling sweat saturated his spine upon hearing Maeve's request that he drive her home at once, refusing to answer anything further beyond, "Now. You must. Now."

She won't be asking that I drive her home if it were a miscarriage, but it must be serious. Frantic, he changed into civvies.

"Nipping out to take care of something. Contactable," Oliver uttered in the direction of the Chief Inspector's desk on his way out.

Anything goes wrong while I drive an unmarked police vehicle for personal use, this dickhead won't stop at Complaints and

Discipline. He'll want his pound of flesh at court for starters.

Maeve's decisive hop into an official RUC vehicle, however camouflaged, was enough for Oliver to grasp that their drive westward would keep him in the dark. Maeve kept her eyes shut to prevent sectarian graffiti from sapping her confidence. Oliver kept his own mainly on the road.

"Is the Royal close enough for you?"

"No. Today you are coming inside with me."

Maeve's frozen smile transformed Oliver's sixth sense into operational. His survival intuitions sirened. Was he heading straight into a booby trap? An ambush? He longed for the usual army escort.

She noticed he was checking for his personal protection weapon and muting his radio. *Under the circumstances, the biblical precedent calls for a slingshot.*

Maeve seized Oliver's farm-strong right hand and pulled him out of the driver's seat, leading him with four short footsteps to her home. At the doorway, she halted, strengthened her grip on Oliver's palm and dry kissed his cheek, integrating warmth into his suspense. Opening the door with her right hand, Maeve pulled him into the view of the she-wolves' pack. The living room hushed, and Oliver – an exemplar policeman – swiftly counted eight pairs of surprised eyes zooming in on their entrance. Teacups froze mid-lift. His visual scan needed no more than the millisecond it took the ladies to assume scornful stares. Catholicism was everywhere: a crucifix on the wall, mass cards, rosaries, religious pictures and mini-statues, plus a small holy water font right next to the front door.

"Child, what in God's name are you doing?" Pale as death and panic-stricken, Eileen rose much too fast, needing to steady herself against the nearest chair arm.

"My being here has nothing to do with God and everything to do with nosiness."

The tense environment plunged the audience of biddies into silent sense-making, permitting Maeve to continue undisturbed.

"Yousuns have been having a grand wee natter about this famous fiancé of mine. Well, here he is, the man himself – an actual, in the flesh, Protestant. Allow me to present Oliver MacIntyre. He works for Northern Ireland Electricity. Happy now?" Her voice dripped triumph.

Mrs Duffy rose first. Forgetting the floral napkin on her lap, which parachuted straight to the floor, she fled the house without forgetting to communicate her silent disdain.

"Shameless little—" Yet every glare recognised the fine-looking man's healthy instincts as he jumped sideways, liberating Mrs Tolan's direct path to the door.

Those still inside caught Maeve's next shot: "You, of all people, Mrs Mullaly? Aren't you the one always going on about personal happiness? Aye, right."

Mrs O'Kane's piercing pitch dominated the mass exodus: "Nothing is ever off-limits for you, you brazen hussy."

To her mother's dismay, Maeve didn't hold back. "Not everything needs to be shared in a marriage, as *you* know."

Oliver's exposé occurred a little before eleven. By midday, most of the Lower Falls was in the know. Ciaran and Patrick's younger sister and the daughter of the laudable (at least until then) Donnellys was to marry a Prod. The shocking news swept through West Belfast and beyond faster than the Black Death and Covid-19 put together.

For days after, Lorcan was wrapped in disgrace as Eileen remained gobsmacked and scundered at the way their spirited girl expropriated command of the events.

If ever there was proof that girls are every bit as fearless as lads, this is it.

But self-comforting brought little in the way of any emotional triumph. Eileen and Lorcan were never a romantic powerhouse.

To me, they exemplified the way long-married couples can come to raise walls between them, sometimes as high as my peace walls. Today, decades post-Troubles, we still lead the world in segregation infrastructure. Can you believe that the number of peace walls within me remains just one short of my centennial age?

Now in the third decade of the Troubles and her marriage, Eileen had a new realisation. She recognised that life would bring tasks too large to perform, yet her children's teamwork was over. All her family dinners and other long-practised rituals designed to keep her children close; all her unspoken expectations they would get on in life, unlike their parents, was now set for disappointment.

Look at us: one more broken family in this wrecked North.

As he sped away, Maeve at his side, Oliver's heightened sense of danger gradually ebbed into professional ease. *That's the end of operational deployments in West Belfast for me – if I live to tell the tale.*

But if I had to identify Oliver's primary takeaway from that day, it would be the one understanding (of few) he'd come to share with the Donnellys: once his Maeve was set for action, overruling her was as pointless as racing time.

CHAPTER 3

CONTEMPORARY PILGRIMS

Landed. Unclear whether in O'Hare or O'Hell. If not for the pilot's Happy Thanksgiving, I'd think it was the Gold Rush westward. Relish the movement. I am still stuck on Mass Pike.

"Texting while driving, Ella?"

"At this speed, Tamir? Wheeling you in a stroller into New York would have been faster."

It's obvious Daniel is nervous about misrecognizing an uncle he never met before in a busy Chicago Airport. You should add something, maybe a growing heart emoji, or—

"Fair enough. I did sleep like a baby. It doesn't look like we moved much."

"My bet: your dreams moved faster." When did DC fall lower than Boston on the list of Top US Attractions, freeing Natasha from family chauffeuring duties to Scarsdale?

"Have you ever visited us in Israel?"

"Not yet."

"No ancestral curiosity?"

A removed fifth cousin still has the same Lithuanian roots. The 'professional backpacker' Tamir claims to be should exercise greater geographical awareness of family origin. Okay.

Reboot. If Mom detects you were obnoxious to a member of her Israeli family, it would be your death by hunger on Thanksgiving – your favorite holiday – so get into its spirit. "Would I like Israel?"

"Emm, traffic-wise, you'd feel at home."

He's right. It took an hour to move thirty miles.

"But Tel Aviv won't disappoint you."

Is it the frequent rocket strikes propelling each of its citizens to become Israel's Minister of Tourism? Tamir said he completed five years of military service. Paratrooper, was it? Artillery? Obviously, listening skills could be sharpened. Shouldn't be that hard when it's just two of you in your intimate Toyota Corolla. But five years sounds more than a standard service requirement. A patriot, and one who likes to wear designer sportswear. If his hair length is anything to go by, Tamir is a recent veteran. You are developing PTSD just by thinking of mandatory military service. Inappropriate to rush and judge 'the whole world is against us' Israeli attitude.

"I'll get there. One day."

"I can see why tourism marketing draws visitors elsewhere."

Shit. Did I forget to pack my flight jacket? Wait, did you remember that because it's olive green, and you were mulling over his military service? A good forewarning that your thought process wouldn't be of use in wartime.

"Though, if you think about it, you winding up in New York and me ending up with a heavy accent are a coincidence."

"Your accent isn't heavy, Tamir."

"You are nice to lie. But our family branch ended up in Israel because nobody on the planet was granting them a visa."

These thunderstorms make the Medford-Scarsdale drive incalculable. There's zero chance of surviving this road trip with only two Gala apples in the backseat. You'll have to offer him one of them. *Two miles to the next exit*: holiday binge-eating will commence in Natick, Massachusetts, not New Haven, Connecticut – a bathroom break and the first fast food menu, however far it'll divert us from the highway.

"With everyone underground, there's no rush settling family scores on who emigrated when and why."

See: with a bit of greasy carb-instigated optimism, this trip is already less excruciating than your driving test.

"Was that your boyfriend you were texting? Girlfriend?"

"It's men for me. Kinda seeing someone at the moment. You?"

"Girls."

Obviously.

"It might not be immediately evident, but I am a love migrant."

"Is that a new visa category?"

"It ought to be. The world needs us more than ever."

There is some truth to his claim.

"Let me tell you. Latin lovers are real. My two solo Montana weeks were perfect after the romantic demands of your southern continent. All regrouped now and ready for Boston's cosmopolitanism."

Shame on my implicit prejudice over Tamir's siege mentality.

"You chose well. I'm seeing an Irish—well, he's Northern Irish."

"Ireland, cool. Recommended?"

Who knows? His unpolished directness might charm the Irish.

"If I get the summer grant I'm applying for, I could keep you posted next September. But for Irish Americans, look no further than Boston."

It's interesting that third and fourth-generation Irish Americans are so proud of their Old Country. It isn't so clear-cut with us Jews, nuclear family notwithstanding. Politicians carry Irishness up their sleeves. So do celebrities. I wonder what Irish culture means to them beyond the St. Patrick's Day festivities and shamrocks.

"Your parents – less than overjoyed about your relationship?"

Why would he think that? Maybe because you are his first Goldin. Another urgent signal for the need to be more welcoming, unless you want him to conclude you're adopted.

"Consider yourself lucky, Ella. The Jewish question would be the first line of interrogation in my family."

So, Tamir may not only be a love migrant but also a love refugee. He should consult your State Department brother-in-law tonight. Maybe Mark could extend his stay. Look at that: the sun is excited that your compassion is sprouting.

"Though, to be fair, sticking to our own was what kept the Jews around. I am kidding; it was a joke, Ella."

I hope so. Either way, Scarsdale should be closer in clearer weather.

"Final plate. I am turning on the dishwasher, Mom. Your china and your daughters salute you for another finely executed Thanksgiving."

"Thank you, Ella. We have all earned the Roman recline."

"In a minute." Wow, six texts in a row?

Ring me when you're finished.
No text first.
So I can talk.
Everything unexpected here.
Uncle, partner and the house is stunning!
You guessed right about Gilli.

Daniel sounds architecturally excited. Is he feeling comfortable over there? As his mother hasn't seen her brother for nearly thirty years, this trip can't be entirely relaxing. Nah, Daniel isn't one to have an issue with gayness. But Patrick's orientation would have been a huge taboo in Belfast at the time. That, plus three decades, is one explanation for why Daniel had no idea.

But other than that, what else was so unexpected? The money? If Chicago is as Irish as Boston, maybe the uncle is undocumented. Over the years, there had to be a wedding, funeral, some family reunion to make the trip back. But he couldn't. It's odd nobody seemed to have visited this Patrick either.

Uh-oh, did he need to flee Northern Ireland? Was it gayness or—whoa, could Patrick have IRA connections? There must be something fishy in this story. Okay, back off. Only your gun-jumping personality and overtime fantasies would pick family scandals first. State Department Mark would jump to correct you: stunning wouldn't be the house description for the undocumented.

"Ella, bring your tea into the living room."

Chicago is an hour earlier. Call him later, when you have more time to listen and less urgency to react.

"Mom, we are newless. If Ella doesn't call him now, what will the breakfast interrogation subject be tomorrow?"

Natasha: not just my lone sister, but the goddess of precision and truth. Finding a husband who mastered family exits early on never retracted her life commitment to outlast us all in Mom's company. But you aren't a nobody either; a resounding success bringing cousin Tamir along. Fits into this family like a glove. Entirely unconcerned by Dad's lack of sentence-endings.

"You're right, Tamir. The Jewish rift between America and Israel has never been wider. There is no beating around that troubling bush."

The guy spares you the post-Thanksgiving philosophical debate with Dad. A lot to be thankful for this year.

"Hey, it's 2am – 3 for you, Ella. You aren't a night owl."

"You didn't pick up earlier."

"Sorry, I fell asleep."

Still in his blue jacket? Daniel doesn't look too sleepy, nor eager to talk. More like struck by lightning. What happened to all his earlier enthusiasm?

"Your uncle must love having you there." Why this distracted gaze? "So, was it fun catching up with the past?"

Not the slightest smile. I hate this impossible to read FaceTime. Well, you're no oil painting either. An emerging zit? It's too early to pay for that overpriced junk food back in Natick. You keep forgetting that every FaceTime could be a phone call, especially at the end of a long day. Nah. Better this way. Daniel isn't his usual forthcoming self, but he *is* permanently sexy. Hearing only his voice would have made me much more worried.

"So, what's surprised you the most?"

"That's a good question. One that I am too tired to think about right now."

I don't see him yawning, but he shot down a direct question on why Patrick never went back. Maybe you can ask it in a way he won't deflect.

"Does Patrick still have the accent?"

"Not only the accent. He lives in a Northern Ireland that ceased to exist."

So. Funny. Tamir's exact words to your parents: "You reminisce over an extinct Israel."

Unlike Tamir, Patrick might potentially contribute insights to your thesis. Wow, imagine he is still a believer in the cause. Wow, wow! Could the questions you prepared for those IRA sympathizers in that Boston pub make a reappearance in Chicago? Didn't they brag about their extensive networks? What did they call that money spinner for the IRA? NORAID. You are impossible, you know that? Take it slow. Daniel barely knows Patrick. He deserves the chance to get to know *his* uncle before contributing to *your* dissertation.

There could be a million other reasons for Patrick's infatuation with a dead past. Isn't that the definition of every historian, archaeologist, and classicist who ever lived? But Daniel said Patrick was in speechwriting. And Gilli, now confirmed as a man, a linguist. A perfect match, though neither is in a money-making profession, so what makes their house stunning? Slow. Down. Now. The detective genre is exploding with material. They could be art collectors, for all you know. Gilli could come from money.

"What's that thing behind you?"

"Australian art. Here. I'll stand, so you can grasp its enormity." It is huge.

"You'd never know Mum and Patrick once shared a household."

"Why? Is your mom anti-art?"

"Hardly. But her taste, well ... So, how was your Thanksgiving?"

Not in the mood for clarifications.

"Fun – and long." It's feasible he went through the entire Northern Ireland in the conversation before you called him.

"I suppose you'll be getting undressed for bed around now?"

"Yes. Why?"

"Any chance you'd narrate the process?"

"Why don't you guide me?"

"Your wish is my command."

A NORTHERN EXODUS

DEAR LOVE HIM, but when old nerves remain raw, any attempt by Patrick to embrace Daniel as his newly found nephew was bound to stir ripples back home. So, when Daniel informed Maeve he'd be visiting her brother for Thanksgiving, Patrick's hasty exodus shot back into Maeve's consciousness. And mine.

Are you beginning to feel that I am a version of my own past?

Keep resurfacing? Influenced by events that refuse to go away? Clinging to my promise not to overly intrude, I'll share only the basics.

In those days, Maeve and Oliver cherished their new reality in one of the (still far too few) mixed areas along Belfast's Lisburn Road. Life in a terraced two-up two-down with polite neighbourly conversations deprived of community-based references provided an ideal nursery for the pregnancy to blossom. Maeve could walk to Queen's and prenatal classes, ushering in new friendships. Fears for Oliver loosened. Still and all, maternal empathy buzzed that her own mother needed her.

Neither her father nor four brothers were up for the task of consolation. Maeve was always the one to understand her mother best. She knew Eileen's preferences diverged from biblical norms (think Abel's priority over Cain, or Jacob's over Esau), decidedly belonging to her firstborn, Patrick.

I can spare Da at least one of Mum's 'our Patrick never done a load of his own laundry. He'll not be able to manage.'

Maeve would agree that Eileen's mothering embodied Emerson's famous observation: 'Men are what their mothers made them.'

Feeling her mother's warm palms trying to guess her baby's sex through her black coat, Maeve silently thanked Patrick's immigration for the window of reconciliation.

And I shared her gratitude. It's no big secret that I was and still am powered by grannies. Especially back then, an ambitious pregnant girl getting her master's degree, and determined to get on in life, needed her mother's helping hand. Thankfully, a parent's hopes for their child took precedence over my issues.

"Babies need granny love."

Right at the entrance of Bright's on Castle Street, as their bags were searched, Eileen was busting to know every detail of the pregnancy. Was she having only morning sickness or nausea throughout the day? Craving salty or sweet?

"You're blooming," her mother enthused, while Maeve marvelled at the huge impact of a barely visible baby bump.

"That cold wind out there always gives me watery eyes." Eileen's explanation for her rolling tears was unnecessary as the waitress brought their teas and slices of apple tart to the back corner of the café. "Those for Patrick know to shed themselves at home."

"How's the McGlade girl coping?" was Maeve's initial step for reintegration. A mere hint from Patrick, and the girl next door, an earnest twenty-year-old, would have joined him on the journey, no preconditions. Had he only mumbled, she would have abandoned her belongings and run after him to Aldergrove Airport to travel with Patrick as his carry-on.

In Eileen's eyes, Patrick was a late developer in the female department. Thus, after hearing the McGlade girl's observation that "nostalgia is a superglue," she no longer settled on a raindrop in the drought from her boy. Before and well after he left, Eileen made her intentions for the girl known, in deeds as much as words, to Patrick and the world's ears. Yet, in the best spirit of emotional complexity, Patrick chivalrously stymied any hasty pre-departure match, leaving Eileen and the McGlade girl the comradeship of heartbreak.

"The girl and your da both think he'll meet a rich American girlfriend."

Maeve could tell her mother was minimising the circumstances for her sake.

"And Da?"

"Coming around."

Maeve knew her choices – Patrick's too (hasty departures make people wonder) – had thrown a spanner into her parents' relationship. But she avoided picturing the drama back at Colinward Street.

Lorcan often ejected, "*I'm* selfish? Your girl has destroyed everything we've built."

"*My* daughter? Inflicting blame makes her *my* daughter, but the lads I gave birth to with equal pain are always *yours*."

Such frequent fights would end with doors slamming. Lorcan would then return hours later, long after Eileen came to herself, and himself intoxicated enough to brush off the guilt.

Eileen had come to meet her daughter fresh from the hairdressers wearing a crimson dress that Maeve didn't recognise. She read Eileen's weighty preparations as a sign that things were looking up. Maeve was right. But this chapter change only came after one row between her parents went a step too far.

"Foolish neighbourhood gossip; that's all you call it? Catch yourself on, woman. We're all in existential danger. Pariahs in our parish, maybe even in the eyes of God."

"Speaking in God's name, are you now, Lorcan?"

"If you don't like my tone, there's the door. You can clear off and camp out with that daughter of yours and her Orangeman!"

Turning white-faced and trembling to her bones, Eileen cried, "You go, you useless layabout! I wouldn't linger a moment longer, only I took vows."

Lorcan approached Eileen with eyes inflamed and fists clenching. An external observer might reckon it a life-and-death situation. But not Eileen. She knew it wasn't in him. Yet, watchful eyes far beyond Mrs McGlade's took notice of the curtain-shut danger at the Donnellys that night. Those with limited street vision experienced the episode via stomps and shouts penetrating the thin walls of their home (unlike the peace walls).

Yes, I won't lie. I am possessed by this segregation, these scars, within me. The mere mention of any type of wall fires those 'peace' structures right to the fore of my mind.

Silence then ruled the Donnelly residence for ninety-six hours of sunlight and darkness, threatened only by the progressive powers of sadness and regret. Ultimately, intimate clemency delivered the final joint match point. With an unknowing wink to Max Weber's famous book *The Protestant Ethic*, Eileen allowed herself a mental jab at her daughter: *Given my limited options, a Catholic spouse must be superior to the emotion-suppressing Protestant, in bed at least.* Once speaking terms resumed, Eileen and Lorcan did not once mention the never-to-be-forgotten incident.

Involved in the church (giving readings, in the choir, etc.), Eileen had high hopes in Father Joe's imparting denominational impact on her daughter's future life. Maeve was equally anxious and excited to see her mum for the first time since the tea fiasco a few weeks earlier. With the many Us and Them upcoming decisions on wedding and childrearing, mother and daughter were keen to devise a mutually acceptable problem-management path.

"From Patrick." Eileen presented Maeve with an opened letter.

The paper's density was thicker than Maeve was accustomed to, and she may have also fleetingly noticed its smaller-than-usual dimensions. But Patrick's blue calligraphy paraded across the white surface, hypnotising her besotted eyes to commence a hungry read.

… Senator Edward Kennedy never flipped Irish America against us. A folk hero's welcome of arrival awaited me. Instant acclimatisation is putting it mildly.

They summon me, a neophyte, into NORAID Benefits all across Chicago. Dinner dances attracting all the great and the good. I kid you not. Fixed-price plates serve Celtic sentimentalism for a pretty penny. Taste-wise, as far from Ma's cuisine as Belfast is to Australia. Emerald-green collection boxes pass around these hoolies, stuffed to the gills with American dollars for Irish Justice. I do wonder if 'greenbacks' isn't a coincidental name.

Speaking of emerald, a local bigwig is working on securing my Green Card. It's impossible to satisfy their thirst for retelling their family's immigration sagas. They pull out wallets with photos (one lady brought three albums) and ask that I identify the places they toured in Ireland. Stone me if I know how many times my hoarse pipes blasted out 'The Rising of the Moon' and 'The Fields of Athenry.' Aye, at times, I pinch myself, but in earnest, it's no work at all to feel unique. Especially when they never tire of pointing out Irish friendliness, hospitality, and wit.

NORAID's headquarters is based in New York. They tell me that only in the Bronx will I know what Irish America's life is really about. But Chicago has nothing to be ashamed of.

They already have me down to speak at a huge function. The organiser's brief: 'Ditch complexity. Wallets open with suffering. Want to make an impact? Tell us about the Famine, martyrs, Bloody Sunday, Long Kesh, and the Hunger Strike.' Should be a walk in the park for a Donnelly, eh?

Da – I am not skint.

Ma – I connected with the local Archdiocese. You said once 'Cha d' dhùin doras nach d'fhosgail doras.' But now, 'no door closed without another one opening' has finally clicked.

Ciaran – Déan deifir! Hurry up, would you?

To all of you, Gra, Dìlseacht, Cairdeas: Love, Loyalty, Friendship.

Your Patrick

Maeve's swift fold returned the letter into its journey-worn brown home. For all his good and fully elaborated intentions, she was concerned Patrick could be taking American freedom of speech too much to heart. An anxious glance at Eileen affirmed the mutual apprehension. Amidst the frequent deportations and extraditions reported, Patrick was careless.

Noted Eileen, "Countless ships were lost within sight of the harbour."

Maeve transmitted her concurrence with a sympathetic double nod and tight lips. "Oliver won't hear a word of it from me."

CHAPTER 4

CONFLICT OVER COEXISTENCE

Daniel left already – unsurprising.

Early morning studio start. Good luck with Rubinstein's Final ♥.

How early do they open MIT's studios? Considering he hates fighting, the lame excuse is understandable. Well, at least the bed earned a good fifteen minutes of someone warming *her* up before the shitty exam. 'Let down' is unkind, but a B for last night's sex level amounts to grade inflation. B-, in view of our preceding squabble.

Fuck. Did I overreact? His response to my research plans in Belfast was shocking. No congratulatory kiss on "I got the summer grant. We can be there as early as June 29th." Skepticism overtaking his face in response to my excitement-activating attempt of "It's a chance to spend your birthday at home."

"My birthday fantasies were sun-kissed and palm-treed."

Even if he never heard of '*Mazal Tov*,' it can't be a big ask to radiate a little 'bravo' from a first-hand witness to the grant's competitiveness. True, we do need to think about his summer, too, in the midst of my hypothesis building. But horny talk isn't a plan.

"Packing the white bandana for your coffee curls and the blue bikini, in case the nudist beach is full."

No. You aren't turning this relationship sexless. Your libido isn't low. It was perfectly acceptable to sit up and ask why his family won't stay around knowing we are coming.

"Would you blame them for ditching rain and the Marching Season?"

Their presence isn't essential, but it would be nice to get to know my boyfriend's parents outside FaceTime. And summer is long enough to give them an opportunity to travel even when their son is over.

"What's the rush? We could head there in late Ju—"

"My dissertation clock. A miracle your ears are intact!"

It's unrealistic to expect that everything he'd say would always be supportive or agreeable. But should his ambivalence be a reason to worry? His internal disquiet was greater than the sum of our conversation. Okay, maybe you *are* stressed out, like he said. He sees you; you don't. And he loves you, that you know. So, what's this unsupportive attitude all of a sudden?

"The Troubles, our conflict, must be Bronze Age in research by now. I thought your dissertation was the present."

Being born in peacemaking Mecca doesn't make him an expert. Unfair to expect a post-Troubles aspiring architect to read the Good Friday Agreement. But he refuses to translate the depressed look that returned with him from Chicago. And he extinguished your bright idea to interview his uncle Patrick faster than a blackout.

When did you see him last FaceTiming his mother? He talked to his dad on Monday after his final.

But then you haven't called Scarsdale in three days either. If the Goldins deciphered it's safer to leave you alone during the exam period, Daniel's parents could be as emotionally intelligent. Five years in, Mark continues to complain to Natasha about our family's unattainable self-disclosure demands.

But it can't be just his finals. What reason made Daniel tense up in response to your explanation that the grant for field research helps you avoid the armchair social scientist syndrome?

"I get your motivation, Ella. I get it. But as part of 'discovering' what's *really* what, have you given any thought to how to detect bullshit?"

Hmmm, could Daniel be making no sense whatsoever for a different reason? Data-collection illiteracy. His interpretative skills need to focus on construction sites, not interviews. Yet, odder than a whale in the Sahara, you'll continue to remain mesmerized by the twinkle in his eyes.

"Knowing Nordies, your interviewees will mostly aim to make you laugh. Or take the piss."

"You can't be interested in a crash methodology course. Wait, are you?"

"Does it involve simulations?"

His licking capacities figured out a long time ago that your vagina has a mind of her own.

He deserves a vacation, and the grant-awarders concurred that you appreciate the value of compromise. Unlike Claude Lévi-Strauss, you love traveling. A surprise Cape Cod escape would make him a jollier local. Hunting an affordable summer deal in that tourist trap would be a fieldwork project in itself. See: polishing research skills could still start early with a later Belfast arrival, even if Daniel escorts you there only until you get your bearings.

FFS, why can't Climber leave even one edible item behind? In light of his muscles, recycling an empty Half & Half carton shouldn't be that heavy of a lift. Great, the coffee maker that you programmed last night was left empty. Emily, too, manifesting the three months' itch – not in losing interest in Climber, but the love affair with food shopping in Market Basket is over. And Daniel's indifference to how food finds its way into this hungry refrigerator is evident: there's nothing left for your breakfast. Don't be a bitch about it. You let the three of them rely on your hereditary fear – no *phobia* – of extinction. At least your boyfriend recognizes that breakfast bowls decorated with remnants of porridge should make it as far as the sink before he departs. That's halfway through the cleaning cycle, and a promising sign of his ability to remember their permanent home is actually back on the shelf.

If Emily tolerates macho apartment annexation, you can too. ESPN as the standard background noise isn't so bad. And Climber's (how long will she call her boyfriend that?) sweaty jerseys as our most frequent air freshener. Don't lie: his ripped *David* abs make up for it big time, especially when he planks in the living room. If Climber dominates beauty, Emily, our social life, and Daniel beats us all at poker, should you be complaining over gastronomic chores in this domestic bliss?

Positive thinking: scholastic confinement is over and done with. There isn't any option to change the wreckage you just submitted as an exam. Being clueless over what Rubinstein aimed for doesn't mean all your guesses turn up wrong. Submitting it brought stability to your shaking hands – that's one advantage already. Exiting these double glass doors vanishes the Fletcher School from your life through Martin Luther King Jr. Day. From here on, you return to this building only to survive the comprehensive exams; then, if you play your cards right, a handful of meetings on the thesis prospectus.

Everyone said comps are a different ballgame but passable with sufficient cramming. Daniel told you that the PhD system in the UK is different, so explaining their importance might get him to open up more about Northern Ireland. He *is* a little weird with his reluctance, especially when we talk non-stop about everything else. Sharing with Daniel how much his perspective could have come in handy in the exam today might help motivate him to explain more.

What an odd choice for Rubinstein to give a one-question final exam asking only to critique the Northern Irish peace accord. The exam itself described that agreement as "a masterfully crafted, equality-driven peace agreement that ended the Troubles." Yes, Rubinstein is eminent, tenured, and freed from job insecurities, but this final exam in her popular Conflict & Coexistence course isn't her finest career moment. What did she expect, asking us to compare Northern Ireland only with those post-peace countries now back at war?

Ugh, you worked your butt off for this 3.97 GPA. A screw-up in the last in-class semester won't only kiss job prospects goodbye, it'll butcher the three semesters' methodical crowning of Rubinstein as your dissertation advisor. What academic misery made her cook up the 'there will be only two A grades in this course' policy, especially in this job market?

This is empty panic. No one in the class came close to your class-participation level. That's forty percent of the grade right there. They all said she likes you, not least that pathologically ambitious jerk Isabelle, who cared enough to call you out on it.

"Think of us, your fellow students, not Rubinstein, as your future colleagues. Nothing makes a better impression than sharing your guaranteed A once in a while."

Well, with this regurgitation of an exam answer, you are safe only if 'people don't always get what they deserve' proves valid.

Whatever the outcome, it won't be any more painful than this Medford weather. Whoa! Brain doesn't need to trigger any leg motion in this tailwind. Hypothermia will crash the phone if I pull it out now. Four-in-the-morning darkness when it can't be later than 4pm. A silent film isn't as colorless as this vegetation. This surgically clean air can only mean our first December Nor'easter tonight.

Don't give up on the exam just yet. Unforeseen is a fact of life. There are multiple plausible scenarios. Rubinstein may surprise and decide on detailed comments in place of grade deduction. She differentiates between intrinsic and extrinsic motivations. On the other hand, your ludicrous analysis could frustrate her expectations so much that she'll go ballistic. Even worse, you're a disgrace to Judaism for contemplating the Christmas holiday spirit as your sole life raft for screwing up a final. Her name is Rubinstein, not Smith. But Christmas is a universal holiday, isn't it?

Christmas maybe, but Chrismukkah has a way to go in Daniel's case. Especially after yesterday, when he pioneered Rubinstein's preference for conflict over coexistence. Emily looked bemused by his "A Chrismukkah party? Jesus. Nearly as brilliant as a frat party inside the campus police station."

"It's an excuse for post-finals fun."

"Mash-ups never work."

Says who? Someone who is one?

"And titles bind."

"In publishing, not the partying business. A few shots in, and no one will know it's even December."

"The perpetual crusade to prove that you are a pluralist should find something sexier than a silly Chrismukkah."

A whole philosophical spiel ensued over Hanukkah as the Jewish example of resisting assimilation and Christmas celebrating the one who broke away. Grumpy and uptight, but you can't deny he impressed you with such unexpected spiritual knowledge. Poor Climber, with his naïve remark, "but don't all Irish love a good craic?" really woke Daniel's Mr. Hyde.

"Oh, you're home? Couldn't find my key."

"It's Baltic; come in. How did you get on with the final?"

"I had a wonderful time. Wow, it's Arctic in here too. Could you lower the storm window in our room? I'll do Emily's."

Give anger a break, especially since he came up with the Aruba winter vacation alternative. He was right that the fun would last longer for the two of us, and someone else would clean up our mess.

"Our room is all set. Need a hand over here?"

"Do I smell my favorite cold-weather cocktail?"

"Aye, I added a wee splash of liqueur and orange peel to amplify the standard hot chocolate and vodka. Here: that's for you as well."

"What is it?"

"Normally, by opening the box, you'll find out."

"Wait. Is it a Christmas or Hanukkah gift?"

"It's Chrismukkah."

CHAPTER 4½

THE EARLIER COEXISTENCE
CONFLICT

By now, you must have wondered about Maeve and Oliver's marriage. Did 'unthinkable' come to mind? Or possibly that they waited for my Belfast/Good Friday Agreement, or went into exile at least until the ceasefires? All reasonable assumptions – that never materialised. Maeve and Oliver ditched eloping too. But before I spill the beans on my daring duo, let me justify why briefing you on that MacIntyre-Donnelly minefield of a wedding day exceeds mere gossip.

I don't underestimate the fallibility of memory. Rewriting histories doesn't suffer shortages anywhere. Everyone upgrades. Emotions, biases, prejudice and even carelessness distort human memory. But these problems are extraneous to my *non-human* state of being. Since every generation considers themselves better than the last, my soft power of influence lies in improving accessibility to the truth. Especially when the truth defies fiction. Maeve and Oliver's wedding, with all its loaded background, is one of my autobiographical slices worthy of an accurate public record.

On that morning, the alarm's bell blasted Oliver's tormented sleep.

Oh, shit! How did I miss the timing device?

His initial panic converted into a successful halt of the ringing clock, but emasculating anguish persisted inside his awakening brain. Migraine music cradled the end of his now awful dreaming routine: monstrous wombs gulping every imagined pair of tits in a Pac-Man-like manner.

Deteriorating daytime desires similarly concerned Oliver thanks to Maeve's transformation into a hormonal geyser. She renounced with a tantrum every appeal to devise a pregnancy-disclosure plan for the families (Eileen remained discreet); immature behaviour in his view, when to the sharp-eyed she was already showing. To avoid bickering, silence became Oliver's go-to strategy. At the time a source of misery, but longer-term this self-taught skill proved handy. Oliver unlocked what could take husbands years of extrapolation, namely a conflict-avoidance path that Maeve didn't misconstrue as ignoring on his part.

As he reposed, the phone's ringtone radiated Oliver's right-side headache over to the left.

How is Dad still in Broughshane?

Edward MacIntyre's deep baritone detailed the developments with Oliver's mother. Oliver deciphered the critical kernel: last-minute hat and shoes crisis. Rosemary and Aunt Beatrice would be driving together directly to the wedding, while Edward would collect the groom.

Brilliant!

Oliver's first clear thought appreciated the time extension, for meeting his father dressed up and ready in his current state was unachievable. But his thrill belonged to relief – a chatter-free pre-wedding interlude. Considering the day's prognosis, any delay in reuniting with his mum was a blessed development. Aye, a son's ingratitude flashed and was swiftly flushed by his hangover's guilt.

Why couldn't I stop at 'just a couple of hours watching the footy with a few mates' on the night before my wedding?

Falling backwards on his bed, Oliver's occipital region met the centre of a responsive feathered cream pillow and his frontal, the duvet.

Eyes shut; his memory thundered Reverend Ian Paisley's 'devil's buttermilk' as alcohol's condemnation. Rosemary – someone on the brink of Free Presbyterianism – couldn't get her brain around her son's insistence on a life fraught with difficulty. "Impulsivity was Reuben's curse," she often said to Edward. "The lad knows his Bible well enough not to rush and marry the first girl he meets."

Thus, once the wedding across the divide shifted from planning into arrangements, little peace characterised the mother-son relationship.

From Oliver's perspective, his mother was focused only on thwarting the scandal of his (inevitably accelerated) wedding day. Yet, for Rosemary, "tainting our family's unblemished Presbyterian legacy" was the ultimate maternal failure.

Her preaching was inevitably standard. "Don't get me wrong, I'll have no trouble getting on with the wee girl; it's *you* I care about. But all of it; my difficult pregnancy and the complications of your birth, your childhood tumbles, exam pressures and your teenage days when we could hardly sleep for worry. Even worse, you walking into danger every working day – it all pales. No, no. Yes. You need to hear the truth from somebody."

"Give it a rest, Mum." Oliver tried, which only instigated further tirades.

"I never thought you naïve, son. You fought like a lion to make Inspector. All the good looks in the world won't impress your colleagues once they find out she's from the Falls."

Oliver noted that not all Nationalists were interchangeable with the IRA.

"Don't you turn your nose up at your mother, Oliver. The dogs in the street know the Falls Road isn't just a Nationalist area."

When Rosemary asked, "What do *her* people make of all of this?" he stuck to half-truths. Yes, he knows what sort of family Maeve comes from. Visiting Maeve's home went better than expected. No, Rosemary won't be asked to spend time with the extended Donnellys. So what if she is young? Yes, it's he who doesn't want to wait. He kept quiet about his sadness over maternal differences. Of course Maeve's parents felt as betrayed, but Eileen was the more supportive mum. Even makes the occasional visit to South Belfast.

"Praise the Lord, you have been blessed with options. With these career prospects, thank goodness we have the fine family farm for you to fall back on as your alternative."

"I have no plans to leave the force."

Oliver always tried, but Rosemary was unstoppable. Dismissing Oliver's endeavours with hand gestures, she also often broke down. How could the fine man they'd raised toss it all in the bin over a girl?

"For the life of me, I thought Argentina would get the Falkland Islands before you'd secure marriage permission from your supervisor."

And when Oliver did: "You think your policeman's life is difficult? Wee buns compared to the family life you are choosing."

Rosemary never needed reminding that earning a reputation comes slowly, but losing it is swift. She continually nourished the MacIntyres' respectable social standing in Broughshane with many personal contributions of her own. A pillar in her community through superb traybakes, crafts for church fetes and membership in the Women's Institute, she also earned 'cultural' bragging rights. By the age of fifty-one, Rosemary had completed the exploration of every European capital not behind the Iron Curtain, bar two. Each itinerary included purchasing a mini polyester national flag on a stick, now part of a round bouquet decorating the mantelpiece in her spacious lounge.

Skipping Dublin wasn't too much of a sacrifice. "Frankly, with the terrorist activity it harbours, it's a disgrace, pure and simple, to call that place a democratic republic," she once commented to Oliver.

That week he couldn't disagree, since Special Branch successfully raided another arms factory near Shannon Airport. But missing out on must-see Rome was excruciating for Rosemary. Edward's erudite explanation that the Vatican was a country of its own, occupying an easily skippable two-mile plot within the Eternal City, wasn't enough. Rosemary refused to spend a penny of their income so close to that Pontifical shrine.

Now, her life's work of maintaining the MacIntyres' status as a hardworking, upstanding farming family, good-living folk, could go to waste.

With half those genes, she contemplated, *Oliver must concern himself early with instilling proper Christian values of hard work and respectability in his future children. If not, Heaven forbid!*

Impending fatherhood drowned out all his mother's fears but one. Oliver couldn't help but share some of Rosemary's concerns over the unsteady future they were inflicting on their soon-to-be-firstborn and any potential siblings.

Anxieties don't necessarily affect couples identically, but Maeve's serenity over the unpredictable was in stark contrast to Oliver's inner restlessness.

"Our primary responsibility is to grow up, let go, and celebrate *our* emerging family," she repeated to Oliver's stressed ears. "Trust the future to choose itself for our children. They'll be grand."

Yet, beyond verbal – occasionally erotically supplemented – reassurances to help Oliver cope, Maeve didn't spare him her thoughts over his mother's 'overbearing bigotry.' Oliver felt locked in a standoff. He reckoned that mother/daughter-in-law troubles, unlike those he policed in his day job, have greater prospects of continuing indefinitely.

In that, the otherwise perceptive Oliver failed to comprehend that his solution-focused future wife had the long game in mind. With Oliver being Rosemary's only child, Maeve was banking on the magnetic powers of grandmotherhood to dismantle, in time, Rosemary's mistrust.

Maeve's first visit to Broughshane coincided with an IRA killing in Belfast. Naturally, she couldn't avoid the stinging comparison between the idyllic village and her wee street just off a busy road next to an interface. Theirs was a large house with spacious lawns, fresh air, flowerbeds and fields just beyond the hedge. Hers, a paved yard out the back with a patch of cement at the front door and the view: more houses just the same.

However, the devastating news report from Belfast offered a unique window to voice her concern for Oliver's safety. In later conversations with Oliver's parents, she casually dropped that Provie killings undermined the Republican struggle. After feeling confident of creating cracks in the distrust, Maeve commented that the focus should be political instead of military. Of course, she was hinting at the open secret of the time, namely that the recent Downing Street Declaration yielded positive results for non-violent Irish nationalism.

Global solidarity demands my shout out to exogenous developments assisting Maeve's forward-thinking approach. For one, Irish America becoming progressively irritable with IRA violence had an impact on internal Catholic attitudes. Secondly, the global celebrations of an end to conflict in South Africa and the since reversible Israeli-Palestinian peace would have left me as the lingering bad egg. That wouldn't have been well received in our then closer-than-ever European neighbourhood.

Yet, for all of Maeve's good intentions, marriage was still an altogether different matter for her future mother-in-law.

A domineering mother, no doubt, old-school too. Rosemary envisioned my Catholic-Protestant divide as a fight between good and evil, but also knew religious sentiments wouldn't change Oliver's mind about Maeve. So her hopes lay in bureaucratic difficulties. She had every right and reason to expect that addressing the specifics of a mixed wedding would bring out the best of inflexibilities and divides within me.

Thus, Rosemary was blindsided by my Mixed Marriage Association locating a sympathetic priest to perform Oliver and Maeve's ceremony. Oliver was convinced they'd found the ideal 'setting the example for others' type of celebrant upon hearing the priest quote Paul's verse on pursuing things which make for peace. The deal for Maeve was sealed as soon as she obtained a dispensation from Father Joe (her local parish priest of St. Paul's) for a marriage with a non-Catholic.

"Yes, he's a maverick priest all right, rocked some boats around integrated schools, but a trustworthy community representative." Father Joe told Eileen and Lorcan, Maeve's never more gobsmacked parents. Their disbelieving objections triggered Father Joe's biggest surprise of all: "I'll be there," he said, patting Eileen's hand, "for moral support."

No, with the hurdles these two are facing, I won't need to blink first.

Rosemary calculated while Oliver's best man Robert secured the Great Hall at Queen's in bionic speed for the wedding reception – extremely tricky for anyone to get at short notice thanks to its prestige and ability to fulfil security requirements. And yet, the well-connected best man and son of Queen's bursar delivered the venue for a Monday evening. The priest was able to ring-fence the multi-denomination chapel at City Hospital for forty-five minutes top. With that, he diffused the 'setting foot in the others' church' bomb.

As the marriage's roadblocks were wrecked one by one, Rosemary, dumbfounded, acknowledged only to herself that her endless reciting to young Oliver of 'Where there's a will, there's a way' had finally come to haunt her.

So, back to Oliver, who was calculating that his father must be nearly at the house and looking for parking. Briefly, he toyed with praying for the day's passing with no unpleasant incidents, only to brush the idea right off as taking the Lord's name in vain. Thanks to much effort, the now upright Oliver managed baby steps into the kitchen. Entirely confident that he wouldn't be able to keep down a bacon and egg sarnie, he turned on the cooker anyway. His dad could use fortification too.

On his path to the loo, Oliver intentionally avoided the unfriendly bathroom mirror. *This special day calls for routine change. I'll shave last.* A hot shower always does the trick. Relieved to discover a less-than-catastrophic image in the mirror, Oliver brushed his teeth twice. *No nicotine stains yet. Now's the time to ditch smoking*, he thought as he applied aftershave in abundance, a few extra drops inside each armpit.

Donning the perfectly fitting silver-grey suit over the bulletproof vest was the simplest task for him. Understandably, Oliver conceived it to be the protective armour to get him through the day. The final step, perfecting his silk cravat, corrected any remaining imperfections in his mood. Precisely at the moment that Oliver felt most pleased with his dignified appearance, his equally smartly attired father rang the doorbell.

Traffic cooperated with their short journey to the chapel at the City Hospital, mostly done in a father and son's understood silence. Thus, Oliver re-engaged with a question he frequently probed but remained short of a definitive answer.

Why have I chosen Maeve over anyone else?

Naturally, his supervisors had engaged in a similar interrogation.

Would our differences inevitably come between us?

Though Oliver's gaze revealed nothing, Edward was hardly blind to his boy's inner difficulties. Upon parking the vehicle, he said, "Wind and tide surprise. A firm hand on the tiller, that's all that's expected of you, son."

Bear with me as I deliver my private hypothesis as to why Oliver chose Maeve. A law-and-order lifestyle comes with a passion to serve, but also with a talent for boldness. Go right ahead with your justified critique. Indeed, that doesn't mean Oliver would wish more of the risky edge after hours. Matrimony outside the community was unpopular with most, to say the least, but unimaginable for an ambitious, or indeed any, RUC officer.

Yet, a job centred on survival trains one's mind for comfort in danger. It's part of Oliver's professional skillset to not know what he was looking for before he found it. From there, it's a shorter distance to self-licence experimentation with status quo disruption. Matching himself with the prevailing norms wouldn't have made someone like Oliver happy. Maeve did.

Seeing his best man Robert awaiting his arrival with four of his close friends turned Oliver's attention to logistics. All five, childhood mates big into rugby, who kept in touch despite diverging professional paths.

"Reliable lads," his dad noted approvingly, as Oliver considered that their fitness might come in handy if guest-escorting duties should require the use of strong-arm methods.

Weddings tend to be stressful, but to keep this one civil during historically sensitive times mandated quite the attention to detail. Don't get me wrong: inter-church cooperation was taking place during the Troubles. I always had my complement of good Samaritans offering pastoral care to share the burden of stress amongst individuals and churches. Yet, understandably, mixed-marriages never gained cross-Christian priority. Thus, the wedding ceremony kept the standard vows, but skipped the liturgical battle lines of a Nuptial Mass and Communion taking.

Right before Maeve walked up the aisle, escorted by her father, and driving all thought other than awe from his mind, Oliver had one final career flash.

Let Special Branch note all vehicle registrations. At least I got to earn the Queen's Police Medal. After today, zero chance of that. Yet, if there's ever peace, I may have just put myself in pole position for promotion. Aye, right.

The lights illuminated Maeve's beauty. But as she walked down the aisle, escorted by her father, the swirling murmurs quickly coalesced into one single gasp. Yes, the big day also revealed the big secret no longer hiding under Maeve's classic white gown.

As a visibly shrunken Lorcan stepped back from his daughter's side, Oliver entwined his fingers with her perspiring ones. The priest couldn't avoid the obvious contrast between the two men. Lorcan's sinking heart curtailed his regular height by three half centimetres, while Oliver appeared increasingly empowered by illegitimacy.

Given the charged atmosphere, the priest opted for the briefest welcome. He rushed as quickly as he could through all the preamble and prayers and straight to the big question – should this couple join together in holy matrimony? The universal response came as a combination of awkward silence with heavy breathing and meaningful coughs.

The marriage vows and exchange of rings followed. Maeve listened to the list of promises to 'love and honour (she insisted on 'obey' being deleted) ... through sickness and health ... for richer or poorer ... till death do us part, so help me God.' Her "I do" came in a trembling voice due partly to 'up-the-spout' symptoms (lightheadedness and nausea). But Maeve's facial expression was unequivocal in its statement: she was taking Oliver as her husband willingly and with a full heart.

When it was Oliver's turn, he welcomed the role with a short but unmistakable chuckle, puzzling the guests, but not me. I recognised his inner revelation: his wedding created a rare Troubles' consensus moment amongst those who are otherwise obsessed with the non-common ground.

And so, he made sure to plight his troth with a confidence. *They need to see it.* He, Oliver MacIntyre, as patriotic an RUC officer as ever was, intends to protect his family from hatred and bigotry from this day forward. Upon successfully completing his verbal duties, and almost before the priest had a chance to intone, "I now declare you man and wife—," Oliver enfolded Maeve. He swept her into the iconic pose renowned as the V-J Day Times' Square Celebration and planted his lips upon his new wife's to the faintest of spectators' cheers. Only then did the priest manage a belated "You may kiss the bride." This was a new twist even for this most progressive of clergymen.

Lorcan had started piling into the water of life before any food was served at the reception, though the majestic vomit climbing inside him had reasons other than the whiskey. He emptied himself straight into the nearest vase of roses with only minor thorn punctures. After tucking the floral arrangement under the white-clothed table, Lorcan felt his blood pressure subside, but nausea persisted. The lie is blown to pieces. Everyone knows RUC officers are on the guest list at this wedding. Now, everyone knows too that his daughter married a Peeler. And is pregnant.

"Look around you," he gurned to Father Joe, who came to console him. "I'm the picture of a buck eejit. The foolish oul' dad, joke of the day. While the pair – not a care in the world."

A compassionate clergyman, Father Joe placed his hand on Lorcan's shoulder. "God's wisdom mustn't be questioned. Confessionals are overflowing with fathers complaining about their daughters' choice of husbands."

Fine words, unhelpful to struggling Lorcan.

Mother of God, how could this be my daughter's wedding? It won't be enough that Ciaran is a no-show; how long will he need to be on the move thanks to this debacle?

Lorcan knew from the moment Maeve opened her eyes that his powers over her were on a dwindling course.

She was never as receptive to my counsel as her brothers.

Standing there, tormented by his only daughter's choices, helped Lorcan ignite one of his rarely performed soul-searching moments. *Centuries of Crown brutality; living through a class struggle and decade of repression, my flesh and blood delivers infiltration into the police's arms. She consumed countless Patrick Pearse quotes while being dandled on my knees. Yet, my offspring, in my lifetime, turns her back on her community and thwarts the dream.*

Subjective interpretation is a human activity. Adults never completely outgrow egocentrism either. If most people find it difficult to take another's perspective in everyday life, this wedding's circumstances presented archetypal mitigating factors. What's more, Lorcan, deep in bitterness and Oliver floating in bliss both, recognised the intensity of British Intelligence in the wedding's activity. Actually, Oliver was somewhat relieved to see them there to ensure his big day could proceed without incident.

That said, both men failed to probe the warranted – how could such a wedding ceremony proceed free of sabotage? The pragmatic reasons arrived years later, producing mini scandals as they came to light, and are best summarised by Napoleon: "A spy in the right place is worth 20,000 soldiers on the battlefield."

Indeed, the British forces positioned their most productive supergrass amongst the wedding guests in the form of none other than the prone-to-professional-discretion Father Joe. Shocked? Trust me, you are not alone, not in West Belfast. Especially not amongst some of those who, over the years, unloaded their sins onto him in the confessional.

Yet, intelligence gathering at that wedding went far beyond Father Joe's community of believers. The full extent of the Dirty War enterprise is still unveiling, so I'll avoid debates on its usefulness, or morality. My motive in raising it here is to remind you, dear reader, that espionage as a professional pursuit dates as far back as biblical Joshua.

All I know is that the MacIntyre-Donnelly day of union window-dressed one of the most successful undercover surveillance operations ever performed during my Troubles. Every strand of security surfaced at that event for a meticulous fact-finding mission. They all came as kitchen staff, busboys, the wedding photographer (otherwise specialising in mugshots), or posing as uni doormen and students in the area. RUC officers connecting with their regular informers, aye, but all other stakeholders found their way there too: MI5, GCHQ, SAS, UDR, Provisionals, along with INLA, southern volunteers, UVF and UDA. Retrospectively, a sample of the Irish Defence Forces may have enjoyed Queen's front lawn and quad that day too.

Together they spent large sums of British and Irish taxpayers' money bugging each other's vehicles, updating patrols; umpteen sources and handlers reconnecting. I am not exaggerating when I say the actual exchange of vows between Maeve and Oliver was the least exciting piece of information swapped that day.

Descriptions of 'fairytale wedding,' 'magical reception,' 'matchless atmosphere' and 'impressive venue' took on a whole new meaning in subsequent security-based conversations. During the anniversary years that came and passed, as Maeve and Oliver celebrated, I wept tears of joy and sorrow at the numerous lives saved as much as taken thanks to that event.

Decorated by silky, slinky and small nightwear, and sitting at the hotel room's dressing table, Maeve examined her newly dressed ring finger.

"Outstanding choice, Mrs MacIntyre," the unuttered line by each one of my ancestors.

So deep in her worries, Maeve missed Oliver's shower exit.

When will it blow up in our faces? This abandoning conformity may have been a step too far, even for you. There was the option of living together.

The flames on the candles decorating the newlyweds' suite fluttered as Oliver moved past them. His nakedness met the back of Maeve's neck.

"I am terrified, Oliver."

"Needless. A high-performing officer is looking after you."

But will you always be around, or will I have to raise this child alone in a council flat in West Belfast? Maeve didn't say, but he saw her fear in the mirror, and his eyes assured her he'd never bail out.

"Trailblazing is never easy. It's too late now, anyway." His mouth caressed her hair gently, taking in its floral scent and breathing out a crowd of kisses. "All being equal, the wedding night is a shared tradition."

Well, it's only respectful to end here.

CHAPTER 5

ENTRY POINTS

"DANIEL, WANNA BET YOU'LL thank me later, big time? Saint Patrick's Day coinciding with Passover – how lucky can you get?"

"Parades and marches – not my concept."

A caring girlfriend should better prep the meaning of a weekend on the Goldin's witness stand, beyond endorsing the blue-buttoned shirt as his outfit. Tamir's now regular household presence incapacitates this kind cousin of mine as guest decoy when the family meets Daniel. He hasn't a clue that his RSVP suspended all other invitations. Equally unaware of the express Scarsdale-Manhattan train, and that our home is walking distance to the station that would rescue him. I'll AirDrop him the Metro-North Harlem Line timetable. Binge-watching dysfunctional family shows could be another potentially helpful digestive for the food-factory Passover Seder.

"If you are that keen on compensating, Ella, a post-holiday blowjob would be the perfect ending."

"Before dismissing as an afterthought the world's best Saint Patrick's parade, please consider this naked truth: Passover limits alcohol to red wine, consumption is prolonged, structured in tiny sips. Wait. Hear me out. It's for your own good. The Goldins are close readers, so you'll experience a never-ending night. The search for solitude was never our strongest suit, but on Passover, we sit like sardines around the oval dining room table. You will be semiconscious with starvation by the time food reaches your mouth. And don't start me on the boredom of reading historical fiction that couldn't be any more foretold. I'm not kidding, Daniel. Be my guest. Laugh your heart out now, but by the time my family is through with you, you'll be begging for a dancing ten-foot, acid-green leprechaun."

"All right, Ella. This sounds like a reasonable compromise: 3:05 in Scarsdale gives sufficient window to detour and purchase some green post-Passover lingerie."

"I give up, and you've relinquished all claims for advanced warnings."

What happened to finding gutsy attractive? You should respect his choices to test his sense of humor's limits.

"So tell me, isn't St. Patrick's like the greatest Irish thing of the year?"

"It's not a national holiday."

How weird when the entire world insists on turning green.

"Not in Northern Ireland and not a holiday in the Mac-Intyre-Donnellys' repertoire."

Is that because he didn't grow up Catholic? He said he attended integrated schools. But don't Protestants and Catholic leaders make pilgrimage to the White House bearing shamrocks for the President on Paddy's Day?

"You see, one of Mum's brothers died on that day."

"I am so sorry. What happened?"

"Not entirely sure. It was before I was born. I never really inquired, and nobody provided a detailed briefing either."

Well, it would have been too good to be true for his family history to align precisely with your PhD needs.

"No point grieving. Giving certain holidays a miss when you are in a mixed family can sometimes be a cause for celebration."

"Speaking of family, you are tonight's star attraction. Nothing thrills my parents more than hosting non-Jews on Passover."

"Even as their daughter's boyfriend?"

"No exceptions! As long as culinary expectations are at a minimum. But I am done warning you about my family, remember?"

"Perhaps my lucky odds lie in ancestors that survived the Famine, eh?"

"Ella, check this out. Mom made green matzoh balls."

Oh, boy. Natasha only carries the lime-green trayful. Will Mom walk in next with green soup but dressed up as Elijah? For a goddess of first impressions, Natasha's green dress can't be a coincidence. And if she dared to claim it never crossed her mind, count on her Mark as your teasing envoy.

Daniel's performance deserves an Oscar. We're only two-thirds through, and this scary family already gave him a billion opportunities to freak out. Is there one topic they aren't keen to talk to him about? A shoo-in with Mom as soon as he noticed her birdfeeder and the daffodils she nurtures by the front door.

"Your landscaping brings the best of the Tudor-style out. And your attractive home needn't worry. I am half Protestant."

Mom should be the one continuing Daniel's drive through Scarsdale. His fascination with the area and the homes would cement her first impression of him.

"This place is amazing. Growing up here had to be a kids' paradise."

It'll be a win-win: Daniel's real-estate queries won't remain unanswered, and Mom is perfect for bringing his luxury-country-village perception back to earth, even inside her new Lexus.

Daniel cracked open far more than just Mom's shell. Just watch Natasha and Mark compete over their infatuation. How do I stop Grandma from forcing matzoh on the poor guy? If only Dad wasn't boastfully showing Daniel every treasured item in his living room's Menorah collection, we'd all be eating by now. They all opened up to him, and quicker than a cooked mussel. Forbidden culinary metaphors in the midst of a Passover dinner – is that kosher? All right, Daniel, I concur. You have earned my busy hand on your thigh. I can visit his crotch from time to time; no one at this table will stand soon, that's for sure – as long as he continues to align his smiles with the above-the-tablecloth conversation.

"It's the magical powers of parsley, Natasha. All credit to the Donahues. Running into them yesterday saved you from eating food coloring tonight."

Oh, no, health freak Daniel doesn't know she is joking. He'll now think that the mega-size *maror* scoop he slurped with the gefilte fish was sheer poison. As soon as Mom returns to the kitchen, I'll reassure him that *maror* is naturally horseradish red.

"If anyone runs into Jemma or Chris tomorrow, remember to thank them for the cooking tip."

"Only the Donahues, or was our holiday menu in the *Scarsdale Inquirer*, Mom?"

"Daniel, may I pour you some soup?"

"Yes, please, thank you, Susan. So what colour are these … balls … normally?"

"As pale as your girlfriend's face."

"Thanks, Mark. This is the precise point at every year's Seder dinner when it hits me: convincing my only sister to marry you – straight out of the Passover Miracles list."

Don't give me the look that kills, my dear brother-in-law. You know you brought it on yourself, giving me your word before the Seder. You promised that the stupidest family joke is out of this year's repertoire: why do we eat matzoh balls in chicken stock? Because fleeing Egypt, the Red Sea's salty waters reached the Israelites' balls. Who owns the last laugh now, Marky Mark?

Yes, me.

"The food is delicious, Susan."

"Two full refrigerators of everything, Daniel. Help yourself to seconds, sevenths, or twelfths of every dish."

"*Chag Pesach Same'ach*: happy holiday! With that, we have officially marked the end of the Passover Seder. Any first impressions you'd care to share, Daniel?"

"Really, Dad? Hasn't he suffered enough?"

"I'm grand. Loving the food and the company."

Daniel is the sexiest when he's kind.

"And compared to the Israelites, not suffering a bit!"

Remarkable: each family member is squarely in the 'falling for those who make *them* laugh' category. I expected less conformity, at least from Cousin Tamir, the Israeli Intelligence officer that he gloats about being.

"I do have a question, Adam, an utterly uninformed one if you have no objections."

"By all means, ask away, Daniel."

"This closing sentence we read: 'Next year in Jerusalem.' That's quite the urgent call—"

"Nailed it, man. Yes, longing for the Promised Land is more like on 'a need basis,' wouldn't you agree, Adam?"

"My generally wise son-in-law is right, overall."

Oh, boy. Dad is assuming his philosophical expression.

"Judaism is captivated with the future. Take the Messiah's arrival – it's a daily wish, with a 'one day' expectation."

Astonishing: Daniel is insatiably and genuinely intrigued by the sermon, beyond decoding that curiosity is the way to Dad's heart.

"But I would fine-tune: for pious Jews, Jerusalem is still very much the actual physical city in Israel."

"I think it may hold true for my MacIntyre grandparents, my Presbyterian side."

How prevalent are born-agains in Northern Ireland? Inside his family? If his grandparents are evangelicals, an agnostic grandson could be a challenge to accept. Is Daniel juggling more identity asks than I factored? It wouldn't hurt getting acquainted with more of the Judeo-Christian traditions in Northern Ireland before July. And you really should start discussing with Daniel where to stay in Belfast over the summer.

"The tendency to seek one's 'Jerusalem' is something you share with the English, I mean, I think, if I recall the words of *Jerusalem* correctly."

"You're absolutely right, Daniel. Thank you for the reminder; I forgot all about that hymn."

Look around you. You are the only one contradicting the group's spiritual tangent. Mom calls Passover 'Jewish psychotherapy' thanks to all its 'why' questions. But the engrossed-in-conversation non-Jew gulps every second of this. Not even slightly nervous about potential comparisons to the Passover's Fourth Son who doesn't know how to ask. Maybe we aren't as singular as we make ourselves out to be, and Daniel's family actually shares our 'Probe to Deepen your Life' family manual? July cannot get here fast enough.

He's asking again: "So, what is the modern Jewish approach for this Jerusalem call to action?"

Dad is so happy to answer, of course.

"For me, the Haggadah, this Passover text, messages the idea of change. Nothing in life is static. Everyone possesses a chance to come out of a personal Egypt."

Natasha is eager to interject. "Dad, you'll remember that Daniel studies architecture. He might be interested in the section on the temple plans."

"Thanks very much, sis. Let's all be reminded that it's Passover, not Halloween, and do our best to spook my boyfriend a little less."

Another year of not overcoming overeating. If Daniel sur-vives tonight's heartburn, he'll manage tomorrow's matzoh brei breakfast.

"Are you peeking into my old drawers, Daniel?"

"Guilty as charged."

Funny how Mom never repurposed my bedroom. Unless I'd insisted on repainting, we would be sleeping in nursery pink. True, the larger-than-the-Hampton-Inn guest room is more than sufficient for their entertaining purposes. But Tamir occupies it regularly now, so she really should start doing something with this bedroom. Maybe my frequent visits make Mom think re-modeling is premature. But even Natasha and Mark, who are here much less, still retire in a room redolent of her person-al history and teenage tastes. Mom is taking 'you'll never lose your place in this family' pretty far, so be more grateful for your emergency returns shelter.

"Just ensuring you haven't edited your childhood because I was coming."

"Why, would you be doing it?"

"Perhaps. You never said you were a debate champion."

Is there anyone in Scarsdale High School who isn't? How would we be a pipeline to the Ivies without it? The trophies look shinier than usual. Did Mom ask the cleaning service to declutter the bookshelf too? *I, Claudius* is still here. They know the Thomas Hardys are immovable.

"I had a serious Escher phase around the same time back in high school."

Is that why I love Daniel's restless doodling? Wow. Could it be eleven years since I bought this Escher poster in The Hague? Nothing captured better that unsurpassed winning feeling in that tournament, where your debating skills felt as boundless as his art.

"I like your family. They are great. So open."

"I like them too, most of the time. But wait. Don't tell me you were a little nervous? What did you expect?"

"No preconceptions."

That's still better than the alternative of him expecting something that wasn't.

"It's nice to see you around them. How you get on."

Could you have chosen a lovelier boyfriend?

"Your father, he's not a fan of one-sentence answers. I guess that was unexpected ... I mean, him being an editor."

"That's so true! I've never thought of it that way." You love that he's protective of you. You adore that he listens and asks for your advice. Be that as it may, it's Daniel's unanticipated observations that blow your mind.

"And the holiday celebration was a nice surprise too. You Jews are interesting people, if a wee bit pretentious coming up with an annual read all about yourselves. Definitely more cerebral than dying rivers green and getting steaming drunk."

"Trust me; there is no shortage of self-congratulatory male-inscribed texts in our tradition. But they are no match for the less pious acts performed by Jewish women. I'll devoutly show you if you join me here in bed."

"Pushkin never welcomes my 'good morning, boy' with this tail-wagging level."

Dad seeks company, and Daniel deep sleeps upstairs. Sunny stroll? Why not? Daniel won't lose his way among his last night's admirers, and you've been missing the Bronx River path.

"Must be the setter's thanks for a fellow Irish visitor. Nifty new harness. Splurging on dog accessories?"

"Insignificant to your inheritance. He's started pulling lately. Chasing cyclists too. See?"

I do; that was quite a yank at my arm. What is that nosy pup smelling in the Donahues' bushes?

"Excellent counter pull. Keep it up."

Good, loose lead is much better. "Come, boy. So, Pushkin tells me he loves the longer walks."

"Hippocratic conspiracy orchestrated by your mother with both our doctors."

Pushkin had become quite the food beggar. He needs these walks more than Dad.

"Straight-shooting here – is Daniel long-term?"

So, the walk has a talk agenda. Farewell to 'bringing someone along liberates you from the dating questionnaire.' But Dad as leading inquisitor isn't the natural tribunal. I must have said or signaled something different last night that he and Mom discussed after the Seder. Your Monday therapy session just earned its first item.

"Why, Dad? Would you like it to be?"

This is a long pause, even by Adam Goldin's standards. Hmmm. With Mom's hand so visible, he's lost namesake's bragging rights with Adam Smith. It's pathetic how his self-selected Eve, known as Mom, teleoperates Dad. Why did he agree to take this on? On the bright side, a twitching Dad channeling Mom spices up this mini-workout. Sunny and seventy degrees could bring us all the way to Bronxville. Too bad I didn't think to grab coffee at Martine's while we passed through town.

"A blended relationship mandates open eyes."

"Every relationship is, by definition, blended: two people uniting, isn't it?"

"Well said, and, as always, splendidly thoughtful. But, among the rare effective parenting consensuses with Mom, we like offering you, and Natasha, the long-term perspective. I only ask you to recognize that forces of tradition press harder when different cultures are involved, that's all."

That's all? What the fuck? If I post a clip of this editor's squirms, it'll go viral among rejected writers. "Would bringing a

Chabad Lubavitcher from Brooklyn last night fare any better on your compatibility scale?"

"There's no need to get upset, Ella."

"Feels like there should be."

"It delights us to see you happy. Raising your eyebrow won't help with wrinkles. You know that I mean it."

Do I, or should I start a stress-reducing technique?

"I'm way ahead of you in the life cycle, so I can tell you of countless times I experienced the inability to anticipate the future."

Isn't he contradicting himself, then?

"My small ask is that you won't underestimate the kinship of a tribe."

Small ask? Is this my father? Unless parsley wasn't the sole new ingredient in last night's matzoh balls.

"A relationship with different cultures is like a ménage à trois. The third partner is the realization that you have been molded by a different soundbox."

I am not even going to start arguing with him about his metaphors that sound mixed to me. But it isn't like me to miss my father's progression into the fanatic that he never was. Maybe age is getting to them? I can envision grumpier, hunched, but medieval Jews?

"Pulling to the middle comes easier within the Jewish spectrum. Just bear in mind that a path with Daniel is bound for unsteadiness."

"Kudos, Dad. Preaching, with Thomas Hardy."

"I don't mean to preach. What did you have in mind?"

Misjudged yet again. Somehow, I thought that he also knows *Far from the Madding Crowd* by heart.

"Ah. You meant Bathsheba's preference for 'steady in a wild way' over 'wild in a steady way.'"

Thank goodness dementia isn't on the horizon just yet. He

does have Grandma's genes.

"Though, her love life might not merit emulating. The difference between wild and feral is oftentimes blurry. Pushkin will pull again as soon as the footbridge is in sight."

Am I shocked to the point of hallucinating my father's terrible love-counseling? Cheap blows like 'you are turning into Grandma' are needless when all this could be killed through his self-proclaimed progressiveness.

"Let's be clear; I feel ridiculous entertaining thoughts of crossing that mental bridge this early. But because you insist, how about approaching my potential union with Daniel as seasoning for the Goldin family tree?"

Good, we're now even with shockers.

"We won't be the first Jews to bring outsiders in." Infuriation aside, I must admit that a startled Dad is a funny sight.

"No need to overreact."

Speak to yourself, and for yourself, Dad.

"I only intended for you to make the mental note that a non-Jewish partner arrives with a burden of transmitting the Jewish dimensions by yourself. Hymns, holiday scents – they won't mean to Daniel what they mean for you."

You can afford generosity over the last word when his arm on your back is a ceasefire. Let Dad interpret your silence any way he likes. You'll archive this entire proselytizing conversation as the first-of-its-kind post-Passover hangover and sugar overdose caused by Manischewitz.

Of course, Mom is putting Daniel to work.

"Yes, all these wine glasses live in the three empty shelves in the glass cabinet over on Tamir's right. As close together as buttons on a keyboard; that's the only way they'll all fit back in."

"Mom isn't the Scarsdale Police, Daniel. Hands-on activity is synonymous with affection."

"Sure. I offered to help tidy up."

"I can help too."

"Too late. Daniel and Tamir smashed every post-Passover clean-up record."

They do resemble synchronized skaters reinstating the dishes.

"Boys, you are dismissed with gratitude."

Siamese twins in their grey Nike and navy running outfits too. But while Tamir is tan, Daniel is blue-white.

"We're away out. Tamir and I are doing the tour of Scarsdale's poshest bits."

"To see the real mansions, run up Heathcote Road. Or if you don't want to get lost, the high school track is five minutes from here."

He isn't leaving here without a kiss goodbye.

"Mom, you know, I was a tad disappointed."

"Again? What was it now?"

"I'm not saying that the psychology of diplomacy can't assist, but sending Dad, really?"

"Sorry. I like Daniel. A lot. Dad's anxieties are his own."

She's serious. Don't over-delight. Freud didn't care for religion either.

"Ready for a bigger surprise? Choosing Daniel would require you to actively choose Judaism, which couldn't be said of any of us."

See: Mom didn't waste a minute figuring it all out.

"The way I view it, Ella, you are the true hope of Jewish survival."

"You make it sound like it's the mark of Cain. No – *The Scarlet Letter* is probably a better analogy."

"Credit should be given to Orthodox chauvinism's crystal bowl. They knew we'd do the better job of ensuring generations to come and placed the passing of Judaism in matrilineal descent."

Of course, Allport and Jung, her beloved Frankl, but also Maslow – all were kinder to the religious experience than Freud. But that isn't the explanation. Mom's Jewish identity is, always was, secular Zionism.

"Mom, why would you think I'd grow to care about something I couldn't care any less about now?"

"Let's not go overboard. Hard to foresee you venturing into Maimonides. But Judaism reforms all the time, and it's far beyond overdue for the female voice to take the lead. Close your mouth, Ella, unless your stomach craves a mosquito or two. It's spring already, and coming in, you left the screen door open, as always."

＊＊＊＊

UNDENIABLY MY OWN wee microcosm, isn't he? Daniel is both communities and neither.

A thousand apologies, I know I promised to delegate. But I held as long as I could with the story of Daniel's arrival. You see, throughout Maeve's pregnancy, I felt I was pregnant with Daniel myself.

How could I not? Following years of life-taking conflict, this new-life miracle would stare directly into my existential dilemma. So, whereas many experts ponder how a family conflict influences a child, I couldn't wait to see how Daniel's birth would influence the family conflict. Born to the combination of his singular parents: what about him wouldn't be a Hollywood thriller?

Well, our Daniel's original emergence didn't disappoint.

As Maeve manoeuvred her ivory Ford Escort away from the crowds building up in my city centre, the labour's process building through her body accelerated awareness.

It's a fortnight too early! (By my calculations, her dates were off). *What's your rush? Your dad and I have complicated your life enough, without choosing 12th July as your birthdate.*

Legit contemplation, given our diverging reading of the 1690 Battle of the Boyne. Oliver wasn't around, naturally. During these years, flashpoints flared for about a week on both sides of the bonfires and parades. His work rota wouldn't permit a phone call, not to mention a quick dash home in between shifts.

The prospect of all that danger and overtime's double pay isn't as attractive now, Maeve admitted to her almost-born, while struggling to navigate away from the parade route.

Wonder why she hasn't used a taxi? Well, you try getting one around there, on that day, in my 1990s. Labour surprises, hence, forces people to buck the norms and to find themselves doing unexpected things.

For the first time in anyone's memory, Eileen and Lorcan endured the entire July in Belfast in place of the customary fort-night's escape to Donegal. No explanation offered, nor needed. The elder Donnellys didn't argue, at least not with Maeve, over her heel-digging. She stayed the Eleventh Night at the terraced house just off the Lisburn Road in place of their Colinward Street home.

Everyone says first babies are always late. Besides, sleep is difficult enough as it is. I want to get what I can in my own bed. Of course I have numbers to ring in South Belfast.

Eileen's tongue-holding surrendered in a single, soft-spoken, "putting your stubbornness on sale would have made the Don-nellys richer than the Guinness family."

Overnight, cramping concerned Maeve. So too, whether her belly muffled for her baby the roars of "fuck the Pope" drifting in through her open window on that muggy night. By morning, abdominal pressure spelt it was time: clear even for a woman on her first birth. *Will there ever be as many pontiffs as their curses last night?* was the thought subverting Maeve's momentary attention.

Lucklessly, she confused one roundabout for another, and, making the wrong turn from Tate's Avenue, Maeve veered straight into a dense neighbourhood celebration of Loyalist culture.

Wanting her life's plan to work, Maeve tried unhelpful soothing.

You've got time. The waters haven't broken. Donnellys always run late. Thirty hours of labour with me almost killed off Mum.

The ghetto blasters were thudding The Sash; Union Jacks displayed all over. In a crowd dressed for the day, Maeve became optically confused, seeing only red, white and blue. None of the breathing techniques from the antenatal classes seemed to help, but Maeve's (inaccurate) counting of the gap in between contractions bolstered her confidence.

They're still half-pissed since last night's bonfires!

Maeve's adrenaline supply wasn't giving up, notwithstanding excruciating abdominal pain.

For fuck's sake, I can't let a crowd of Orangies stop me from getting to the Royal.

Her entire family was born in the Royal's maternity unit, and Maeve was determined to facilitate that entry-level clan eligibility for her children. She spotted a passing RUC mobile patrol operating out of the Lisburn Road station.

As soon as I mention Oliver's name, they'll help.

But the pain paralysed her.

No! Please, baby. Don't push. Not so fast. I want your Daddy to be there with us.

A stab overwhelmed her stomach. Maeve's face tensed in convulsion, and blackness overtook her mind.

At 12:45pm, Oliver caught a transmission on the police radio from the city's Village area: "Female motorist, semiconscious, in advanced labour suffered minor collision injuries with a large wheelie bin. Due to the ongoing incident at the Royal, an ambulance is transferring her to Belfast City Hospital."

Oliver wondered how a love for Ulster could surpass maternal responsibilities. *That hormonally bewildered Loyalist should thank her lucky stars to have our seasoned rescue team on hand.*

Maeve didn't need to elevate her eyelids to detect the parental assembly in the post-natal ward. She continued to feel groggy and drained from her ordeal and the painkillers, but the heaviness of her plaster-casted right shin returned her to consciousness. So did the sensation from the lightning-shaped red scrape decorating her left cheek.

"They said they'd reduce the painkillers."

Oliver was by her side, topping up the glass of Lucozade she'd incessantly consumed since the emergency caesarean the day before. The besotted grandparents, who hardly spoke to each other at the wedding, marvelled at the wee wonder – first grandchild for both sides.

"Och, such a totey wee man!"

"Wouldn't you just run away with him?"

And such like, until the baby started to fuss, triggering a nurse approaching the cubicle to lift him from his cot and soothe him.

"Quite the tale your family will get to tell your beautiful boy someday. But it's feeding time now. Mum and baby need privacy."

Maeve's eyes signalled Oliver to escort the two sets of parents out. He'd be more useful in the corridor umpiring the baby-oriented détente. "I'll call if I need you."

The nurse drew the curtain around Maeve's cubicle. "There's your hungry wee man. Think you can manage?"

Given her condition and the fact that she was a new mum, the nurses checked on Maeve frequently.

"Just give me a shout if you have any difficulties." The midwife dexterously fixed a pillow over Maeve's incisions and placed the baby on her chest. Maeve made eye contact with her pale, wrinkle-faced mini-man. His intense stare stimulated her smile, and she gently moved back his tiny blanket to rediscover the teeny clenched fists.

"My baby, my son; *my* precious boy." Whispering, she pressed her child to her engorged breast, and the hungry infant latched on almost immediately.

After an initial nipple pinch, Maeve's body felt soothed by the bliss of meeting her baby's needs. The receding breast fullness helped Maeve divert her attention to the conversation going on out in the corridor between her mum and Rosemary.

Yes, those two new grandmothers were in uncharted waters, but the duty to help out called.

"Oliver must have a month's worth of messages from Supermac stockpiled and won't have a baldy what to do with any of that food." Maeve heard Rosemary say, as her mother replied, "It's no bother for me to cook up some dinners for them. Stew, maybe a nice piece of ham."

And Rosemary agreed, offering to make a steak and onion pie (Oliver's favourite), litres of potato and leek soup and her lemon traybakes.

Culinary arms race.

The fathers had greater struggles with common ground. Walking the labyrinth of conversational banalities, they agreed the baby was a fine strapping lad. Neither could wait for the bell to signal the end of visiting hours.

Everybody wished to avoid the hazards of the volatile situation. These were my early days of scouting peace; a time of some tentative ceasefires. My Belfast was opening up, and nightlife was a possibility. I seemed almost normal!

The National Question – that is, whether I would remain part of the United Kingdom or unify with the Republic of Ireland – was being actively deliberated behind closed doors. At that point (and to this day, actually), specifics were still up in the air.

So, for many people, had I been a normal society, these then groundbreaking political developments would have been the 'go-to' conversation subject next. Especially when personal issues of Daniel's baptism and education were on the table. Instead, the uncomfortable but civil conversation between Lorcan and Edward subsided, and the two men became lost in their thoughts.

When Maeve and Oliver chose to live in South Belfast, Lorcan counted on the upright Catholic St. Bride's School to keep the faith strong in his grandchildren. But after overhearing Maeve mentioning Lagan College to Eileen, the prospect of a grandson emerging from an integrated school mortified him.

Earlier that afternoon, on the walk to the hospital, he griped to Eileen: "You heard Father Joe about Lagan College: creeping Unionism."

"Five Gaelic phrases and you're the Minister for the Gaeltacht," she returned. "Would you ever stop giving off? Leave the poor girl be."

Keeping the uncomfortable silence didn't negate Lorcan from indulging in self-pity concerning his co-grandfather.

Sharing his name with the Father of Unionism, Edward Carson. I'm astounded that Carson even tolerated the word 'Ireland' remaining when this place was created.

Lorcan's point punched my own soft belly over the polarising powers of my given name. For Catholics, I am the North, or six counties. Over the years, some have gotten used to my given name as an unideal compromise, a neutral option.

Yet, retrospectively, I ridicule myself for periodically toying with a name change. Futile torments they were, for the simple reason that my afflicting label proved a teeming fountain of lifelong personal friendships with other anguished lands. My dearest mentor South Africa – there's a no-brainer. But loads of lands labelled with cardinal directions became my dearest friends as they, too, were homes to humans fiercely rowing over national paths. Remember East and West Germany? The two Koreas to this day?

There are more examples, of course, but I am digressing from Edward and Lorcan, who, in that corridor, looked like patients en route to open-heart surgery.

As a senior member of his local Orange lodge (marching the day before), Edward felt humiliated by his new grandson's potential proximity to the IRA. *Rivers of bloodshed, not an inch towards that United Ireland, yet they refuse to accept that the United Kingdom is unbreakable.* A Bible reader, he was terrified about letting his new grandson walk the desert of disbelief. *A baby can't be choosing his destiny*, Edward thought. *If something happens to Oliver, or they split up, his Catholic credentials will airlift the bairn straight onto the Falls Road.*

Oliver saw the mothers absorbed in food and baby needs, the fathers embracing silence. He counted on the baby truce to last the quick duration of his visit to the loo, especially given the public location.

They all saw him walking back slowly. A little lad, five at most, dressed in his Manchester United football kit, right down to the matching red socks, was ahead of him in the corridor. The boy's grandad held his right hand as the lad hugged a new football, probably a gift for his baby brother.

"Sports could be tricky."

Catching Lorcan's comment, Oliver's anxieties broke loose. *Everywhere else, sports bring people together; only here, we let it shackle us to a bitter past. Why can't they bloody grasp that neither of us intends to turn? Cold War ended, Germany unified, Oslo Agreement signed. Why does it take so long to create common grounds over here?*

Audibly, Oliver uttered, "That's a long way off. Six years at least."

"Don't bury your head in the sand. If you don't, society will make judgments for your ch—"

"Lorcan, you promised!" his wife interrupted, saddened that her husband would never be a Solomon. "Make yourself useful and bring the car round while I say cheerio to the wean ... and Maeve."

"Go in too, Mum," Oliver said, taking Rosemary by the elbow.

Eileen and Rosemary's entrance coincided perfectly with the end of Maeve's nursing.

"Your two grannies are partners in crime, Daniel."

Maeve searched and found the healthy sadness in her mother's eyes.

Eileen knew. *She couldn't go as far as naming him Declan, but she memorialised her brother with the 'D'. She listened when I told her, your brother won't be remembered if we won't put in the effort.*

Tears sprang up in Rosemary's eyes too, but for different reasons. *Daniel MacIntyre, born on the Twelfth – a child who chooses well!* But aloud, she only said, "Daniel! What a proud, solid, biblical name."

Maeve beamed with love and pride as she gazed into the infant's eyes. "He's perfect, and growing up in this lion's den, Daniel will need God's help, from wherever source it comes."

Ad infinitum, mothers know best.

BOOK TWO

CHAPTER 6

CHASING CURIOSITY

LANDING, AT LAST! "Daniel, what do you think of 'Into the land of a hundred thousand welcomes'? Is it catchy enough to kick off my beautiful new travelogue?"

"Please tell me the cliché is attributable to apprehension?"

Is the negativity because you are as nervous, Daniel?

"You'll have to experience your first romantic vision solo from the slow lane because I've got an Irish passport. See you on the other side."

Don't overthink this. Chaperoning his girlfriend straight into his family's arms entitles Daniel to shared stress. Now that he's Scarsdale's honorary citizen, it's easy to forget your own nerves back at Passover. He thoughtfully gifted you this gorgeous leather-bound notebook to serve as a journal/travelogue, inscribing it with *Some thoughts are better handwritten. Your Daniel.* No, it isn't counterproductive to over-romanticize Ireland. If not for explorers' fantasies, half of this planet would have persisted undiscovered. Mild arrival-phobia is fine; overwhelming hysteria, inappropriate. A PhD expedition acquainting you with an earlier Daniel requires much less of you than the astronauts currently traveling through humanity's last frontier.

"When I left for America, Dad made me recite Dickens: *'I am disappointed. This is not the Republic I came to see. This is not the Republic of my imagination.'"*

"Another fine example of Dickens' wild imagination."

See: he's never stopped finding you funny. And he's told you a million times over how much he loves that you make him laugh.

"Misperceptions are a rich slice of the local humour."

Nice of him to keep me posted. Count blessings and ignore illusionary fears. This *is* a soft landing – five weeks in long-sought Northern Ireland complete with matchless fieldwork edge supplied by your cross-communal, super-sexy boyfriend. How is confidence not topping any other brain activity?

"So, your dad's a police official with a secretive bookish side?"

"C'mon, Ella."

"You c'mon. Be nice. Fill me in on *something* about what's ahead."

"Stop. You're being a melter. Your surprise was one of my plotted pleasures. All right, all right, if you give me back my elbow, I'll reveal this much: it's a dead cert Mum will be waiting for us at the Europa Buscentre. One of her life's mottos is 'It's better to turn up two hours late than two minutes, because then one had a reason.'"

Why wouldn't Dublin Airport be indistinguishable from other airports? JFK and LaGuardia have the same fuel-emission scent. An extreme fantasizer would expect a countryside aroma or sea air to welcome them in this arrivals hall. But you would find such a sensory experience schmaltzy, right?

"It's chilly out here."

"Take my jacket. A typical early July morning. It'll soon warm up, all the way to a balmy Irish summer of, oh, about twenty degrees. Celsius. On a good day."

The Belfast bus, finally!

"Got your wee tickets? C'mon ahead." Friendly woman driver with a *very* strong accent.

After sleeping through an entire transatlantic flight, how is Daniel so exhausted? We're barely ten minutes on the road, and everyone all around you snoozes. So much for your plans to earwig Northern Irish conversations. Fingers crossed the bus driver shares your vigilance. Well, at least all of us are participating together in the perfect shelter from this eager rain. Let's hope Zeus collaborates and stops this flood as we approach Northern Ireland.

Hmmm, distance is in kilometers over here, not miles. If only America gave up world defection, you could decipher what '*Belfast 145km*' means for the road ahead. Sleeping Beauty next to you promised that green mountains would replace this flat road after the bus passes Dundalk. Your geographical grasp even sneaked in a cameo that impressed him before he drifted off.

"El Paso is a helpful analogy, Daniel, though I know enough of the Troubles to call it Bandit Country."

"I think smuggling predated the Troubles, but you are absolutely spot on; war redefined 'wild' in that Wild West."

And what's to complain about now that your itinerary gained a guided tour? "Sure. We'll try to organise a tour. If not before I leave for Cambridge, maybe one of the Donnellys? They know the area better than me."

Camera setting should be on 'Burst' after Mom's warning text greeted your landing.

Do what you need with Prof. Rubinstein. As a Goldin, you are our imagination for that land ♥.

With a sister who is the next best thing to being anywhere on the globe, this might be your single chance as the family's documentarian.

Yippee! '*Welcome to* ~~Northern~~ *Ireland. Speed limit in miles per hour.*' Distance to Belfast in miles too. Your orientation problem is solved, even if politically motivated paint bombing of a traffic sign wouldn't be the standard tourist welcome.

Wow, this is a plant universe, exactly as promised – a love affair with every shade of green! iPhone photography isn't reproducing the vivid verdant hues of this meadow. 'Live' camera mode isn't capturing the scenery either. In the city, umbrellas would create helpful photoshoot focal points, but what are these faraway dots anyway? Cows ... no, sheep. Horses? Who could reach animals grazing so far up? How are they brought back from such a distance? Noise pollution – another unlikely city issue for this energetic grassland.

Maybe video taking through the water droplets on the bus window could give a little perspective to the depth of this infinite horizon. Good, 'Landscape' mode doesn't blur the grass as much. Light isn't great, but in this sun-rain interactivity, I should watch for rainbows. That would make the overused Ireland's cliché a sign that you aren't overly starry-eyed about this trip.

Oops, low battery. Time for a new activity. It'll take Daniel longer than the next hour to resume consciousness. What should you do? Writing in your travelogue could usher motion sickness. But the 'plausible scenarios' internal monologue is something you normally enjoy. Toot your own horn as Option One. Daniel's folks could fall madly in love with you. Sure, they seem sort of helicopter parents; they couldn't wait for his return, but that's normal, and they were always friendly on FaceTime. It's unavoidable that some comparison to former girlfriends would take place. With that impending welcome, you'll sustain positivity by enunciating the gratitude they deserve for making Daniel.

The cashier in Cape Cod praised the Magritte enamel brooches for his mom and the Dalí melting-style alarm clock for his dad. Daniel concurred. Natasha wanted the same gifts for Rosh

Hashanah this year for her and Mark. There's no better seal of approval.

Option Two. The 'divided-on-affection' approach to our relationship, by definition, puts one of Daniel's parents on your side. Your own dad gifted you with a head start on this one. Piece of cake.

Option Three is to recognize that *both* parents could be wary. You could be the American girlfriend provoking the fear of an only child's potential immigration. True, Daniel once said, "My Granny's favourite Irish adage was *Nil aon leigheas ar an ngra ach posadh* – the only cure for love is marriage." Surely, they must know about their son's attitude to institutions and conventions. However, they may be unaware that we are yet to sing any happily-ever-after tunes. And they did get married, and Catholic Maeve did take Protestant MacIntyre as her last name.

If ambivalence is the case, ignorance is bliss, and you'll embrace the mental coma of no inquiries over what his parents think of you. It won't be unprecedented. Daniel never asked you what Mom and Dad thought of him.

"Rise and shine, Ella. The bus stops round the corner."

Yay. Belfast isn't raining. "That's your mom."

"Aye."

Video chats don't do her justice. I should be so lucky to showcase such three-dimensional hotness in my early fifties. Or is she younger? Never mind that, it's positive psychology that you need to keep up to help her like you. And she deserves applause on the edgy yellow in a layered dress. The short brown hair and sexy long legs make her the sunflower of this gloom-stricken street. There must be quite the look-at-me office dress code at the Human Rights Commission. Hang on. She had to take the day off. Even if it isn't warmer here than in Dublin, you didn't schlepp all the way to Burlington Mall to buy this copper top for nothing.

"Here, put your jacket back in your backpack. You're turning out to be a clone of your mother."

"So I'm told, by Mum's side. Dad's side doesn't seem to notice."

Oh, she spotted us. And she's excited. Her heart must be jumping too.

It's natural for her to go for his tight embrace first.

"Check out the longer hair! Suits you, son."

I agree. Bizarre first words, but his presence makes her really happy. Proper French manicure for the classy sapphire ring on the right hand. I hope her squeeze isn't blocking the blood flow to Daniel's arm.

"Looking well yourself, Mum. Pleased to see you're starting to dress down."

Playful vibe between them. Definitely La Vie Est Belle sprayed all over her 5'9 feet towering over you. Too bad I didn't know that when Macy's had its 'spend over $35 Lancôme Gift' back in May. Unless it's fillers or a facelift, she'll have superb advice on skincare and exercise.

"What a delight to finally meet you in real life, Ella."

She may be a germaphobe, or perhaps gripping onto Daniel makes her unable to embrace you, but this is a genuine smile. "A pleasure indeed, Mrs MacIntyre."

"Christian names dropped into the Atlantic mid-flight?"

Is that the same as a first name? Must be. I don't think I ever called her Maeve. Maybe I never needed to. Two minutes in Belfast, and progress is already evident.

"I got a parking spot nearby. Ella, let me help you with your bags. We'll miss the rain if we hurry."

"Where's Da?"

"Headquarters summoned. You wouldn't expect that to change over a year."

"You upgraded your motor. Niiiice."

"Aye. Splashed out on a new Audi. Because I'm worth it.

You're on the insurance, so you can give it a spin. Ella, sit in the front."

"Are you sure?" Stop wasting energy on insecurity. She isn't fake-nice, and she's entitled to feel nervous too.

How did it get to 6pm? I have news for the moron who claimed it's hard to fall asleep far away from home. Oh, God, what if jet lag made me snore right here in this study? Clearly, zero effect to the British/Irish coffee Maeve served upon arrival. But even with the mishap of mistakenly assuming they have a disposal in the kitchen sink, Maeve appreciated your help with the post-meal dishes. That unlocks huge prospects for fixing potential transgressions with your lemon chicken and orange lentils. No. It'll be better to start with the Mediterranean lamb, your signature seduction dish. There's nothing Daniel loves more, and shopping for ingredients will bring you sooner to St. George's Market.

A home displaying the patriarch's medals and plaques of honor in the study should appreciate the Goldins' kitchen military training. But the 'guest' category in this South Belfast house won't include you for much longer.

This isn't a tiny house, even as half the square feet of your home. For a city home, it easily swallows Natasha and Mark's Georgetown townhouse. Beacon Hill presses together English-style brownstones that cost a fortune. The open kitchen and dining space isn't small at all. Joining your Costco run, Daniel already decoded that the size of American houses and lawns shocks Europeans. As do portion sizes for baked goods. He halves the sugar in his delicious brownies because "America supersizes everything." Anyway, forget real estate assessment and move to things you are better at: personalities.

Performing interior decorating, whoever placed this modern navy-blue sectional made the library this study's focal point. Overwhelmed by chatter won't be this room's first impression, unlike the Goldin's family room where furniture facing each other serves that purpose. Here tidiness takes the lead, so how did Maeve and Oliver tolerate Daniel's scattered clothes all over the floor? Love, just like you. Interesting: the books are arranged alphabetically, the shelves separate fiction from non-fiction, and all of Oliver's police awards are in the non-fiction half—

"Hello, sexy snoozer. Looking for a book?"

With so many, it's going to be a tough choice. Daniel showered and changed to an ironed blue shirt. That's a going-out cue. Maybe keep the leggings ... but he ditched the sneakers, so maybe not. A bedazzling refresher might be the way to go. You could ask him—

Uh-oh, this ginger-haired guy who just bounced in will haunt Daniel straight to the ground.

"What about you, big man?"

"Shite, Michael! You scared the fuck out of me."

"Hey, Ella. Remember me?"

"How could I forget you, Michael?" Though he has ditched the soul patch, and the glasses.

"So, are we all good to go?"

Not before I shower and change.

"There's a gaggle of groupies been missing this man here. Haven't the wit to know better."

Okay, fast thinking: the white skirt, magenta sleeveless top, turquoise choker, over-the-knee black boots because you don't know the distance you'll be walking tonight. No A/C inside. But the outdoor temperature? The sheer black jacket should be at the bottom of the suitcase; take it just in case. Stud golden triangle earrings are fine where they are. Daniel will be happy you're seen wearing his gift, and it's more important to focus on make-up and hair. Shit, this will take a while. Oh well, Daniel and Michael's friendship could use the extra time.

"What kept yous? About time!"

So, the rowdiest bunch in the pub is Daniel's social bubble. Aaron, no, that was Jonny, or was it Will? Not the slightest chance I'll ever recall this shooting range of names. Except Hannah – cannibalizing hazel eyes independent of the overdone eyeliner. Unable to match the right foundation to her skin tone, yet awfully friendly to Daniel despite being invisible in his stories. But if his mortified reaction to her far-too-long embrace is anything to go by, Hannah won't be the name to memorize. If you have to talk to her, flattering her glossy black hair would be friendly. Crap! She caught you staring. Smile in a way that won't disclose she educated you on why masks were obligatory for executioners.

"Let me get this round in." Michael's voice is strong enough to shout over the throng. "What do you fancy, Ella? This pub is famous for its gin selection. Some decent local artisanal varieties. Or a cocktail, perhaps? Go mad."

"It's on my itinerary to test whether Guinness tastes better in Ireland."

"Some would argue this isn't Ireland."

Excellent start. Your boyfriend's best friend is now convinced you are the American tourist joke. Even a casual drinker knows a trendy bar will feature microbrews.

"There is a local craft beer called Titanic Town; want to sink this one?"

"Thanks for not laughing at my unoriginality."

A new round already? You haven't even started to decipher the local protocol. Sober, all this joking and teasing is out of your league. Nine months with Daniel wasn't long enough for the speed of this ball-hopping conversation. The loud music is no help with comprehension abilities either. But Daniel is too busy in conversation to notice your 'help' look. At least Hannah is off his radar. Impossible to refuse the approaching round. Maybe a highball? Heavy on the ginger ale and lighter on the vodka? A glass in hand is helpful to uncross arms.

"Game of pool, Ella?"

Michael has sensed I'm floundering. And he remembers I play. His list of best attributes is longer than friendliest and most observant then. Rescuer, calming, a head above Daniel, who is oblivious but at least enjoys his natural element.

Doesn't look like Michael is dating anyone from the group. Reasonable assumption, though, that he's having sex with women.

"There's a game area upstairs."

You want Michael to continue to like you. It's too early to suggest that regrowing the beard would add definition to his rounded face.

"Stairs are at the back."

"Thanks for suggesting we head up here. I was a little out of my depth."

"Early days. You'll be grand. How long will you be around?"

Maybe Daniel shared and Michael simply forgot? He's as popular up here as he was downstairs. You can't expect him to keep track of every piece of information he hears. It's the better option than Daniel briefing him on all your little secrets.

"Let's shoot a few. No need to call."

Despite hovering over the table instead of leaning, Michael is methodical even in uncomplicated shots.

"No, go ahead and run the table. I'm enjoying your talent."

Wow – how did he pull a clean pocket despite that elbowing drunk getting in his way? Impressive.

"Daniel tells me he'll be giving you his version of the Troubles' Tour tomorrow."

Michael remembers our short-term plans.

"Is that the usual thing?"

"There's a standard tour; loads of companies do them. But I doubt that's what you'll get. Er ... you know, because his family never ticked the right boxes back then."

Shit, not the 8-ball. Michael's talent of maintaining a winning streak while being the life of the upstairs party is something you don't see every day.

"Back at uni we slagged off the conflict-resolution folks. Told them we were onto their dirty little secret; that hate enclaves were their doing to remain academically relevant."

Your billiard inferiority is abundantly clear. Needless to share with Michael that you haven't a clue what he's talking about.

"You'll be in good hands with Daniel."

That's the plan.

"But at some point, you might want to do the formal tour. Sure, it's all tourist hype, but the Black Taxi tours conducted by the ex-paramilitaries do offer an interesting cross-communal angle. After the IRA veteran tells you his side of the story, he'll drive you across the peace wall and hand you over to his Protestant doppelganger for their version. I take it you're here to suss out why we're all so screwed up, right?"

Why do they all think it's so funny?

"Sorry, I didn't mean to laugh. I was imagining the look on your face as you try to make head or tail of their accents."

You want to spend as much time as you can with Daniel while he is still around, but Michael is growing on you.

"Any other pearls of wisdom?"

"On peacebuilding? That's your subject? Not a baldy, to be honest. My Dad once said that disengagement was the best way to keep out of the Troubles. Problems weren't equally distributed to prosperous leafy suburbs – if that makes sense."

Don't hammer. He already looks scared enough.

"You can't be falling for this fella's bullshit offensive."

It's as clear as the vodka he schlepped along that Daniel is thrilled to be back.

May he forever keep the superpowers of these lips.

CHAPTER 7

EXCEEDING EXPECTATIONS

OUCH, OWW. FAREWELL TO the forgotten highs of a painful headache. That's Daniel's voice downstairs mixing with aromas that I won't be able to digest. How much bacon frying can one breakfast produce? Well, it's 10:55, so brunch at the MacIntyres' might include unfamiliar items. If the bed is still warm, maybe Daniel's exit woke you to this migraine. Is the bed warm, or are you freezing? Huh. Only socks. Yet, no flashback on undressing. Setting your body clock to Belfast time needs to happen fast. That will require a realistic differentiation between capability and desires. Okay, you'll reattempt the out-of-bed challenge only after revisiting how we ended up back in his bedroom last night.

We tiptoed upstairs; that's an easy memory. But afterward? Eyes shut might help to work out some bearings into your blackout. Daniel claimed a wanking world record on this bed. That's not a figment of your imagination. Begging that you be his 'naughty girl' was real too.

These muffled voices and sounds aren't a hallucination either. Is it the fry-up, or running water, or both sounds intertwined? Once they finish setting the table, you may be able to pick out a word or two from that three-way ping-pong.

Sleep deprivation isn't an excuse to appear unrespectable for his dad. The police are always the police – even after reforms replaced the RUC with the more trusted PSNI. Coming up with this lucid observation, you must be more coherent than you think. Yeah, right, but matching the number of last night's drinks with glasses of water should relieve some of this hangover. Where is the bathroom? There is one on this floor. That's where last night you couldn't work out the complicated shower, which now gives you a reason to worry whether you still smell like drink.

When did last night reach its end? While in this bed, Daniel offered a description of his teens. "Sometimes reckless, often pathetic, always horny. All still valid."

Perhaps you'll remember more sitting up. Still way too fast, even with the headboard as support. Last week's period should have left a couple of Advil in my purse, but where is the purse? When it reappears, make sure the sunglasses are inside, for a dark alley would be too bright in your condition.

Grey is a bedsheet theme, but the multi-colored squares on the duvet are a fun touch. Did Maeve remodel the room for Daniel's homecoming? Not a remnant of a torn celebrity crush poster, unless it hides behind the wall cabinets. He probably didn't have a smartphone back then, so what was Daniel jerking off to?

Oh, that does bring back the FBI-style investigation you put him through on why he never mentioned his gatekeeper, Hannah, before. She definitely looked emotionally unprepared for me, but my presence made Daniel incapable of surviving the conversation with her. Was that the reason for Michael's upstairs move? You know it wasn't. Michael sustained much more than his original good impression. But Daniel's "You can't be troubled by competition!" was disappointingly belittling. And why would he use the word 'competition' if she weren't?

Yes, I should have expected that a sudden jump out of his cuddle to validate discomfort about Hannah would end in knocking my knees on these cupboards. It's a small-enough and dark-enough bedroom for rushed movements to end in pain. And it gave Daniel the optimal situational escape, but fetching ice for my aching knee was also a very Daniel-like considerate thing to do. Not to mention the TLC tongue for my visibly offended nipples. Hmm. Knee remains a swollen tennis ball, albeit painless. Urgent care can wait. The murky weather not only balances the indoors, it also cooperates with a cut jeans day and inspires the grey pair with the purple blouse.

Perfect! Yesterday's glass of ice is today's life-saving water, right next to the Panadol tablets Daniel said are the same as Advil. 11:05am should be more than eight hours since last night's dose. Liver damage is a done deal; just chug two, no regrets.

My jealousy wasn't backing down as fast as Daniel hoped if he had to reassure me with a trite phrase. "Life is made up of three parts, Ella: was, is, and will be."

I didn't fall entirely hostage to his kissing tricks if I said that Hannah's frosty glares gave 'green with envy' a whole new meaning.

"I'm more than ready to compensate for any compatriots' aggravations."

And he did.

Ouch. Damn it. Now, how will your left knee justify the identical daytime collision with the same cabinet – what's wrong with you?

Was I appreciative enough to Maeve on her hospitality before Michael whisked us away yesterday? Oh, God. The stakes of not screwing up the 'Dad meeting' are only getting higher. Pick one thing, one object to help with potential flattery.

Yuck. Daniel should consider himself amazingly lucky to have grown up architecturally inspired in these dull surroundings. My current state of appearance appreciates that light fixtures aren't a make-or-break home accessory, but that isn't the item for the compliment you are searching for. Hey, there's a complete

James Joyce collection on the bookshelf. Are these books here because of Daniel, or has his old room become Daddy's upstairs library branch? A well-conserved, mostly leather-bound canon that would make the 'Best Fifty Books of the English Language' list somewhere. With the smell of bacon infiltrating the room, no point risking sniffing mustiness just to check if the leather is authentic. I'll just believe that, as a product of Anglo-Irish education, Daniel read them all. Maybe he'll show me his high school while he's still around.

Okay, quasi-erect, semi-mobile too. Thank goodness for my never-to-disappoint jeans – no matter what I did the night before needing to fit inside them. Will it be the purple blouse that enjoys daytime Belfast first? Maybe the white? Would hyper-fashion-conscious Maeve approve? No, the black, under the blue-and-white-striped jacket is your today. No necklace; the single pearl earrings require the least amount of concentration.

Maeve and Oliver must be rolling their eyes at Daniel downstairs. Some serious make-up removing work is becoming urgent, but not now. Stick to a quick face wipe, concealer, a touch of powder, quick uplift to last night's smoky eyes, and neutral lipstick. Walk into the Miracle but spritz a bit behind the ears, once on the back of your head. One thing you cannot risk is perfume shortage.

How could I have missed this Louvre-size photo exhibition as we were lurching up this staircase last night? On the bright side, I haven't broken any of them. Memorizing who is who in his family will be a project. Carefully edited wedding photos on display. Maeve went for classic, I see. White lace, beading, train, the best of the traditional wedding gown. Hey, she was a natural redhead, well, reddish-brown. Kudos for managing the fading. Even short and all brown now, her hair remains vibrant.

Whoa, yesterday Daniel looked like his mom. Apparently, he's the spitting image of his dad. Unfortunately for me, not as buff.

But Oliver's grey wedding suit won't win boldness as its description. Daniel would never wear it, not even in the nineties.

Hmm, a pretty frozen moment for these two 'I's' becoming one 'We.' The lovebirds are cheery; the rest seem as though they never met a smile. Ooh, look at that adorable bow-tied baby! I wonder how long the white shirt stayed that way. And a few years later, still as gorgeous in his school logo blazer and tie. Looks like they keep school-uniform fashion across the ages here. With his spaghetti body type, this uniform wouldn't keep Daniel up at night worrying about body image. Now you have your explanation for why he doesn't have a problem spending much of his time naked. His hair is too short in every photo. I should ask Maeve if that was in style or whether it was a way to enhance his oceanic eyes. Freckled as an Australian Aboriginal artwork, or did he have chickenpox that day? Ah. This must have been the racket that got Daniel into tennis. But which grandparents are gifting him with it? Granny's gold cross necklace and Grandad's shorthaired pointer are useless cross-communal clues.

Perhaps a light cough before barging straight into their kitchen conversation. Are they talking about last night's Hannah? Is she a barrister already? Yes, Maeve is absolutely right; Hannah should focus on a London-based career. Great. Now your upset stomach is a rollercoaster.

"Ah good morning, Ella. Nice to meet you at last. Did you sleep?"

No hugs might be a MacIntyre family policy. Tidy in his commander's uniform, still impressively jacked, but formal Oliver is also a little shorter than Daniel's six foot.

"Hope you have an appetite. I had to crack on with my fry-up duties because I'm away to a conference shortly. But I didn't want to miss the opportunity of meeting you."

Daniel's fantasy meal.

"Sorry if my sleeping in held you back. All evidence to the

contrary, normally I'm an early riser."

"Dad, you finally have that partner for your crack-of-dawn runs."

"4am tomorrow, Ella?"

"For goodness sake, you two! Let the girl get over her jet lag first."

I hope she isn't loading all those sausages and eggs onto my plate. Oy, mini pancakes too? Not a grilled tomato – even starving, I'll avoid one. Well, you could work your way through those mushrooms. With so much fat and carbs around, their treadmill can't see 'Off.' Ever.

"Well, you're looking the better for a night's sleep. Hope you found the bed comfortable. Don't wait for us. Tuck in."

Daniel is chowing down so fast. Is he even taking time to chew?

"It looks yummy, but far beyond what I can eat right now."

"Daniel confirmed you eat pork."

I need to reassure Oliver, fast: "I eat everything that moves or stands. Normally."

Stick to the toast and rearrange the rest around the plate to evade a crisis.

"With the ambitious itinerary our Daniel has planned for you – the city by day and my family by night – you'll need plenty of fuel."

Is she getting up to bring me more food?

"Wee top-up on your tea?"

Ah, tea you could handle.

"Feel an urge to drive, Ella?"

Of course, I forgot cars here are reversed. My seat is on the other side. Hey, yesterday I didn't catch that the Audi has a manual transmission. So, it's not only confusing that they like; complicated is a local favorite too.

"Your dad typifies policing."

"Hoping you mean it in a good way. But what makes you think so?"

"He looks the part. Compels compliance. Some family subtext back there too, right? C'mon. The Goldins would disown me if I missed your father's head drop as soon as your mother mentioned we'll be visiting her brother."

"Hah-ha. You are an irresistible investigator, babe."

"So will you be – as an interpreter, that is."

"You Americans are so direct."

We are? Geography works in funny ways.

"I suppose I could give it a shot. But don't get too excited; I'm not sure I know anything interesting."

What's with the constant dodging about his family?

"Let's see …"

Hope his relatives are quicker responders, otherwise I'll never write a PhD.

"I suppose marrying each other exemplifies my parents' courage. Even post-ceasefires, their marriage wasn't the launchpad to the Deputy Chief Constable post Dad occupies now. But, no, I can't spoil all your fun, Ella. Just a few more hours of delayed gratification till you meet—"

"This is cruel and inhumane treatment, Daniel."

"Enough nosiness. Wind your neck in. But before you do, look to my left. That's City Hospital where I was born. Though the Jubilee maternity unit is gone, replaced by a building younger than me."

"Okay, let's compromise: not the whole picture, a couple of family paint strokes. You can do that for your girlfriend, right?"

"A short trailer is as far as I'll go."

Homecoming turned him into a tough negotiator. He hasn't been this cagey since visiting his uncle in Chicago back in November.

"Uncle Ciaran is a local Rockefeller now, but as a young Robin Hood I think he had more of Dad's respect."

The perfect note-taking moment catches you with nothing to write on. He'll think I'm not listening if I type on my phone. Excellent memory is all you have going.

"Mum denies this, but I may have overheard talk at some point that Dad came close to arresting Uncle Ciaran."

"Seriously?"

"When you see where my uncle grew up, it's not that bizarre."

Guide, research subject, boyfriend – the alignment of your personal and political is more than you could ask for.

"Is that where we're headed?"

"Nah. We're doing Loyalism first."

You're the boss.

"If I had to guess, it was Ciaran's transformation into a Champagne Socialist ... never heard the phrase? Self-described socialists living opulently."

What's wrong with compassion and sensitivity by the rich?

"These days, Ciaran loves living like the lord of the manor. But it's not his money that Dad finds odd, more how he earns it. Property and pubs rather than campaigning for justice. I think a Pat Finucane or PJ McGrory would have made Dad privately much prouder of his brother-in-law."

"Who are they?"

"Let's put it this way: a solicitor's reputation in the North is as atypical as this place."

Why do they have all these fancy names for the same profession? They're all attorneys, aren't they?

"A good Belfast lawyer could have earned a reputation in other ways than just by stealing other people's clients."

Does Hannah know about Daniel's antipathy toward the legal profession? Best wait for Natasha and Mark to share with Daniel that they met at Yale Law School.

"You'll need to know about Finucane. He's a Troubles symbol. An icon for some. Loyalist paramilitaries gunned him down having tea in front of his kids."

That's why the name sounded familiar. The Sinn Féin politician must be his son. I should add to my questionnaires something about trauma and the unseen wounds of post-conflict. It wouldn't hurt asking interviewees about healing and forgiveness. And resilience.

"We're cruising into Loyalist land. Tribal street art is about to resurrect your cherished conflict."

Daniel perfectly timed his sardonic warning. Not a Guernica, but the masked UVF gunman in the mural points his gun straight at me. A black and white street canvas with a God and Ulster call to action is emotive. How many people around here are still living the war in their heads? You read billboards when you are stuck in traffic. Clearly, someone over here invests time and money in order to tap into, transmit, or reinforce an unsubtle message. Daniel could be right that passing daily through murals makes people inured to seeing them. But this one is freshly painted, so at a minimum, locals would unconsciously notice a change in the scenery. Is it done to maintain loyalty?

"Susceptibility to advertising, Ella." You don't need Natasha's voice inside your head to emphasize the involuntary impact of street displays. Advertisements make you buy into a brand whether you are aware of it or not.

So, what's the brand on the Lower Newtownards Road? The red hand is on every mural. Is that the no-entry signal to Catholics? But the hand on the STOP traffic sign is white. I think it's white.

"Daniel, what's the red hand standing for? I've seen it on the flag, but why is it on every mural?"

"Never heard the legend? Back in the mists of time when Ulster was without an heir, a boat race was set up between two chieftains. The first to touch the land wins the kingdom. When one chieftain realised he was losing the race, he cut his hand off and threw it to shore. And lo! The new High King of Ulster."

"Yikes, is that the Northern Ireland 'caught red-handed' moment?"

"Sorry, Ella. I am laughing because you are hilarious."

Not hilarious enough to get him to unwind. Or maybe he's just jet-lagged? Of the two of us, I am the one who wants this tour.

"Our next stop, West Belfast, will illustrate how both sides appropriate Irish culture to their own ends."

You should do right by Daniel and reduce your judgment of him. Sarcasm might be his way of communicating that he's above all this. But as a guide, he should be able to stomach it. Every history has monuments that are difficult to accept in hindsight.

"That's Cupar Way ahead, your first official peace wall. Belfast is here to disprove that the Berlin Wall was the last to fall on this continent."

He has good reasons to be heavy-handed with the irony. It is depressingly high. Wow, homes are so close to the wall. Tiny yards completely overshadowed, some even covered in steel mesh.

"Don't you find it astonishing that *Love thy Neighbour* is recited in all our churches, yet no one listened?"

Good point.

"Think about it: an enduring love of walls is one of the few things uniting the communities they split."

Daniel earned every right to be defensive. Would you enjoy driving through stuff you object to?

"The Republicans always had the upper hand in conflict imagery. Coming up is the Falls Road's most accomplished artwork."

"Wait. Could you slow down? I'd like to take some photos."

Unlike your fast-paced boyfriend, the vehicle ahead is interested in Bobby Sands. Hopefully, it'll take its time until this crawling tour group gets out of my frame.

"Mum's childhood home is a stone's throw from here."

The dark joke is clear; less so is why he isn't taking you to see it. A direct ask would embarrass him if he's ashamed of his roots. I'd never thought he'd care about such things, but there is an unmissable class difference between his neighborhood and this area.

"I am circling a bit because there's something I'm looking to show you."

Don't make a big deal about not seeing the house when another of this family's homes is coming tonight. He won't be too informative anyway; so far, the only thing he's shared was that his mother was the only girl in the family. Michael's advice to book the tour for the area was dead on. That guy knows your boyfriend.

"Don't worry. We'll not run out of Republican murals. Not on these streets. God forbid, future generations should be oblivious to the real truth."

Am I hallucinating that Daniel's uptightness on the Catholic side outdoes East Belfast?

"Found it."

"Palestinian flags. Why are they here?"

"Flegs as they are known by local conflict junkies, and yes, Israel's mistreatment of Palestinians is a Nationalist cause."

So what if you are a Jew? Daniel must have prepared his Catholic relatives – he knows you are a liberal and distraught by Israel.

"Now, switch your view to the other side of this interface for the flip side of the story. How do you like these Star of David flegs alongside the Union Jacks?"

What's happening here?

"Rest assured, Ella, whatever transpires in Cultra tonight with Mum's family will be balanced out when you meet my cucumber-sandwich-eating Protestant grandparents."

What *is* he talking about?

"It's a known fact in certain parts of this country that your long-lost Thirteenth Tribe made it into Antrim."

"I thought Loyalism was all about being part loyal to Britain, but it's for Israel too, for real?"

"Unloved children come together, don't they?"

True. Israel is the global unloved child.

"Unionists feel they got undeserving stick from everyone. Look over there: you might notice red, white and blue, but I see divisions on a kerbstone."

That's a good navigation tip. Green, white and orange indicate a Catholic neighborhood. Last night was too dark to notice, but the Cathedral Quarter should have had the rainbow flag on its pavements.

You knew, even before he turned into this cynical tour guide, that Daniel would already be in Cambridge by the time you get around to visiting the Orange Order and Free Derry museums. Yet, macabre joke aside, there is something in Daniel's explanation of the absence of a museum for the Troubles.

"A museum requires consensus on what should be placed inside. It might not be accidental that our cross-communal Titanic Museum celebrates a ship sinking on its maiden voyage."

"Then that leaves *you* the opportunity to design the Museum for the Troubles."

"I wouldn't hold my breath. Anyway, your thirst for barriers must have made you parched. Ready for a pint?"

"Aren't you still detoxing last night's?"

"You barely touched the Ulster fry, our local cure."

Everyone at breakfast noticed, then.

"The second-best hangover remedy is a dirty big lunchtime

pint to restore the equilibrium."

Your lack of enthusiasm only seems to inspire him. It's not like him to be so inattentive.

"What if it would contribute to your research?"

"How?"

"My compatriots get off on pigeonholing each other. Tribal identifiers are unconcealed to local eyes. And ears. But you, Ella, lucked out with an imperfect, and thus unreadable, Northern Irish example."

Now he's completely lost me. Is he both communities ... or neither?

"Sure, shops and petrol stations, nobody would know or care, but filtering is still very much the business in bars."

"And how would one know?"

"By the distance between the eyes, clothes, rhythm of speech."

"You're bullshitting me."

"Well, it's always better to be safe than sorry in July. My mixed background is your security ticket anywhere in Northern Ireland."

Until now I wasn't worried. I can't tell if he's serious or joking.

"Daniel, you can't get inebriated on me. I can't drive this car."

"One pint, max, and a bag of salt and vinegar crisps."

Sourness is the last thing my mouth needs.

"Och, Ella. You have to admit that a free parking spot right in front of this drinking establishment is a sign from God."

That's what he is seeing. I am seeing rough lunchtime all-male drinkers lurking and smoking in the pub's entrance because they don't have anything else in life. Good, I think he's finally getting my look.

"You're right. This place is minging, borderline dodgy. I have a better idea: The Sunflower. The last pub in town to still have the original bomb-proof grille round the door. You'll love it."

CHAPTER 8

VIVID COMPLEXITY

"WE'RE ALMOST THERE, Ella. Wait till you see the place. It's spectacular."

Hopefully, Maeve, the destination also arrives with a less defensive son of yours.

"Aye, dead on. As you well know Ma, spectacular at Uncle Ciaran's can sometimes come with dire—"

"Shut your bake, Daniel MacIntyre! I counted on your uncle's new security gadget to unleash the apocalyptic forecasts, not before."

"Seriously, an iron peacock for an electric gate? Your brother doesn't do things by halves, does he?"

"They also upgraded the home gym."

Oliver estimated ten minutes to get us to Ciaran's house. Maeve corrected that it would take closer to twenty, or thirty. He didn't prove her wrong. Unfortunately, this longer drive was too brief to neutralize Daniel as the miserable person in the backseat.

"WOW."

"It's lovely along the coast here."

"Unreal." Like being in a car commercial.

Maeve said this inlet is called a lough, but the view competes with the best of Martha's Vineyard lookouts. Your Northern

Ireland reading list lacked a tour book, obviously. Who knew? Not you, and your over-focus on the shipyards and the Troubles.

OMG. Ciaran owns a white palace? Luxury didn't need to stretch too far from the city bustle to settle paradise. Three floors, three chimneys, a three-car garage, three sets of windows on each side of a classical arched entryway. Is the Holy Trinity the inspiration for this harmonious if OTT design?

"Ah, it's the man himself back from the Land of the Free! You're looking well on it, lad. Come here!"

Bear-hugged by the uncle, kissed by the aunt, Daniel will need my make-up remover for that crimson lipstick.

Ciaran is as confident with fashion as he is in demeanor. That's an unmistakably tailor-made paisley shirt with contrast cuffs. Burberry dark-wash jeans look equally cut to measure, and Gucci loafers ... what else? The home gym sees Ciaran frequently.

"Where's your manners, you ignorant nephew, not introducing this beautiful young lady? I'm Margot, a pleasure to have you with us, Ella."

Classy golden dress. She is the couple's people person. Probably the best customer of her tanning salon business.

"Hope you don't mind the over-excited pups. So you're a dog person too?"

"Hey puppies! We have a setter. They are both absolutely gorgeous."

"Badly behaved, manic and shedding all over the new carpeting, but they'll settle. Come on ahead; everyone's waiting on the patio."

Kudos to Margot for walking with elegance in turquoise killer heels. Geez! The back of the house is the seafront. Please be a night that lasts forever. What more could this mansion have besides a pavilion, tennis court, and a manicured lawn? Fun: fifteen guests, give or take, to mingle with.

"The long-absent eldest nephew is going to be monopolised

for a while, just to warn you. So let's get you sorted with something."

Your first private property's full-size gazebo bar, manned by a professional mixologist. These white clapboards could have been shipped directly from New England. And what a view of the Antrim coast and the hills beyond he has while working this classy bar.

"Your home is stunning, Margot."

"Scotch? Cocktail? Bubbles? Name your poison, Ella."

Charm must stay alert when this family constellation is also your research candy store. Aside from asking for water, a foreigner should be able to get away with the wrong drink.

"Chardonnay would be perfect, or any red too; whatever's the easiest."

The two older guys next to Ciaran busy catching up with Daniel fit the uncles' bill – so, which of them is Malachy and which is Colm? Following Margot over to their circle is the right thing to do when she carries the silver tray with your white wine and their espresso martinis.

"We'll be waiting forever for any of this lot to do the formal introductions, so let's make it super easy for you, love. These rogues are his three uncles and two of his ten cousins. Zac is ours; Jason is Malachy's. The rest are scattered 'round the globe, including our eldest, Declan. But a big reunion is planned for August. You'd still be around? Brilliant! We'll have a repeat get-together then."

All of them are dressed up by Hamptons standards. Thank you, Daniel, for your thoughtful nudge toward the floral dress. The white denim would have been too laid back. Now I know why he borrowed Oliver's striped dress shirt (a cut above his usual blue polo style) and tucked it in with a belt.

"Sláinte! Here's to the returned Yank!"

"Hi, I'm Zac. Interested in a short tour of the place?"

He noticed I was standing here like a spare part, listening, and understanding nothing of their banter.

"I'll take you, pet."

"And don't forget to show my girlfriend your 1916 Proclamation."

His suggestion means Daniel won't be coming with us … grinning Margot should be nice company.

"Amazing, I never saw such beautiful carving on an oak staircase. How old is this house, do you know?"

"Built 1911."

"Don't spare me any detail, please. My dream job is to give tours at Newport Mansions."

Margot didn't get my reference, but it's more interesting to hear how they have brought this house into its 21st-century condition than to clarify. This is also a museum when it comes to sculptures, looks like they love gold-framed landscapes too.

"We needed to move with the times."

Is Margot talking about home improvement or history?

"When we first arrived, the place was in a desperate state. But the oak staircase is original. Banjaxed, but you'd never believe it now. This house was never just bricks and mortar to us, truth be told. Back when I first knew him, Ciaran didn't own as much as a rusty pushbike."

She's handing you the chance to talk about the past.

"I hope it's not too personal to ask how you met?"

"Love at first sight. In a total kip of a Fleet Street pub. That's in Dublin. I know, big cliché."

Easy to see how Ciaran's commanding presence would be attractive. Slightly plump Margot probably knew how to do glitz and glam really well really early on. Manicured nails, perfect eyebrows, fake lashes, some work done too, but a down-to-earth girl.

"Aye. Passion always wins out. That's human nature, no

different in them days either."

You can't risk prying too early. Let her talk. Bide your time. For all you know, she might be talking about the personal, not the Troubles.

"When this place came on the market, Ciaran jumped at it. I was more cautious. But he never hesitated. Sure we can afford it, he kept saying. Our once-in-a-lifetime opportunity to create a forever home. Of course I gave in to his pestering, and no regrets. This is our baby now."

That's far more glamorous than Dad's version about our home. Mom hates it when he brags that living there ensures they stay married because she'd never leave the house. But this place ... it's a statement.

"Did you live in Dublin before moving here?"

"No, West Belfast, three doors from Ciaran's folks. They're no longer with us; you didn't know?"

If she only knew how little Daniel tells me about his family.

"Eileen, his ma first. God rest her. Cancer. Da, two months later. Probably of a broken heart, the poor man. Can't fathom it's four years next month. Och, a terrible loss."

"Daniel gave me the Troubles tour this morning."

"Had you travel back in time, did he? Och, dreadful days those were. Ciaran mostly on the brew, like most young men then, working off and on, home one week, away the next. Kept disappearing faster than reading glasses. I suppose that's why this place means so much to us. Hope Daniel showed you the new Belfast. It's lovely."

Margot couldn't have communicated 'closed for questioning' any clearer. Exercise patience, especially because you can recite Professor Rubinstein sleepwalking: "Wars don't start without social support or at least tacit local consent, however fucked up it might appear to an outsider of that society."

"Are you familiar with *Architectural Digest*? It's a very glossy

American magazine. Your master suite would have made their cover. They'd love this black and white theme."

Sublimation is the only thing stopping me from dropping straight into this enormous bed.

"How do you pull off this incredible fragrance? It's like entering a flower shop."

"A cheap and cheerful trick: pillow mist."

"Do you ever wonder about the people who lived here before you?"

"Not really. Last stop on our tour is the newest addition: his and hers walk-in closets."

As an American, least interesting to me, but she has clammed up again. Margot doesn't want to touch the past, and you need to return to the happy place of complimenting her McMansion. Effortless, when this bedroom includes a panoramic vista across the Belfast Lough.

"I could sit in the tub all day admiring this view."

"The Lough and the Antrim hills are just as spectacular from the patio. And we better get some grub into those lads of ours before they start yapping."

She is eager to get back to hosting. Better to have Daniel request binoculars for you; your camera is downstairs too.

Interesting: everything is based around a large front hallway. It was three—no, with the grand piano, *four* reception rooms that we passed. I wonder who plays in this family.

Margot and Ciaran did a super job transforming this historic house into a modern design without destroying its character. Unbelievable, this dining room is the size of a boardroom. Mom would have cashed in all their savings for this combination of high ceilings, crown molding, and mahogany paneling. Impeccable preservation of stained-glass windows throughout. I know – Mom will have an instant image if I describe this room as larger than the 'I Got Life' scene in *Hair*.

Too bad. A tour of the kitchen would be impossible with all these caterers bustling through the cloud of steam.

"Ella, come sit here. It's a long way to sunset, but you're in the best spot to catch it. I'm putting you between Daniel and our daughter Katie. Baby is teething, though, so she may come in late and leave early."

This view doesn't need curtains, not even these royal-looking blue ones. A Windsor Palace replica can't be Ciaran's dream home; perhaps ancient Gaelic nobility shared the same lavish taste in drapes.

"Mahatma Gandhi would renounce vegetarianism for this roast." The bearded uncle is Colm, I think. Margot basks in his accurate praise.

"A working holiday, Ella, so I hear."

Why are Daniel's cousins discomfited by Ciaran's comment? Maeve also stares at him as though he shouldn't have said it. Turning your head for Daniel's reaction would be too obvious. Oliver is on this side of the table too. Unfortunately, that negates your ability to decipher what he thinks of the Donnelly side of the family sitting across. The only catchable sighting of him is the non-alcoholic drink by his half-eaten meal.

"Yes. I'm a PhD student. Doing research."

Phew. Ciaran is smiling wide, and there's a merging laugh around the table. Nothing wrong with being nervous, but knowing they have no reason to be a hostile audience should relax you.

"For the record, Daniel isn't the first in this family to welcome visiting professionals. And even marry them."

So, Uncle Malachy has the white hair and the Norwegian journalist wife. No, you didn't imagine Maeve appreciating her brother's diversion.

"Just to warn you, Ella. Way back when, my mum Eva reported the Troubles for *Aftenposten* and look at the Troubles she got into."

Daniel had mentioned that Cousin Jason would be the joker.

"Ahem. I am not that ancient, thank you, son. As you know well, this place remained a story after the referendum."

Do Norwegians also use upward inflection at the end of sentences, or is it something Eva picked up locally over the years?

"Ella, you'll come to see: this place is one tough nut to crack. It left me no choice but to extend the terms of my assignment."

No, she'd kept her own accent.

"We credit Eva with the Hume-Trimble Nobel Peace prize." Peacemaker Margot is uncomfortable that this family has a past and plenty of internal dynamics. She also worries when the catering crew refills Ciaran's glass.

It would be ungrateful to blitz Eva with direct questions now. Five weeks could fit in several coffees, even with a busy journalist. With some luck, Jason is around throughout the summer. Colm's pleasant tendencies are the perfect backdrop for a revealing interview too.

"So, what is it you're after, Ella?"

It's not like you are on the witness stand: Ciaran is just a model Alpha. Inattentive to his wife's anxiety, he leaves you little choice but to answer.

"New perspectives on peacebuilding. Though I'll confess, I'm still searching for the manual at this point."

"We need to get you some results then."

"They're barely a day here, Ciaran."

"If the Good Friday Agreement resolved every issue, my love, Ella wouldn't have bothered her barney to come, would she? Would you now?"

"Give the girl a chance to eat her food while it's hot. Daniel, you haven't said a word about your year away." Poor Margot tries to change the subject, but Ciaran is uninterested in that trajectory. All the more respect to Mom's insistence on being kicking distance from Dad at our dinner events. Involving Daniel could take an interesting turn. I wonder if his loving uncle knows about Daniel's 'I'm above all this' attitude.

"You're Jewish, is that right?"

Shit. Is Ciaran an antisemite?

Is it just me or did the room go silent?

"This is supposed to be a convivial knees-up, not a feckin' funeral! We need a bit of craic. Daniel, why don't you share that old Jewish joke, eh?"

"Which one?" He's reluctant, scared?

"Which one? Och, he's too young to remember. Right then. A Jew danders straight into a Belfast bust-up. 'Whose side are you on?' 'I'm Jewish.' 'Aye right, but are you a Catholic Jew or a Protestant Jew?'"

"That's really funny, Ciaran. I plan to remember it."

Either it's the oldest joke or that, unlike me, everyone plans to forget it.

God, his eyes are piercing. Thank goodness for Margot's skillfully transforming 'saving room for dessert' into 'dessert saving the room.' She must be used to staging interventions to avert volatility. Meringue and strawberries with cream is my favorite too, a common ground with Uncle Colm.

"Your people retain our deep respect."

Wait, what? If that's him tipsy, a drunk Ciaran must be quite the sight.

"Contrary to general perception, Israel is not entirely the evil empire for us."

Whatever Ciaran is talking about, it can't be good.

"No, yes, we venerate how you revived Hebrew."

If I share that despite years of Temple Sunday School, it's a language I know nothing of, Ciaran will be really disappointed. No one is sharing my confusion, but 'on edge' is pretty universal.

"Over here, we have a long road ahead to revive the Irish

language, not like in Israel."

Did someone just groan, "Not this again; too early in the night to bring up the Irish language"?

"Is it, Malachy? If anything, I am sharing with Ella our cultural connections."

Dad, or possibly Mark, might know what the hell Ciaran is talking about. Crap! There is more confusion to come if the catering manager is lighting the patio heater while her team carries trays of coffee and truffles outside. Maybe Margot wants to adjust the seating arrangement when Oliver didn't say one word the entire dinner, and Maeve mostly spoke with her eyes.

Hey, Daniel definitely intended that yawn for Oliver, our designated driver, and Maeve nods back. Am I witnessing the MacIntyres performing their mixed marriage 'abort' drill in real-time, for my sake? Or for theirs?

"Is this the early riser or the jet-lagged Ella?"

"Oh, I am sorry, Oliver. I was doing my best not to wake anyone."

"Cuppa?"

Yes, you are planning an in-depth interview with Oliver, but it'll be a huge mistake to miss this alley-oop pass into what he has seen in his career.

"May I ask your advice, Oliver?"

"Fire away."

"I am paranoid about writing an uninformed dissertation."

"Well, worrying won't get you anywhere. It's my local angle you're after? Okay, but I can't think before I've had my first cup, can you?"

He delivered on his promise of good tea. And of course, I'll deliver on my promise to him to keep our conversation confidential given his very public role.

"Yes, peace transformed policing. Comfortable taking notes

on your phone? Very good. Look, crime control requires the community's cooperation. But around here, professionalism wasn't enough. The PSNI, our post-conflict police, had double resistance to overcome: Republicans with decades of police distrust and Unionists who felt cheated—oh, good morning, Daniel. There's tea in the pot."

"I thought you planned to grill my dad next week."

Am I embarrassing Daniel? Oliver is open. Mom said that most people want to get their stories out. And he looks like he's enjoying my questions, especially the straight-up ones. Why is Daniel so weird about it?

"Did I make it before his rose-tinted description of our citizens in uniform?"

He's more worried about his father's answers than my style, then.

"The Dirty War is no longer a secret, is it, Dad?"

"Intel exists in any self-respecting conflict."

"It doesn't legitimise infiltration, Dad. It didn't for the half of the family Ella met earlier."

"Don't confuse oil and water. RUC's crime control, unlike the IRA's, was within law-and-order boundaries. Why are you smiling, Ella?"

Oliver misses nothing.

"I have an academic *déjà vu*."

"A counter-terrorism course in university? Which textbook was used?"

"I should have some of the class notes right here on my phone … *Always a fragile balance between combatting violence and the use of force …*"

"Go on. I am all ears."

"*Civil wars are brutal … contested definition of 'victim' …*"

"*Does the 'informers are part of the intelligence war' come next, Ella?*"

Unless you are projecting, Oliver seems to like you too.

"You must have graduated from Fletcher! Look at that – I forgot that we discussed Northern Ireland in this class."

"Let's hear what you learned about us."

"*Should governments talk to terrorists? Guided by politics, Thatcher allowed the death of Maze prisoners. The Peace Accord acted as blanket amnesty. Victims left to bicker over accountability. IRA achieved the Irish Republic in 1921 but fell short of delivering unification.*"

"That's the whole lot? Sounds more like investigative journalism to me."

Oliver is right. Makes one wonder about the value of university education.

"Go on, Dad. Enlighten Ella on why you would do a daft thing like even consider voting DUP. I still can't get my head round it. That's the hardline Unionist Party that—"

"I know the DUP, Daniel." It's my dissertation that he seems increasingly indifferent to, in stark contrast to his helpful father.

"Let's not get carried away. Of course I'm far from thrilled about the DUP, but Ella must know Democratic Theory. Many moderate Unionists are conflicted, but the DUP remains the show in town by sheer number and influence. Will the UUP ever have a big seat at the table? The well-intended Alliance works on things I support, but took too much of a turn away from Unionism. Plenty amongst us are still searching for ways to listen to each other."

"A 6am kitchen party for which I didn't get the memo?"

Party's definitely over now that Maeve's joined.

CHAPTER 8½

LEGACY OF THE PAST

"I NEED TO KNOW, Ciaran. How radicalised was our family?"

That was Daniel earlier today barging unannounced and without Ella into his uncle's solicitors' practice in my city centre. Please forgive me; I wasn't planning to stick my nose in at this juncture at all. But when one's greatest fears materialise, needs must.

Upon dropping Ella off at Falls Park for the West Belfast walking tour, Daniel embarked on his own self-guided circuit of the Garden of Remembrance at Milltown Cemetery. The Republican Plot was a first for him, which is how the fallout from the inscription happened. Yes, Daniel discovered that *Declan Donnelly died on active service. March 1994. Age 18.*

It's only right that I explain.

"Daniel! Big man! What brings you here? Left the lovely Ella back at the ranch?"

"No, but I'm meeting her in a bit."

"Och, that's a pity. I'd have treated the pair of you to lunch. You have time for the busman's tour anyway. We just extended into the third floor. As an architect you'll be interested in our clever use of the space."

But Daniel's interest lay elsewhere, not in Ciaran's newly designed 35,000 square foot legal kingdom. His uncle's love of material possessions and proud Irishman's taste were evident by the Donegal paintings and wolfhound statues carefully placed throughout. Borderline cheesy Celtic touches aside, the design's restoration of original architecture impressed Daniel more than he expected.

Within earshot of Ciaran's many minions and two partners, the chat was pleasantries: the family, how well the weather was holding up ... you don't need me for those details. But once they were back at Ciaran's private office, Daniel began to cross-examine his uncle. He started by mentioning the gravestone, then shot that question right at him.

"It was a different time, lad. A culture of dying. Things resolved at gunpoint."

The conversation wasn't going according to Daniel's plan. Ciaran, known for his open and demonstrative nature, stayed tight-lipped as Daniel battled emotions.

"Everyone sacrificed for a normal life, and for the cause. Declan was our family's price. Hang on; I need to take this phone call. Back in a tick."

Ciaran couldn't sprint out fast enough.

What was happening to his life? Daniel was shell-shocked, his thoughts spinning. *How many of his uncles were Provies? What's being hushed up, and why?* Patrick always kept to generalities, always glossed over why he left.

Was Patrick an active IRA member?

Though, being gay had to be a liability around here back in the 1990s. For all he knew, the IRA could have packed Patrick off as a security risk and Patrick never forgave that backwardness. And why wouldn't he independently leave? It's only recently that an openly proud life became easier in Belfast.

Or, was Patrick involved? Wasn't he writing speeches for some Irish organisation? Daniel couldn't recall for which one. Chatterbox Ciaran had always evaded all his direct questions about Patrick. He shut them all down with the standard spiel on how the post-Troubles generation hasn't a clue how bad it was for Catholics back then.

So why didn't Patrick ever come back? Just being a hardcore Republican wouldn't keep someone from visiting or attending their parents' funerals – especially if that person was no longer an undocumented immigrant. Marrying an American should have resolved any lingering visa challenges, if there were any. He seemed well connected in Irish American circles. Loads of people with these views lead perfectly legal lives.

Was he estranged?

Or still on the run?

Is Patrick prohibited from setting foot again in Northern Ireland?

His own mother was even less forthcoming. All events pre-Good Friday Agreement were encrypted.

Was being secretive his mum's strategy to get ahead in life? Mixed marriage wouldn't hurt advancing through the ranks of the Human Rights Commission, could even be potentially helpful. Especially for someone like her who day and night promotes assertive advocacy. But a Provie connection might be too much reality. His mum wasn't the type to be sidelined.

Patrick was never to be discussed, except making it clear she vehemently objected to his Chicago visit.

"No, I don't have Patrick's contact details."

He really annoyed his mum with that request back in autumn.

Without Ciaran, I'd have never gotten to Chicago in the first place.

Yes, she doesn't like Ciaran's living-large lifestyle, but Mum's mixed feelings about him go beyond that. Her relationship with Margot never fit the good/bad absolutes either. There is intimacy between them, but only to a point. Now, looking back, Daniel suspected an agenda between the sisters-in-law to ensure no family disconnect. And specifically with him, Mum was always soldier-ready to guilt him into feeling that talking about her brothers puts her in a terrible position.

Dad must know the full story. His dad was always cordial – and guarded – with Ciaran. Only the very occasional slip of the tongue insinuating that something lurked in Ciaran's past. Was Ciaran merely a supporter or a participator in active terrorism? Perhaps he was just a thug on the wrong side of the law?

Daniel was proud that his parents never thrived on conflict, polar-opposite to the unhappy DUP-Sinn Féin political marriage. Yet, his parents' endeavours not to stir the pot left him a man who doesn't know his family. Now, the Declan he'd never get to meet nor ask about is a stop on Ella's Troubles Tour. His bright, tenacious, dissertation-driven American girlfriend, who thinks asking questions is life's strategy.

"You're getting all wound up for nothing."

Finally, Ciaran is back. Daniel couldn't stem the flow of his questions.

"Enough, Daniel! No, the past isn't trapping you … violence is long over. Catch yourself on – you're completely overthinking this. Seriously. No way Ella would make the connection, if she even sees the stone … the tour guide only ever talks about the hunger strikers."

That was as much as Ciaran gave in to Daniel's outburst before he succumbed to his own emotions and darted out muttering about needing to use the gents. Daniel was shocked at the sight of his normally bluff and hearty uncle consumed with feeling. But the motions displayed were not those associated with irritation or anxiety. Rather, Daniel noticed, his uncle was consumed by regret.

He understood it to be another lost opportunity for the truth about the Donnellys when Ciaran took twenty minutes to return. And when he did, Ciaran was on his mobile, again, nattering on about litigation.

Ella will be waiting.

With a "Sorry, son, crisis brewing," Ciaran rushed out once more with only a wave between them.

Shutting Ciaran's office door behind him, Daniel left, still utterly unaware of a decades' old Saint Patrick's Day morning when four Donnelly brothers made their way via the A1 towards Dublin. Given the travellers' identities and the security along the way, the journey would nearly have been faster on foot.

Ciaran was in the driver's seat. He wouldn't let his brothers drive.

This all needs to be controlled. "If you want to see the parade, all of yous, that bottle stays hidden until we're over the border."

Warranted vigilance. An all-male car was a tough border cross. They needed to stay under the radar.

"For fuck's sake, knock it off, dickheads. You'll draw attention." Ciaran grew exponentially irritated at the bickering twins in the backseat.

Jesus, until what age will these two eejits continue to fight over farts, smoking and open or shut car windows?

An all-clear wave at the checkpoint and an uneventful border crossing revived Ciaran's amiable nature.

"I need to make a stop before Dublin."

A mile or two past the border, he veered off onto a small and twisty side road, still up in the hills.

Colm, riding shotgun, fuelled annoyance through the previously prohibited whiskey bottle.

"Christ! Will we ever get there? What for?"

"None of your feckin' business," Ciaran said as he rolled down the window. The younger Declan and Malachy were drinking too, and the smell was getting to his head.

"We'll be too late. You said we wouldn't miss a bit of the Paddy's Day craic."

Ciaran had promised. A rare outing for the brothers; first time for the younger three in Dublin. He promised Margot an early arrival too.

Not looking over my own shoulder for a bit would make a nice change too.

The passengers quickened their impatient whining. The twins were quarrelling again, kicking the back of his seat. It was like driving with toddlers, Ciaran thought, and in response, accelerated.

With alcohol in their blood, the teenage horsing around accelerated too. Now Colm was sucked in too. One wrong head-turn to shout at his squabbling brothers and the high-speed movement shaped into spinning wheels in a flipped-over pancake of a vehicle.

Ciaran's open window threw him out free.

An active Provie commander, he immediately recognised the fumes of leaking fuel, the ticking engine.

All three had lit fegs!

Smell was the first thing a slow-to-regain-consciousness Ciaran discerned. Fresh grass, overtaken by nauseating coppery meat. Next, he noticed the crackling sound of fire. Writhing in a fog of pain and clouded vision, he detected human movement.

"Malachy! Malachy, are you okay?"

Ciaran's body struggled to rise. Attempting to advance towards his brother's sobs with a massive effort, he soon stumbled over what felt to him like a warm body.

"Colm!" Ciaran howled frantically. "Talk to me, brother." He shook his senseless brother with every last shred of strength in his muscular arms until Colm stirred.

"You're alive! What? Speak louder, man. For fuck's sake talk slower."

"Declan."

The clearer Ciaran's vision became, the more his thumping heart hurt his chest.

My history is scarred by heart-rending scenes, but the horror emerging before Ciaran's bleary eyes was amongst the worst. Three battered brothers, comprehending that this grassy spot in the mountains carried what little was left of the fourth. Aside from his right boot, not a single body part to bring back to Belfast.

"What the fuck? What the bloody fuck are we to do?" Colm shrieked while Malachy was inconsolable.

"He is a martyr of the Troubles, dying in the service of the struggle." Ciaran was calm now. "He's coming home in a proper military burial, of course." Ever the leader, his reverential tone kept distress at bay.

"Have you lost the plot?" Malachy's anger managed to release an owl's cry. "A gunshot wound to our heads is what we'll be getting."

"Know this: Declan *will* be remembered as a fallen volunteer." Ciaran's mind was set.

"They'll demand an explanation that we can't give. What were we doing in this back of beyond out of our patch—"

"Enough with the whining. I was sent here. Now, we've a job to do." Ciaran went into autopilot. "We need to stick to the same story: shite visibility, crap road, an explosive device possibly with my name on it. Either mistaken identity by the Brits or someone knew I was coming this way, to the safe house."

"You're actually going to suggest a leak?" gasped Malachy.

"Aye. Let them think that. Father Joe will ask no questions when he does the funeral."

"You're out of your mind! We'll end up in the ground with him!"

"Changes nothing. The realities of combat aren't news in Connelly House. Wartime accidents are as old as war itself. The life lottery took Declan's instead of mine. As for the Brits, they'll deny everything. Too embarrassing all round."

"There won't be an investigation? We have an RUC brother-in-law now," Colm reminded Ciaran.

"My professional ties aren't news to him. An investigation is the last thing he'll want for his career. Or his marriage."

People believe the narrative that suits them best, I've found. But Ciaran sounded hallucinatory to his two incredulous brothers.

"Our parents deserve Declan eulogised with the memory of a fallen Oglaigh na hEireann soldier. For now, I'm away to get help and start organising the rest. Yours jobs – say nothing and stay cool."

Under a rain of gunfire befitting an H-Block prisoner, a bruised Ciaran lowered his brother's casket into my newly ex-cavated void. Aye, that misty spring day worked overtime to crystallise memories. The meticulous Republican choreography produced a respectable funeral cortege. The Fall's Road funeral route was fertilised by the crowd's tears. Bereted volunteers with balaclavas cradled Declan's tricolour-draped coffin, serenaded by a lone piper's lament. A bouquet of sedatives muffled Eileen and Lorcan's letting-go through the closed-casket funeral and the wake. Their wounded sons Colm and Malachy consumed similar dosages of painkillers to limp at least a short distance on their own two feet; masked men their proxy pallbearers.

Declan's dignified arrival into my loins yielded one of the final upsurges in IRA recruitment of my Troubled days.

In the weeks that followed, a consensus reigned over how moving and beautiful the funeral had been, all thanks to Ciaran. His role in arranging everything; his moving eulogy; his care of his parents and younger siblings during those difficult days.

But Ciaran's haunted mind never rested since. The Donnelly's single sacrifice for Irish freedom amounted to a fatality in a car accident caused by dangerous driving and lit Marlboros.

You may rightly counsel that time heals all wounds, but Ciaran challenged that popular logic. After all, he was one of my most determined, willing to shoulder whatever it took to drive the Brits out of his precious Ireland; to be interned, starve, befriend death.

Instead, his Cain-like actions planted a hedge of armoured RUC Land Rovers on the day of the funeral – the same streets Ciaran had strived to sterilise them out of.

Inside one of these armoured vehicles a devastated Maeve sat alone. She insisted on being part of her younger brother's final send off, but invisible. The full Donnelly plate didn't need more 'shameful daughter' whispers and accusing glares.

Oliver, of course, was relieved she'd agreed. The last thing he wanted was to explain further the family he married into. Especially not to his own parents, whom he and Maeve were scheduled to see that Sunday in Broughshane. He just hoped his parents missed the news report, so he wouldn't need to lie.

Watching her family mourning, Maeve harboured a volcano of anger towards her older brother for immersing so many of her brothers in the IRA.

But, deep inside, my ever-hopeful girl admitted only to herself: *Declan's death honoured us with life, for there was never a better path paved for the Donnellys back into the community.* Former pariahs, now forgiven, despite the wayward daughter who betrayed them so cruelly.

But she also knew that on Colinward Street, that greenest of days, St. Patrick's Day, was thenceforth pitch-black.

CHAPTER 9

"FROM THE NORTH DISASTER

WILL BE POURED"[1]

HE'S SINGING ABOUT THE Antrim Glens. Daniel's first chants in the five days we've been here. Huh. All he needed was an awe-inspiring view to revive his romantic self.

"Confession time: I had a bit of a hidden agenda having you walk Carrick-a-Rede Rope Bridge ahead of Broughshane. Dad's parents are traditional, so it's best to discover the countryside with the unsteadiness metaphor in mind."

Crossing a rope bridge sticking out into the Atlantic is a first for me, but not the metaphor. The whole wide world is a narrow shaky bridge; according to Rabbi Breslov, the trick is not to be afraid!

Now that Daniel is relaxed and enjoying coaching you, sharing with him the Jewish version can wait.

"Granny, in particular, worries about family values."

Uh-oh, are your religious credentials in the way on this side of the family too?

"She often overcompensates on any potential religious voids in my upbringing."

"Sounds to me like a very boring family dynamic."

"Depends on how you look at it. But keep your excitement at

bay as we are shown our separate bedrooms."

This postcard of a sex stop must not go wasted then. But too many families crossed this bridge with us. Maybe we could continue the walk to the edge of the cliff and make love there? Scotland is too far to be able to peek.

"Any other dos and don'ts to keep in mind, Daniel?"

"You can't heap too much praise on Granny's cooking."

"Consider it done."

Hopefully, this incredible landscape produces more veggies on her plates, making it easier to go overboard on the compliments.

"So, do you feel compelled to switch personalities during family visits?"

"Umm, I never thought of it that way. I think I had a broad sense of diverging habits from a young age, without full self-awareness."

"What would you call it, then?"

"A nice childhood."

The visit to Ciaran's was a snippet; too short for any firm conclusions. You need to respect his wishes not to talk about it now. It wouldn't hurt you to get more reading done before asking him about religious differences. Is it Catholics who baptize and Protestants who christen, or is it the other way around? You don't want to appear totally clueless. Especially when these feelings of complex reality and nuance keep creeping up on you since we arrived.

"Our darling boy returns to the fold! Hello, hello! Oh, how we've looked forward to seeing you again! Your granny's ancient heart couldn't last out much longer."

Elegant, cream-dotted blue midi dress.

"And you must be Ella, even more bonny in real life."

Her naturally grey hair is flattering, and the understated pink lipstick is in good taste too. I wouldn't be surprised if Mary Berry is Granny's fashion icon.

"Granny, you're looking beautifully turned out, as always. And I see you've not let up on the garden either."

Geez, these roses' scent is almost overkill. And the lawn, mowed in meticulous stripes. The shaped spheres of shrubs – perfect, Mom would diagnose 'borderline obsessive.'

"Och, we have to keep our end up. When you live in the Garden Village of Ulster, Ella, the bar is set high. And you know your grandad loves pottering away at it. Keeps him out of mischief. The heatwave has been hard on those freesias."

"Is the man himself around?"

"Edward! For the life of me, he was right here, getting in my road with his fussing and impatience. I sent him off to make himself useful. Must be in the greenhouse. Edward! They're here!"

Handshakes (man-hugs aren't popular here), greetings, and there are always pleasantries about the drive and scenery. Daniel's grandparents both look young, even though they must be around eighty. So trim and energetic. And tall. Edward, with his full white head, dresses smarter than Dad. Adam Golding would never wear navy golfing pants, and would never have them ironed with a sharp crease down each leg. But the subtly striped shirt could be a golf gift he'd like. It's all very matching. Probably by Granny, acting as Edward's personal stylist. I'll ask Daniel later if his grandparents always coordinate outfits.

"After all your gallivanting, you'll want some liquid refreshments on a warm day like this. Daniel, you'll be pleased to know I'm still making my homemade elderberry cordial. The tree is not the tidiest thing in the garden, but every summer, it earns its keep."

"Here, I'll give the children a quick busman's tour first. Sprouts over here, should be ready for Christmas dinner. But my lettuce is a dead loss I'm afraid this summer and I can't fathom out what's eating the beans."

The perfect seating is organized in the patio under a pergola fragrant with more than roses. True farmer's hands on this grandad have prepared this chilled-to-perfection elderberry cordial.

"I hope you brought hollow legs. Your gran has been cooking for the five thousand."

Thank goodness we are finally standing up from this dinner. I thought my folks were feeders. The overcooked lamb will sit in my stomach long after the 11pm sunset Rosemary promised. Is it roast for guests all over Northern Ireland? That will mean freedom from potatoes only once I'm back on American shores.

The gold-framed velvety chaise longue back in the lounge has my name on it, but Granny insists we watch the sun go down back on the patio.

"I do love these bright nights. I was praying you'd get a good day." At last Granny can put her feet up. Praying must have been the easiest thing she did today; refused every offer to help with tidying up, of course.

Not a leaf out of place even in these pots. Never knew that window boxes can cause perfume overload outdoors.

"So, what's the latest from the Holy Land, Ella?"

Why would Edward confuse me for Reuters?

"Not a peaceful moment for your people over there."

Here we go again. The *other* long-standing conflict keeps popping up everywhere. Oliver criticizing West Belfast Nationalists for removing the plaque of the Israeli President's old home wasn't random after all.

Yet, nobody cares to ask if I wish to answer for the Israel I've never visited in my life.

"Undeserved criticism. What does the world expect? For the Holy Land not to defend itself?"

Just leave Edward's point unanswered. He won't get the irony. Why would he? You didn't, until Dad's history lesson on Jewish resistance in British Palestine. And then you continued an independent Google to fully understand. When Daniel unwinds again, he might even get a kick out of the Israeli Michael Collins who turned Prime Minister; and those militant Jews self-describing as Zionist IRA. If you interview anyone from Sinn Féin, that camaraderie would be one unexpected shock from the country they keep criticizing.

"As if Israel doesn't have enough on the battlefield, now they have to deal with all that Tik-Tok propaganda."

"I have never been to Israel."

"Really?"

Re-sync with his disappointed grandad ASAP if you want Daniel to keep on living.

"Not yet. But I am so curious ... how was Daniel as a kid?"

"Energetic as a wee terrier. He kept us on our toes."

"Och, he was a wee dote. Not a bother ever. And he's grown to become a fine young man."

They adore him, and he shares the emotional bond.

"You can't but have noticed he's the spit of our Oliver at that age."

"A son in the RUC, I am sure was no picnic, I mean with the Troubles and all."

"Heartsore with worry we were. Years of sleepless nights. Oliver could have chosen a life on the farm you know. This is a fine farm of land, but ..."

Of course, why wouldn't land be significant for Northern Irish farmers?

"But he'd always wanted to be in the RUC. Always law and order with Oliver, even as a wean. I suppose he had a strong sense of duty from when he was no age and that is no bad thing."

Nod and smile. It's important for Daniel that you make a positive impression. He won't survive a question about Oliver marrying Maeve. And their answer might not tell you much anyway. Think of Mom's horror stories about Grandma, when these days Mom can do no wrong by her.

"Back then, everyone lived in fear for their children. We were more fortunate than many of our neighbours. Some lads moved away to the mainland; others were drawn to Loyalist organisations. Our Oliver always held the line."

Except when it came to marriage.

"Grandad, I never thought of it that way."

Me neither. Now you know why he became a policeman. Too solid and motivated to be a rebelling teenager who would join friends toting paramilitary guns.

"Edward exaggerates. Oliver wasn't always serious. He had a charm about him and a way with words, just like you, Daniel."

"I put you on the spot loads of times, Granny. Like when I asked if this farm was stolen from Catholics?"

"That was later – when you were briefly a stroppy teenager. We forgive you for that."

"But we did ensure you knew this farm was settled by your Scottish forebears four hundred years ago."

Is Edward getting emotional?

"Removed the stones, drained the bogs, made it productive. MacIntyres have lived and farmed this very land all this time. Keeping it in the family."

Someone must break this awkward silence, and it won't be you.

"I am exhausted, Grandad."

Really? That's what he chooses to say when they just opened up? In our twenties, and coming from the US, aren't we supposed to be the vivacious of the quartet? It's the fourth night in a row where Daniel's jet lag discontinues your questioning. Well, he knows them, and you don't. Rosemary and Edward do look a little tired, so maybe it was considerate, not unhelpful Daniel.

They aren't tight-lipped, and clearly, culture matters. You'll be able to revive the conversation tomorrow; a question on Scottish settlement should do it. Better yet, ask Edward to show you those kilts in the family tartan he went on about at dinner. Perhaps overly provocative to inquire if their farm was part of the plantation of Ulster and if the first MacIntyre was a Scottish mercenary. But family interviews ought to prioritize how communal memory played into the Troubles. And you must get the story behind that flags arrangement on the mantelpiece.

It's Daniel in the bathroom.

"Jaysus, your hands are icier than Siberia, Ella."

Someone woke up on the wrong side of his lonely bed. I am a little morning tired too, but not causing those around me to feel bad. Maybe brushing my teeth will help him snap out of it and snog. Didn't know bathroom cabinets were an American thing. Where do they store stuff?

"Shite. It's bleeding a fountain now."

Like that wasn't the exaggeration of the century.

"It would be nice to survive a simple morning shave unscathed."

"Why are you making me feel weird?"

He isn't rushing to respond. You seem to be the only one concerned over three sexless days.

"Is respecting my grandparents' wishes that big of an ask?"

"Your grandparents appear unconfused about our virginity."

"Then it shouldn't be that difficult to control ourselves."

Who wants to make out with this grumpy version of a boyfriend I used to know anyway? No, you are better than intuitively imagining that Daniel changed since he came here.

Optimism is the only mood to get you through Rosemary's mega fry-up. If the growling is anything to go by, we were supposed to be eating an hour ago. Give it a chance – the grandparents might prove the recipe for Daniel's friendlier being.

"Ah the youngsters are up and about. And another gorgeous morning. Well-rested?"

"Oh, yes, Granny."

Daniel becomes happier on a full tummy. And no one will hear you complaining about the 4am chicken coop concert.

"Nothing like a full farmers' fry-up with eggs hatched this morning to get the day off to a good start. I'm sure you young people have rebuilt your appetite."

With so much food, could anyone ever reach the rebuild phase?

"We can't allow you to explore the beginning of the world on an empty stomach."

"Granny loves Thackeray's description of the Giant's Causeway."

"Thackeray didn't do the Causeway justice."

Edward isn't a Thackeray fan, then?

"Why don't we let these two reach their own conclusions, dear?"

Ah, there he is, pacing impatiently on the doorstep. I want out of here too.

"Heavens above, Rosemary, it'll be lunchtime before they're away."

"We'll not keep you any longer. A wee something for your lunch in case you get peckish. Safe travels, and don't be rushing back, though rain is expected for later."

Maybe it's your bombardment of questions. Ever since we arrived, he's translating, explaining, and ferrying you around. If he wants out, why wouldn't he just ask directly for a day off from your dissertation? Yes, everyone else is excited to help, but it could be that the sequential family gatherings are getting to him. On the drive up yesterday, he made a point about talking to the wrong people.

"You want to find out why the place is dysfunctional? Talk to ordinary people. My privileged friends and family won't teach you about Us and Them in Northern Ireland."

Okay, so he wants to steer his family away from my dissertation. Unclear why, when Edward makes Chosen People remarks, and Ciaran broadcasts his United Ireland aspirations. But I love him too much to become the cliché of couples going at each other to feel successful.

"Are you ready to see one of the world's most beautiful places?"

As spectacular as you always imagined, and Daniel's moodiness won't ruin your bucket list. But why is he being so weird? I don't ever remember him like this.

"What's the history of the Giant's Causeway, do you know?"

"Every schoolchild knows – a lava eruption, 60 million years ago. Then there's the legends on the Giant Finn McCool. And the tourist trap that this place became lined up a visitor centre."

That stop could insert some interaction into this walk.

"Though you'd be shocked on how uninformative it is."

Why go to the trouble of building it?

"In the abnormality that is Northern Ireland, you'll find there a creationist perspective on the origin of this place."

Not that shocking for someone who follows the local cultural debates. But this isn't the time for political commentary. He won't be able to keep up his grumpiness much longer because Victorian literature was your teacher: natural beauty does magic for romance.

"Grandad used to bring me here when I was wee. We should hop on these basalt columns ASAP if you don't want to experience more people than stones. Right here, his huge palm would take my little hand, just like this."

Finally. So nice to feel him again.

"Helping me onto the pillars, he'd proclaim in his best announcer's voice: 'Son, let's walk in the footsteps of giants.'"

"It's crazy beautiful here, Daniel."

"Quite special, but careful. See? Columns might look steady, and then you slip."

"Inconceivable that the Troubles took place among such breath-taking scenery."

"I am not a cognitive environmentalist."

Is that a profession?

"But I doubt much blood was spilled all the way up here."

That is something you should be fact-checking.

"But Vietnam was exotic, and beautiful too. And is there anywhere more appealing than Pearl Harbour?"

Your imbecility is giving him good reasons to nit-pick. "Point taken. But I mean, it's hard to square off local friendliness with the harsh history." Uh-oh. The right eyebrow raise isn't the response I was looking for.

"We are remembrance specialists. Don't read fine dining and coffee culture in Belfast as a genuine transformation."

Is he intentionally mixing his messages? First, he complains that I am obsessed with the past, now he is pulling the history card. Anything I say annoys him. Did the relaxed-in-his-skin Daniel stay back in the US? How necessary is it to point out he didn't want to be here for the summer when he's leaving for his posh Cambridge in two days?

"You see, around here, history isn't only a school subject; it's one's inheritance."

"But you told me—"

"I told you that you are looking in all the wrong places."

Stop the hysteria. It's not like Daniel to be hurtful. You are overreacting with all this blood rushing to your face. Nothing you did back at his grandparents merited his sudden insanity.

"Check out our sports teams, schools, holiday destinations. Investigate people's baking preferences, tastes in music. That's contemporary boundaries."

Still unhappy with the earlier dispassionate robot? Now you have a Daniel liberated from cordiality. What the fuck is wrong with him?

"How do you not get it? With your background."

"Excuse me?"

"Okay. Look ..."

I am looking but seeing nothing except a person I don't know.

"... Your relaxed approach to dating a gentile, for one."

What? How is this relevant to anything now? Ever? And why can't he stop rolling his tongue inside his left cheek?

"What the fuck is happening, Daniel?"

How long does it take a human to exhale?

"I can't do this anymore."

"Can't do what? What?"

"This. Us. It doesn't feel right. I'm sorry. But it's a dead end."

Legs cannot tremble at such seismic speed when the horizon is as clear as glass. The wind, the breaking waves and this carousel of gulls are all screaming your screams. 'YOU. FUCKING. ASS-HOLE!' cannot stay in your throat forever. Where did he dredge up the nerve to decide for both of us? Why aren't you yelling at him every curse that he deserves? How are you stumbling with-out moving? Shut eyes only contribute to deepening the ocean, not steadying you.

"No, Daniel! Don't you *dare* touch me anymore."

Could his shitty excuses expand the Causeway under my very feet? Where is this Causeway's end? It's as boundless as his cruel-ty. These basalt columns will reach Scotland if he doesn't shut up. Why am I soaked? Is his nonsensical blabber capable of drench-ing? Is it pouring, or are these my tears? I can't see anything in this storm – except the futility of trying to change his heartless mind.

CHAPTER 10

CRISIS MANAGEMENT

A DIRECT FLIGHT INTO the sun would be dimmer than this phone's contention it's 4:12. Which is it? If it's the morning, then there's no chance of you being the sole nocturnal shipwreck on this island. Are these insomniacs untangling the clues of their miserable existence too? Let's see: odoriferous underarms, gross stains slaughtering this once-proud *Choose Love* purple T-shirt, and an Everest of chocolate wrappers. It's not forensic science to infer you have inhabited this shithole of a flat for a few days now without a single knock on the door.

Unless your tears deafened the sound? Nah, that's impossible. Daniel, the jerk of the century, won't come, and poor Michael needs his own recovery after the Causeway Rescue Mission. Your Survivor's Immunity Challenge is to decode whether you are here longer than the five days it took Daniel to dump you. Welcome to your new reality, Ella Rivka Goldin: your crisis-as-an-event matured into crisis-as-a-process.

Astounding how your therapist times her vacations with when you need her most. When she asks, you should proudly relay how your feminist self still emerged during life's tragedy. Yes, yelling that you aren't returning to Belfast with Daniel was manic, but Daniel deserved every second of his desperation. Michael, whom you insisted could drive you back, must be too traumatized to return to Northern Ireland's premier tourist attraction for the foreseeable future. Outstanding anti-depressant performance while installing the sorrowful you over here in his cousin's empty flat.

"As you can see, he's a skint student. But the lavish accommodation is free all summer. Wait, there's more good news: nothing leaks."

Obviously, Michael's sales talk omitted Daniel's love for you.

He's a sweetheart to gather and bring over all your junk from the MacIntyres'. But he could have skipped the welcome to your new abode cup of tea destroyed by milk. Untouched. And now, look at that: the curdled liquid has degenerated just a bit less than you. Yuck. One Northern Irish favorite you are now exempted from.

Fair assumption that from here, Michael sped to the nearest pub. His description must have gone viral amongst his drinking buddies: "She's in bits. I thought she would have legged it straight back home. Instead, she's holed up in that flat living off Wispa bars." He had to unload the fiasco on someone.

How could I miss Daniel's attitude reversal? Because even a master-psychic would have been shocked, that's how. Routine couple's issues aren't a justification to lose steam. How did he get to decide for both of us that our relationship is over? Great, just as they began to enjoy a dry break, now your eyes are re-joining the haters' list.

Crying five days in a row without an ounce of new realization is pathetic. You need a better plan to prevent the development of early cancer. At the very least, inject into your shattered life a touch of positivity. Remember Michael's heartwarming biblical stand-up attempts?

"You should feel right at home settling into Belfast's Holylands, on Jerusalem Street of all places. Is that fate or what? The downstairs flat is his friend's, empty for now, so you've the place to yourself."

Whether or not you deserve a badge of honor for your resilience, it won't be the *Jewish* victim prize you'd be claiming. By our victimhood standards, not even eligible for the nominees' list. If anything, you are a Jewish trailblazer. Surpassing good old Moses, you made it inside the Promised Land. On second thought, is that such a wonder? The Hebrew Bible underestimated every one of its female protagonists.

Hey, broad daylight at 5am. And people dare to say the weather is dreadful. Now look at this chateau: Michael's cousin likes his walls empty and his plants dead. A carpet could have shielded the dust pollinating the wooden floor. But maybe his heart similarly broke and rugs reminded him of the love ripped from underneath his life. That brown wooden structure hasn't been a desk to anyone in quite a while, and the low-cost white chipboard bookshelves seem just as lonely. A student district of Belfast? Still too unmotivated to get out of bed and find out.

Daniel's exiling you out of his life was unnatural, unethical, irrational. Though it's the trusting self once again setting you up for heartache. Why didn't self-preservation instincts kick in? The minuscule odds of expecting a breakup amid his grandparents' love-fest is one reasonable explanation. I should have legal rights against his breached promise to complete one of Europe's Top Ten Coastal Routes. Now I'll have to look up Dunluce Castle on my phone.

Why do you even want him back? Wouldn't a brilliant architect choose the ruins of a castle as the ideal backdrop to ruin his girlfriend's life instead of the beautiful Causeway? Location is everything.

By any measure or scale, my ongoing breathing is a miracle. You shouldn't rule out that sharp survival skills enabled your sleep on a mattress thinner than at an undergraduate dorm. Well, the absence of his pushy legs and occasional snores very likely assisted. Not that you will need it, but unlike your old dorm, you are sleeping in a double bed.

Embroiled in radical delusion over a boyfriend of nine months – how could this happen to me? 'The village fool': did that sum up your state when he proclaimed, without a shred of crimson, that our 'us' was irrecoverable? And how pathetic to preface dumping you with a lecture about identities.

"Unshared history constrains our choices, Ella."

"Only if we let it."

Anything you said made him pull further away.

"Don't be naïve."

I was naïve? After arguing he's all above it, is it any wonder he reminded you of a toddler making no sense to his bewildered parent? When did all this irrationality happen to him? Out of nowhere pulling that Jewish card.

"Blending cultures isn't as easy as you make it out to be. It's mind-boggling that a few good decades of success could make American Jews forget all their history."

How was that relevant to anything?

"Identities constrain."

Nothing of this fear of commitment back when he met my parents, befriended Tamir, or joined my DC visit to Natasha and Mark. Were we in a time-traveling relationship?

Shit. To lose him now – after all the hard work getting him to master each and every one of my sexual furnaces – what a bloody loss, a bloody waste. Yeah, fucking bloody. Why not? You have suffered enough here to British-slang your bleeding heart—oh, no! No. No. Did I miss my appointment with the CEO of the Centre for Democracy and Peace Building? SHIIIIIIT! It took me forever to get on the diary of the Director for the Council for Integrated Education. Fuck! Fuck!

Okay. Stop. Now. You know how to breathe; you know grounding techniques, so do them all now, one by one.

What the hell keeps me in this god-forsaken place? Not a single item here is mine. Never physically, and no longer emotionally. Home? Should I? Hmm. Not so fast. That option is a mere plane away anytime. Shortcutting a decision on something you worked so hard for isn't you. This is every Behavioral Economist's fantasy. Survivors differentiate by the ability to adapt to the unexpected quickly. Consider it this way: you have lucked out with an opportunity to implement every takeaway from last year's Crisis Management Seminar. The faster you embrace this open-ended situation, the quicker you get back on track.

On track? There isn't one person around to delude that you have begun processing what just happened. At best, the horizon includes an expedition of grief. If you don't muster an intrinsic value to stay here, three months of background research slide down the drain, with your dissertation on their back. How is that as your future?

But how for fuck's sake am I to do that? You need to think! You love decision traps, don't you? Bragging to your therapist about your imagination – well, now it attained its real-life chance. She'll ignore your "it's the worst timing" and demand that you pragmatize your emotions. Sense-make this disaster your utilitarian way. This is Bentham's land, for now, at least by those who defined themselves as British. So what might make you a little bit happier? An interlude from spending time with your depressing self should be a small step in the happiness direction.

Movement forces you to think. That won't happen before serious damage control. You are festering at an industrial speed. Quite the chutzpah in your state to complain about the flat's appearance. Though, this isn't a room with a view either. A very ordinary small-city street, being rained upon once again as it stirs. Funny, not only yours, but none of the other apartments on the street have screen windows. Don't they have mosquitoes?

No, I should leave the window shut. Even the everlasting rain is powerless against the Holylands' mighty sewer. Or is it just the smell of overflowing dumpsters? Irrespective of potential cultural appropriation claims, an area shouldn't rush to claim Zion's highest sanctity when garbage collection isn't a priority.

Weedy hair is shouting for its curls back, and you don't need a visual to know that your red rabbit eyes will require far more than improvisation. Is it any surprise that Daniel didn't want someone with the potential to decompose so quickly? Why would anyone?

That's so unproductive when you need an open mind to every possibility before deciding what to do with your life. Find a distraction away from the mirror. A middle-of-the-night phone call will give the Goldins a heart attack. Just recite something all the way to the shower. "Friends, Romans, Countrymen ... I come to bury" my love for Daniel; definitely "not to praise him" in any way, shape, or form.[2]

Well done. Switching on the bathroom light is a first you should be proud of.

"Hello, hot shower, this is my body. We need you."

How sweet of Michael's cousin to leave Extracts. For Sensitive Skin too. That should help dignify my entry into the nearest decent hair salon. There must be one nearby. Maybe I'll ask them to take off an inch or two.

This city is no London. Look at that – freshly painted *Continuity IRA* crossing out Union Jack graffiti. Unlike modern electronics, the past resists depreciating on the Ormeau Road. What would happen if I grabbed a spray can and crossed out this black CIRA with a personal contribution of never-before-seen street art: HBU = Heartbroken by Ulsterman. Now, wouldn't that be a conversation starter for boundary-obsessed Belfast?

Did British soldiers understand every acronym decorating their street patrols back in the day? Daniel may have caught me as unprepared as Westminster when the Troubles broke out. Actually, more like betrayed Unionists after the Sunningdale Agreement, or perhaps as expendable as they felt when Margaret Thatcher signed the Anglo-Irish Agreement. No, I am probably experiencing something similar to Nationalists' vulnerability after Brexit. Nuh-uh, more like the sold-out Unionists after Boris Johnson took the helm.

Why am I complaining? Bruised by disbelief is Northern Ireland's comfort zone. Funnily, a United Ireland – unimaginable in their lifetime for Uncle Ciaran and Auntie Margot – could be the least shocking development this place ever saw.

When someone you thought was a soulmate disappeared into thin air, you have some nerve passing judgment on the unplanned and the unforeseeable. The first To Do at home is to delete my organ donation – the brain anyway. With such distorted bias, it would be harmful to any progress already made in neuroscience. And to think that reading mysteries consumed the bulk of your adolescent days. Yet you missed every clue.

Hey, I have been here before. That's that trendy part of Ormeau Road. Either you aren't as disoriented as you think, or you discovered a personal Lilliput. Well, even if this Post Office were open, it wouldn't be delivering a post-visit thank-you card to grandparents in Broughshane.

That's Daniel's favorite café chain, which is far from a signal for you to begin guessing what that son of a bitch might be doing now. Yet, a half-empty café with carry outs toted by people on their way to work is your best space for an 'alone together' situation. Personal tectonic change won't negate good coffee. Rehearsing being the person Daniel used to love can't hurt.

"Hi, a large cappuccino, please, for here, yes, thanks." The corner table has eavesdropping capacities that could help keep depression at bay. It's never a waste to sharpen your accent-deciphering capabilities.

What the hell: "May I also have a blueberry muffin and that

chocolate croissant?"

Be my guest, barista. Join the universal Masculine Embarrassment Club on feminine bleeding and attribute the carb-binge to that time of the month.

"Would you have any Advil, by any chance?"

"Pardon?"

Remember, they call it something different here. And this is not a 7-Eleven, so why would they have painkillers in a hip café?

"Never mind. Just the bakes and coffee, please."

See: there is a tomorrow. The simple communication with a guy who looks ten years younger than you and now confused and alarmed already makes you feel infinitely better. The music, too, speaks volumes of truth about the sort of days life brings. Was Van Morrison's mother a psychotherapist too?

No, no, no. You two must know on some level that your behavior is crossing the line of public affection displays. Get. A. Fucking. Room if you don't want to be responsible for flooding South Belfast with my tears. It's 10am. Don't you work? No way he is saying anything that funny. Who is he, the entire cast of *Saturday Night Live* in one guy?

Geez, I am so lonely. As long as Daniel didn't cross the sleeping-with-someone-else Rubicon, I could get him back. Enough. Whether he had, or he hadn't, you long ago crossed into pathetic. And it's too early for a new boyfriend when you don't know why the last one dumped you in the first place. Like anyone has ever gotten a good answer to that question in the history of humankind.

You know better than to rationalize his escape as a suffering artist's quest. How many times did he say that you fertilize his creativity? And believed every piece of flattery you imparted. It's entirely your fault for under-sketching how much of a muse you were to him.

Okay, you are as caffeinated as you'll ever be to revisit your epistolary barrage. Wait, should you agonize over your individual texts when deleting the entire conversation requires four quick taps? It's a stretch to call it a conversation when your texting storm didn't await replies. You won't have the luxury of blaming drunk texting, nor a friend doing it on your behalf when none are around. But maybe there was something in the texts suggesting what I could have done differently; a hint why he pulled the plug out of the blue. No one breaks up without having a reason.

How urgent is it to collect another reason to feel regretful in your abandoned state? Eat something before the analysis. You need to fuel your courage. Evidently, the pastry chef was unmotivated while sprinkling this dough with either sugar or chocolate chunks. As you scroll, keep in mind that you were never the type of woman to need a man to save her, even when you are all alone in his country. No, you won't be looking for something comforting in these texts. Nothing entertaining, just an understanding of why he didn't give you a chance to change his mind. And, of course, the disgrace you first need to feel to start healing.

So, deep breath. Texting storytime:

Never thought of you as cold-hearted, Daniel MacIntyre!

Just put the phone away. It isn't as though Hemingwayan gems blazed through your fingers, or that he journaled anything useful about what he had bottled inside.

Whoever oversaw the blueberries was a lot more generous than the chocolatier. If you didn't want blueberries, why did you buy it? You could pluck them out as part of 'he hates me, he hates me not.' Oops, shit. Now one is a stain on your beloved orange shirt.

You need to accept reality for what it is. Just scroll all the way down to his last text, eradicating excuses to forget:

You have Michael. For <u>anything!</u>

Selfishness that puts a wildcat to shame. Even uses his friends. The real idiot here is you. Most of the time, he just took you for granted. Hours, yes, you wasted days listening to his complaints, comforting him over his unappreciative professors. And scorched earth policy is how he reciprocated. Those capricious 'unfollow' clicks while weeping in Michael's car on the way back to Belfast might just have saved your life.

I should be so lucky to rely on Emily, or any of my girlfriends, the way Daniel tossed me over to his friend. Perhaps Maeve's goodwill could decipher his behavior. But did she even like me? No evidence to think she thought I was great. No evidence the other way either. She was friendly, helpful in a busy 'no time to chat but feel free to raid the biscuit tin any time' way. Oliver was more open. Who gives a tiny fuck if it's because he is an Israel-loving Protestant? But what could he contribute when Daniel is much closer to his mom? Does she work nearby, or is it Oliver's headquarters that is around here? But relying on accidental brushes isn't really planning, is it? What's wrong with me? Strategizing is my bread and butter.

"Excuse me. Hi, may I please see a breakfast menu?"

He is still scared of you.

"Uh, we don't really do cooked breakfast. Just what's written up on the board behind me, and the buns here, if there's anything else you fancy." He looks apologetic. Not nearly as sorry as I am. "I think we do soup later on. I'm still new. Not sure if there's anything other than sandwiches. And cakes."

"So a salad is out of the question then?"

Earth's greenest island without a single plant-based food. Why are you terrifying this no-fault barista? Well, he must be calculating the ensuing tip. No, because they don't really tip over here in places like this. At least that's one small detail Daniel managed to relay before vanishing.

"It's fine, no problem. I'll have that cinnamon scone. Could you warm it up, please?"

Heartbroken, you could still exercise some civility around indistinguishable baked goods.

Okay, melancholy isn't a good enough excuse for cognitive simplicity. This unfolded *Irish Times* is a lucid omen for your career—

Is that my phone?

"Hey, sis."

"Thank goodness, Ella! If you kept this texting regime going even one more day, I'd be on tonight's plane. Mark already looked into flights."

Have we been texting?

"So, can you please take me through your last three days? Coherently?"

What's the date today? Maybe it was just three, not five, days of wasted research time.

"What did you think we'd do after you fobbed a gazillion calls from Mark, Mom, Dad, *and* me with those 'I'll call you later' auto-replies?"

Was I evading their calls? Shit! How many times did I call Daniel?

"Are you there, Ella?"

"I am here."

"How are you, honestly?"

"Navigating the fog of impetuousness."

"It's reassuring that your humor is back. So, have you made up your mind already?"

What is she talking about?

"You do remember that we'll all understand if you come home."

If I am unable to recall a Goldin Intervention, an awareness vacuum carries some advantages.

Natasha's resolute efficiency cages you; might as well make the most of it. "So, how would you advise me to make that decision?"

"Rationally."

Is Natasha trying to remind me that I am here because of my PhD, not Daniel? You know she'll discuss both sides either way. She'll understand succumbing to feelings, but she conducted graduate school research as part of her joint JD/PhD and knows the value of a travel grant. If I return to Medford now, could I really decipher from afar how fanatical local politeness is the wrapper on a Northern Irish history of brutality and suffering?

"I get the difficulty of returning early with all that Northern Ireland means to you."

For someone who forges ahead with action, this is considerate of Natasha to say.

"At the same time, you need to be realistic."

"It's more like smoke and mirrors I'm experiencing. This place is indecipherable. Right now, I am in a charming café. They have the best pubs. Yet they continue to segregate their young and their dead. Neighborhoods too. It's like Grandma's eternal love advice of 'stick to your own' repeatedly re-enacted. Rationally, I need more time."

"To be honest, Ella, after our last conversation, I am relieved by how well you articulate thoughts."

"So, what do *you* think, should I stay or come home?"

You can hear her wheels turning with "Ella understands by doing." She is as wired as you to come up with Dad's Jewish rule, *Na'ase ve-nishma* – do it to discern it.

"Are you still at that free flat?"

I guess I shared that too, but not how disgusting it was.

"Okay then. Promise that you'll inspect your personal warning signs, not only professional paradoxes? Even a mini-wobble, and we're on the next plane over."

CHAPTER 11

IN SEARCH OF ORACLES

BELFAST OFFERS A WHOLE new take on 'when it rains, it pours.'

"Where are you for, love?"

"Holylands, Jerusalem Street. Thank you so much for stopping. None of the taxi apps are accepting requests."

"This is my lucky day, so. There's a wee towel you can sit on. I am trying not to drive a submarine."

'Torrential' would also be the Alliance Party's description of my interview-turned-cross-examination. Arthur, the East Belfast Constituency Manager, may still be at the window to ensure I left the area. You'll have to mea culpa your excessive combativeness in the thank-you email.

Arthur realized you are a novice. He also had that annoying local mixture of admiration and condescension towards Americans. But the interview should have been more dispassionate. Yes, his "Look, peace and progress take time" got to you. But your task was to listen, gather data, and block unhelpful triggers, certainly not to jump the gun with, "But it's been decades, Arthur."

He barely touched his water during your query onslaught. Next time, more small talk at the start of an interview to get interviewees to warm to you and feel at ease. Break down the barriers. Remember your ingrained impatience, and your nationality.

He was older, lived through the Troubles, and is allowed to be critical of an American looking in.

"Was Rome built in a day? Having peaceful streets today is an achievement. That said, it is a long road ahead."

"But for a bridging-the-divide party like Alliance, isn't the slow pace frustrating?"

"It's called peace *process* for a reason. We try to be a voice of wisdom, but it's an uphill battle. The Troubles are a thing of the past. Enough people don't want to go back in time, but other people still live there. So it takes longer to concur on what peace means and what the future should look like. The now shouldn't be your snapshot. Look at today as part of an album. Incomplete, but infinitely better than the carnage and fear."

You should have accounted for the power-sharing infrastructure stacked against his party. They *are* too weak to make a difference in Northern Ireland's dysfunctional politics. The multiparty power-sharing executive precludes their ability to exercise the standard small parties' disruptions. How much can be done in the first place in a system that is constantly stalled by 'petitions of concern' and collapses for years at a time on sectarian grounds?

Unlike Oliver, Taxi Lady doesn't vote at all. "Nah, 'scuse my French, but I can't be arsed voting for any of those muppets up on the hill. Bleedin' clampits gurning about Irish street signs and money for Ulster-Scots and bridges to Scotland. Tit for tat point scoring on shite ordinary people couldn't give a fiddler's fuck about. Meanwhile the NHS is banjaxed and my old da is waiting years to get a new hip."

"Thanks. Keep the change, please."

In an unscripted twenty minutes, she taught you everything on political disengagement. Thank goodness the grant covers taxis; weather Armageddons are a gift to your research because any taxi driver older than Google Maps has a GPS brain predisposed to details. But even in the span of a sunny ride, taxi drivers should be able to answer most of your interview questionnaire. And more.

Weird. Nothing in the flat could have produced Pearl Jam's music. I definitely switched off the entrance light exiting this morning. Did Michael's cousin break his promise to stay away? The mysterious visitor forgot a duffle bag at the entryway.

"Ella, right?"

Should I shake his extended hand?

"Ben. Michael's mate."

Is Michael the local unofficial real estate agent?

"Hope you don't mind; I'm crashing at the empty flat for a bit. The ceiling in my place caved in. Lived to tell the tale."

It's a relief failing to remember seeing him before. He looks over twenty-one but younger than Daniel. Was he briefed on the drama?

"I was about to open a beer. Join me? Though they are a wee bit warm."

Geez, his section of the duplex is even grimmer than your upstairs dump.

"And if you fancy fine dining, I've got Chinese takeaway, more than enough for two."

Cinnamon stubble suits Ben's roundness, but the pleasant efforts and chancing glances – futureless.

"Have you been living in the Holylands long, Ben?"

"A couple of years; trying to live on the cheap to keep a lid on the student loan. It's handy – don't need a car – but not the most salubrious. Stay on until the students are back and you'll see it at its liveliest. The residents who own houses here are driven spare; constantly onto the police, but nothing changes."

"Leaping over broken bottles daily, I can see why."

"That's just a tiny glimmer of the glass exhibition accumulated here during term time."

Funny: naming a place 'Holyland' automatically brings on a troubled fate. You lucked out with the name Ella, whether people know it means 'goddess' in Hebrew or not. Rivka – forced by family history and sounding like you are from Crown Heights in Brooklyn, less successful. The act of naming has so much baggage; wouldn't it be simpler to invent new titles for everything?

"I'm guessing Damascus Street or Cairo are the migrants' magnets?"

"Ha-ha, nice one. But true."

How much is Ben informed?

"Visiting this island shouldn't be wasted on politics alone. That's what you're researching?"

He's sweet, so nip it in the bud.

"Don't just take my word. Hollywood thinks Ireland and Irishmen are life-changing for Americans."

How many of the dozens of cheesy movies is he thinking of?

"I am fully committed to overcoming those stereotypes. Sorry. I shouldn't have said that. I am usually not this bitter."

Great. The imperishable tear fountain is now terrifying him too.

"It'll be okay, Ella."

So he knows. "I promise to try to believe you."

"For what it's worth, my summer isn't fun and games either. The only research assistant position open was for a professor writing another endless book on Plato."

Hanging strips won't leave marks on these walls, but a picture or two could assuage the tragedy of entering your domicile.

Why jump to the conclusion that situating Ben directly underneath was Michael's skillful signal that Daniel isn't coming back? Ben could be desperate for an American visa but, at the same time, the difference-maker for your on-life-support fieldwork. You've lost so much time already. Age-wise he's post-ceasefire and optimal to engage the pointers the older guy from the Alliance party made on the changing demography and identities. Even if philosophy-at-large has dwelled on the same questions for thousands of years, Ben could know something you don't about the Belfast/Good Friday Agreement.

Messing up *everything*, Daniel also obliterated all the interviews lined up with his relatives. But maybe his opposition to leveraging his middle-class connections carried some logic. Maybe his influences shouldn't filter your understanding, especially as he insists on being the exception, not the rule. Daniel's friends feel they are beyond the Us and Them approach, but it's not like they've figured out where this place is heading next. Grandma's Yiddish idiom 'a fleeting guest notices everything' is a good reminder of the value of your fresh perspective.

Countless sapiens probably heard from their fathers, "There should be a better way than this one" upon deciding to switch course during fruitless hunts. Your list now includes Belfast's taxi drivers, in addition to a few politicians. Well, more like community workers now, but who knows, one of them, one day, may become the region's Barack Obama. A few senior bureaucrats agreed to talk to you too. You have a GAA game and the East Belfast Protestant band visit next week. Feminist groups are easy to find, and each of these contacts would lead you elsewhere. No, these aren't shortcuts, but survival strategies for a hyper-arid academic zone.

Before I returned to my grim quarters, I should have added to Ben, "I'll see you soon, neighbor." Oh well, life *can* change in the Holylands.

CHAPTER 12

HUMAN INTELLIGENCE

"HENCE, OUR TITULAR PEACE allows for Republicans to fore-see a unified Ireland inside the United Kingdom while Loyalists stomached doses of British marginalisation."

Accomplishing the out of bed and into the 9am lecture merits self-congratulation. A feat over and above venturing into Queen's University medieval-style red-brick quad with its neat greenery. This 'Ulster's Brightest Critic' is someone Auden never met when he maintained that "a professor is one who talks in someone else's sleep."[3] Irrespective of his Michael Jordan-level performance with a pointer, the summer students are smitten.

"Christopher, please, it's a perfect time to spice things up with your counter-perspective."

August 4th is midway through this lecture series, so a first name basis is admirable but not entirely surprising in an audience of roughly fifty people.

"Thanks, Professor Campbell."

First-row Christopher came all the way from New Zealand?

"Basically, if I understood, you'd like us to stop praising your peace agreement?"

Christopher is too far down to catch the face or the clothes enjoying this gorgeous red mane. Bold Professor Campbell looks like he could have been a redhead once. Christopher might look like him more than you'd like to think if Campbell is beaming at his unequivocal imitation.

"I do indeed. You didn't make Belfast your summer home for a dishonest reflection, did you? Our peace agreement was a legal work of art kicking off an unscathed future. True, Joshua faced an easier job in Jericho than uprooting the mental walls dividing us. But it's long overdue to eulogise our peace for what it *wasn't*: a path for reconciliation."

Campbell's deliberate tone has note-jotting all over it; what are you waiting for?

"I suppose I sound like a broken vinyl. Is that a discernible metaphor for young ears?"

It is – vinyl has made a comeback. Interesting that so many professors have a metaphoric mind. Or do they speak in metaphors because they think it'll help us understand them better?

"Anyway, precise diagnoses are essential regardless of how much one can't stand the results."

It's impossible to type every word; abbreviate now and finalize during his air intakes. Oh, a visual. Why is he pointing at a NASA photo of planet Earth in a lecture on peacebuilding?

"Can you even see these two specks on the slide? Britain and Ireland, our two competing Zions, never stopped treating us as irresponsible punks unable to share a playground."

Poor guy. Working so hard to start the PowerPoint for one image. The letters on the slide are too small to read this far back. He should stick to what he knows: metaphors, and leave technology to the engineering faculty.

"Little wonder then that they cooked up a sub-zero freezer for our identities, labelling that an opus peace agreement."

The peace-loving audience is on my side, bashfully metabolizing Professor Campbell's belligerent poise.

"By all means, Bethany, please pollinate us all with your productive hesitations."

I *am* the only newcomer in the audience.

"Thanks, Professor. Aren't you asking too much of the young Good Friday Agreement after centuries of intractable hatred?"

Tsk, tsk. Yes, Bethany is hypnotizing. But leaning back sloped and frozen as a ski trail is above and beyond the need to think of your reply, Professor Campbell.

"I am the last to credit the Troubles with futility."

Anyone walking into this hall right now could confuse his drumming of numbers on the whiteboard for a math lecture: 1607, 1641, 1649, 1688, 1690, 1798, 1803, 1848, 1867, 1912, 1916, 1922, 1969, 1971, 1972.

"These aren't only years. They are permanent scars on the Isle's CV. The Troubles deserve credit for ending the fighting. For now. Please, our partaker in the cheap seats at the back, your raised hand has been awfully patient."

He means me, I think.

"Yes, please, but if you would introduce yourself first."

My voice will break. "Ella Goldin. Ahem." Campbell is too far down to notice your shaking body, and he was gracious in answering your email. Get a grip. The objective is a short question. "I am a doctoral student from the Fletcher School at Tufts University in Massachusetts—"

"Welcome, Ella."

"I'd be interested ... ahem ... I'm interested in your perspective on the contribution of international actors."

Is he slow to reply because this was the dumbest question? Why didn't you prelude with an apology that the series may have previously touched on that? Yet the others don't seem to lose interest.

"Of course, your charismatic Clinton and bureaucratic Brussels added photogenic flair. But more importantly, cash." He isn't through quite yet. "Now, contingent on one's point of view, all should remain pleasant in the UK, or a United Ireland, as long as the corresponding currency supplies funding." Charting full speed still. "And, circling back to Chris's earlier point: now that we are peace exporters, it's imperative, no, fair, to share our brilliant post-conflict formula: a pot of gold combined with politicians mastering imminent institutional collapse."

Great. Campbell's office number is on this door. Here goes. "You found it."

His cheeks are far more flushed up close.

"How did you hear about our summer programme, Ella?"

"Your Best Summer Show in Belfast reputation precedes you, Professor Campbell."

"Hardly likely. After all we did invent the Twelfth in all its glory. But I am happy to be a fool for undeserving flattery."

"Thank you for carving out the time on such short notice. Wow. Your office is beautiful."

"Now that's high praise indeed from somebody who must be no stranger to serious academic institutions back in America."

A good start with someone who keeps his three-button jacket fastened as he takes a seat in his armchair behind the desk, leaving you the distant sofa. He is slim enough to pull it off and look comfortable.

Best to keep your carefully worded questions inside the folder. Diagnosing anything interesting about this place requires his unbroken lecturing. Nod, smile, play fascinated (which won't be an act), and drop hints that you read his books. You need him *and* his contacts.

"So, you have been honey-trapped into researching our own wee country too?"

Lighting his vape is a good sign. Your ears and brain are already into their third hour of hard labor. Now lungs will have to do their part.

"Em, let's see now ... one-and-all, academics are frame-work-junkies. The best Northern Ireland could still offer, I suppose, is the opportunity to enunciate the long-silenced irony of peacebuilding. It's nothing more than organised dynamics to sustain animosities."

Invigorate your nod, so he'll proceed.

"Our complexity isn't complicated if one envisions a hungry lion: monetarily satisfied, we periodically roar but at decibels acceptable enough to remain uninteresting."

He's vulgarly pretentious, but it would be counterproductive to interrupt Campbell now.

"Which to me only magnifies the senselessness in our decades of pain. Would anybody answer for the shattered lives? How could they, when the culprits here – and everywhere – go to occupy clout faster than a runaway bride? Lost lives, physical and mental crippling – these are conflict incidentals; the collateral damages never accounted for."

"Yes, but I have to ask. Coming from New York in particular, it's difficult for me to argue with Belfast's sense of safety and security."

"But for how long, Ella? Complacency is the enemy of critical thinking, isn't it? Search for Northern Ireland's malfunction beneath the surface. Disenchantment, stagnation, decay, neglect and decline are fuels for tenacious sectarianism."

"I think there was a knock on the door."

"Ah, Chris. Two minutes, would that be all right?"

"Where were we? Ah, yes. I was about to offer you this postscript. I continue to wonder who *really* deserves the credit balance for quiet streets: the peacemakers, or the security forces that insist they counter-terrorised the IRA? Perhaps you'll supply the answer, yes?"

This rain refuses to accept August as summertime. A marketing no-brainer making this tea-obsessed land about coffee too.

Ebony & Ivory, not a bad name choice for a street corner café. A great place to dry your hair, and the vacant overstuffed armchair right by the window is your sign.

The yummy cream here justifies a second large Americano for a debrief of your conversation with Campbell. As your nineteenth interview, you could grade it as academic progress. Far from bleak disappointment, because the learned Professor disrupted some of your thinking with a splash of honesty. You are beyond the need to religiously adhere to script, but your tragically tight schedule requires doing better in keeping conversations on target. Far too much rope for Campbell's smug authority and far too little in terms of research-oriented answers. Any experienced interviewer would have interjected. "Dissatisfaction with status quo should lead people to change their situation." He didn't have *any* self-critique, and nothing Campbell said offered solutions to his disillusionment with peacebuilding. True, it's not your place to call him out, but he is tenured at Queen's Political Science Department, not Uppsala's. His academic tower calls for some applied conflict-resolution research and reasoning.

"Where is *your* scholarly responsibility, Professor Campbell?" Yeah, right. But you aren't the evading type either. Could Northern Irish men be mesmerizing you into becoming a passive spectator? Nope, this isn't the time for excuses. You should have done better. A place that saw so much struggle should inspire resilience. If a mini sugar cookie has energized you to jog – in the rain – all the way back to the Holylands, it shouldn't be so hard to copy Barbara Walters.

"Damn it, can't you look where you are driving? All warmed up inside your precious Range Rover. Not a care in the world for drowning pedestrians." See: your voice is growing wings.

Yay. Ben is home.

"Hiya, friend! On my way from Queen's, I noticed the Irish Tricolour."

"Here? You're joking."

"Point taken. The peacebuilding lecture made me think about the white in the middle of the flag—"

"Look at you, Sherlock, getting all the basics."

No, Ben. You are the nicest. Unfortunately still not my type.

"Beer?"

"Sure, thanks. Wasn't the white in the middle of the flag supposed to suggest peace?"

"Thomas Francis Meagher's 19th-century idea of lasting truce never registered. Here you go. Today's beer is actually properly chilled for a change."

"Everything I thought about flags has become irrelevant since I arrived here."

"Flegs! Fuck 'em! Let's drink to that."

"I mean it, Ben. The Union Jack seemed an inclusivity ad: bringing all the Kingdom's parts into such a perfect design, until I got to know Northern Ireland."

"Aye right. It's been a pleasure to serve as your eye opener and your bottle opener. Sláinte."

Oh, no! You didn't. You couldn't have slept with him. Did you? Ben is right here, half-naked and dreaming like a baby. Your bra is open, and this isn't your lovely bedroom … but I only remember kissing him. How did we end up like this? What made the uninterested you do it?

This empty vodka bottle is one clear explanation. So, how come you only remember one beer? Two? No three. Still, far from facilitating this nothingness on the situation.

What is wrong with you? Well, the answer won't make the first draft of an obscure mystery novel. But something other than his long-acclimated flirting had to kindle this mess. What was it? Brain, work with me here! What happened?

Fragments are flashing back … yeah, Ben suggested toasting

the history of power-sharing between Protestants and Catholics.

"One drink per attempt? This would consolidate your research. I'll prove it. We'll start in the seventies, with Sunningdale."

"That Agreement didn't deliver anything."

"I beg to differ, Ella. Worthy of some recognition as it is known as the Belfast/Good Friday Agreement for slow learners."

His knowledge level was surprising; or was the surprise alcohol-assisted?

"Okay, Anglo-Irish Agreement. Knock it back fast. We can't offend the Loyalists longer than it took Thatcher to sell them out, not for peace, but for a total omnishambles."

Yes. After that shot of Stoli. That was the moment Ben started looking smarter and funnier than usual. Bordering on adorable, leaving untrustworthiness all to Daniel.

"Ready for the next one? This toast borrows from the inimitable British peace playbook. I have 'no selfish or strategic interest' in getting you blitzed, and nothing but full respect for your rights."

He heavily outperformed me in political awareness. And drinking capacity. I paused at that point. Was my eyesight getting bleary?

"You can't stop here, Ella. The nineties British declaration of intent to withdraw is toasting material par excellence. That Westminster messaging made all the difference for the Provies."

By the time we got to the Belfast/Good Friday Agreement, I no longer took in the agreements he brought up. Ben insisted they were kosher, though they sounded like a Scottish university and a hilly castle of some sort—

"Ella, you okay?"

"Sorry I woke you. I should head upstairs."

"No, please stay. I'll get you a glass of water."

"You must think I'm totally off the rails—"

"Not on yer Nellie! The single thing that comes to mind is

that you are equally irresistible, teary, or cheery. I'll get you tissues too."

"Please don't tell Michael about any of this."

"Don't be daft."

You need to smile back. Ben deserves to misunderstand that Daniel was all you saw in him.

CHAPTER 13

A WAR OUTLIVED

"Mom, are you hearing me? Rubinstein emailed! No. Stop saying I'm overreacting. An August check-in from your dissertation advisor is worse than walking the Cliffs of Moher on a windy day … Well, you should, soon, it's incredible … Yes, the tour was fun, too short … No, I'd give it more than a weekend and spend time in Galway not just Dublin … I'll send you the photos later … Mom, please, it takes Rubinstein ten seconds to respond to my emails. Remember, I need to sound theoretically sophisticated and advanced in my fieldwork. Muting the laugh would help my self-esteem … Thank you. This is what my cold sweat managed so far."

"*Hugely kind of you to reach out. Ideal timing too: the longer I am here, the more enigmatic Northern Ireland's equality question becomes. Though, recalling the Conflict & Coexistence final back in the fall, it should make far more sense to you.*"

"Did you catch my unsubtle flattery there, Mom?"

"I taught you well, child. Go on."

"*In broad strokes, legal equality is a Northern Irish obsession. Justice, equal treatment, parity of esteem are sacred categories. Justifiable as seeking fairness is, it's confusing when such claims have simultaneously worked to solidify segregation between Catholics and Protestants. I realize that sounds paradoxical, particularly to an American ear, but the Northern Irish non-discrimination frenzy has produced a cost for solidarity and coexistence."*

"Mom? Are you still there? It sounded like you're busy elsewhere. Yes, okay, sorry, I know you're capable of starting a dishwasher while listening. This comes next."

"Both communities are unabashedly strategic in their communal goals. The only policies they seem to agree on are affirming their unique – and competing – identities."

"Still there?"

"Still here, but no longer with you, I am afraid. What do you mean by 'strategic'?"

"Politics is used to entrench differences instead of bridging divides. Oh, no! Wasn't that discernible from what I just read?"

"Take it easy, Ella. Professor Rubinstein is a trained sociologist, isn't she? Why don't you test all that on Natasha, our family's sociologist, remember? And utilize your mother where I can do some good. Did you touch trauma?"

Like my DNA would permit that omission.

"Today's adults were the Troubles' children, a group particularly trauma-prone. Yet, the variability in diagnosing trauma factors (e.g. age, gender, support, social class and coping skills) makes it challenging to link current symptoms back to a Troubles-stunted childhood."

"Sometimes, you really, truly, manufacture reasons to be proud."

"But—"

"No buts, Ella. Traumas differ from one person to the next."

"But—"

"A local therapist could suggest feedback around trauma diagnosis."

"To me or you, Mom?"

"Hah-ha. Adam, your parentally traumatized daughter is on

the line … The younger one. Pushkin brought him in just now."

"Wait, stay on, Mom. There was one more point I wanted to run by you."

"Why haven't mixed workplaces brought greater integration? Every law requires cross-community representation and equality, but all are powerless to ignite any curiosity to mix. 'I don't discuss identity with co-workers' was the most common answer in my interviews."

"Is that really as novel as you make it out to be? How often do you discuss politics with your friends, and with how many of them do you disagree politically?"

Mom has a point.

"Tell me this, Ella: how integrated are their schools?"

"Mostly not. Segregated neighborhoods too. Why?"

"An inclusive mindset will filter faster in the yet-to-mature brain. Okay, Adam, I surrender. If I don't hand the phone over to your father right now, my wrist will break. Stay in touch! I'm here to help."

Well, you knew that sooner or later, his 'I knew it all along' speech would debut.

"Last night, I edited a piece on why people overestimate low probability

events—"

"Dad, I knew it! Casino Daniel MacIntyre. A sure loss at the end."

"That's not a bad analogy, Ella. But I am not saying I didn't buy into your winning hopes. I liked him. We all did."

Mom is right. Rubinstein would probably welcome a psychological dive into the conflict's legacy. If their packed bars are anything to go by, prevalent post-conflict mental health issues are entirely plausible. Who knows, interviewing a pharmacist in addition to a psychologist might also present the opportunity to obtain some weed for personal use.

Wise up. Since when do you do weed? You have four, not forty days left in Belfast and six days until your face-to-face with Rubinstein, when she expects to hear a testable dissertation hypothesis. You know she hates meetings without an advanced outline that needs at least a couple more days to become legible. The data-organizing future has dawned. Panic should halt your hunter-gatherer research frame of mind. No more interviews except for the three community workers already scheduled. At least with that you are covered cross-communally, one from each side, and the third working in the interface around a peace wall.

Leaving this horrible flat should henceforth be solely for the purpose of purchasing food and an occasional raspberry chocolate-chip ice cream. If ordinary folks in those encounters are amenable to conversation, ask only the questions you now recite in your sleep. Focus on the bright side: indoor writing minimizes the chances of running into a certain someone who by now may be back in Belfast, preparing for his own return to the US.

This is the last Google search ensuring that 'psychological cost to ending a conflict' plus 'the Troubles' won't thunderbolt something obvious your interviews overlooked. Shit, the searchable videos alone add up to more than seven hours of screen time. Why did you have to beeline to the most researched place in the universe for your dissertation?

Okay, this clip hashtags victims' groups. You'll watch it now to help avoid any pitfalls when you meet with the community workers. The rest could keep you company on the plane back home.

Opening shots of murals, what else? That's Belfast, all right. Predictable interfaces aren't a promising start as your silver bullet. What was that local term Ben mentioned for their stuck in the past approach? *Whataboutery*, I think it was. Dad would enjoy learning jargon to describe the constant blaming of who did what and when.

Hopefully, this fourteen-minute and thirty-six seconds video isn't another example of those.

I am David Walker and I love the town I call home.

I can relate, mainly because your dirty-blond cuteness stares directly at me. The psychedelic shirt does wonders for the toned torso. Works well with the undercut hairstyle too. He must be about Daniel's age.

Belfast has lived through real highs and lows; a booming, rich, industrial city in the 19ᵗʰ century followed by 20ᵗʰ-century darkness. A hundred years on, my personal history aligns with its 21ˢᵗ-century revival.

He might know Daniel—

I grew up in the Protestant area of North Belfast.

Unless he went to an integrated school, unlikely that their paths would have crossed.

I now live here as an adult exhausted by the whole green and orange divisions, but my neighbourhood remains segregated. I often wonder, why doesn't the conflict fade away?

My question exactly, bro.

I started by asking a couple of my neighbours, who represent the legacy of our past. Brian, who lives two streets north in a Nationalist area, once was a legendary IRA gunman. While Jill, who's only two doors down from me, is a victim of their bombs.

Pretty good cliffhangers.

Brian, what are your deepest scars?

People focus on what you lose during conflict. Life, loved ones, the physical injuries, PTSD. But to be honest, my mental health was more than fine during the Troubles. When I joined the IRA, I was convinced I had a job for life. I'd either die for our ideals or end up permanently behind bars. Never contemplated this becoming my life.

What did the end of the conflict mean for you?

No warrior is ready for the business of peace, David. It's unnatural to switch from soldier to survivor. What caught me off guard? I was unprepared for solidarity vanishing faster than snow off a ditch. For all the pages he wrote, Tolstoy would have done better by us to whistle-blow the psychology of it: together at war, sidelined and medicated at peace, now that's premium takeaway for Republicans.

Brian does chain smoke, and looks like human wreckage tortured by the past. His problems could very well extend beyond substance abuse to a whole range of traumatic stressors. Isn't anybody looking after these people? I'll ask the community workers about ex-combatants' reintegration.

What was it all for? Being on the run, sleeping in a different bed every night. For what? For what? My reputation evaporated a bit slower than my marriage. Ending the armed struggle left us behind. Unskilled for civilian life and damaged. For a while I'd get young lads coming here, thinking they're on some sort of feckin' pilgrimage. Convinced they missed the Republican boat, wanting to be soldiers. Looking action. I chase them away from my doorstep, telling them you'll not see me fighting again. Telling them to go get an education. Become apprentice plumbers. Sorry David, but if it's a positive you're looking from me, I can't help you out. My legacy is not having a fecking clue where my own kids ended up. And the only positive from that is that they knew nothing of the grief this useless war caused.

Hmm. David must be walking over to his other neighbor. He could have enhanced his documentary with some background music instead of standard street noise.

My name is Jill. As long as you won't reveal my age, David, I don't mind your camera capturing my wrinkles.

Did you forgive those who hurt you, Jill?

At the beginning I said I'll never forgive. What good did the memories do? I got cancer. I skipped therapy. They offered. No. Why bother? 'Come to terms with your trauma,' they'd try and persuade me. But no amount of therapy would fix my body, my life. No amount of therapy would answer the only question that mattered: why? Why shopping for a dress all them years ago, my left leg was amputated by a 500-pound bomb? I try to forget, to blot it out.

What makes Jill forget?

And would you say you are successful ... at forgetting? Or forgiving?

Of course not! I don't know how the Queen did it. Shaking themuns' hands after they murdered Mountbatten. Couldn't bring myself to do that.

So, Jill, give us a window into the treatment of victims.

Don't get me started.

You can pause here. The legacy of the conflict haunts David's neighbors. Not to minimize Jill's pain, but your anxiety, worry, and impending deadlines should motivate you to get to understandings. Yet, here you are, still on first base on why it takes so long to recover from war? Paramilitaries' manipulations and threats can't provide the sole explanation for why identity markers persist. There needs to be some independent interest, something within the broader community that keeps divisions alive.

A one-on-one with Rubinstein on her unrelenting office chair is going to be a bloodbath. She knows you have Internet connectivity. The only way to buy additional data-generation time is to reply to her email hinting at your empty-handedness while you are still over here. But why can't I formulate a doable dissertation hypothesis already? It doesn't need to be something you care about as long as it is something to write about.

Ditch breakthroughs. Drop Fletcher's superstardom dreams. Honing one thing, and one thing only: the production of two hundred pages that three people would find passable enough without an overload of 'if you had only looked at ...'

You need to think it's possible.

CHAPTER 14

ANTI-SOCIAL BEHAVIOUR

OMG, THAT'S HER!

"Maeve."

Daniel's mom, marching frictionless in a navy skirt-suit and tan heels. Of course, the red handbag is a mix that matches.

"Maeve!"

"Oh, Ella. Hello. What a coincidence."

Your distressed smile is good enough for me, now that orbiting your Alfred House's office in the rain like it's the sun itself finally pays off.

"How good to see you. How are you getting on with your work? Leaving for home soon, are you?"

Why wouldn't she remember when it's the same day her son departs? Noticing I caught her watch-glancing is perfect. Guilt is all I have going anyway.

"Got time for a coffee?"

"Just about but—"

Bingo.

Don't risk a packed Harlem Café; Nero will do fine. This branch never runs out of cream.

"It'll have to be quick. Mental at the office today."

Her escape plan won't get in the way of your leading her to the steady table. Even if it's larger, it has only two chairs, so no one would be able to join. The wobbly one at the corner risks unnecessary interferences. You need Maeve's full attention.

"So, your research, going well?"

"Getting there. Talking to lots of people about their experiences. Learning a lot."

"That's good to hear."

"How did you and Oliver make it work?"

"Ahem ... sorry, this latte is roasting. Uh ..."

Good thinking bringing water to the table too. Now, start over. You have a job to do, and she can choose to answer, or not, as she pleases.

"Sorry, I didn't mean to put you on the spot."

I know that you know that nothing proceeded as planned for me, including our scheduled interview in your office at the Human Rights Commission.

"The more I researched, the more your family's unique story fascinated me."

She's still in her discomfort. She needs more breathing room.

"I don't mean to pry. Still very much in the midst of synthesizing the logic of this place. Your angle would be extremely useful."

"Does anybody really know how any marriage works, Ella?"

Please don't make me feel like an interrogator. The number of times I tried to run into you exceeds Northern Ireland's centenary by a mile.

"You are reading too much into us."

Am I? A lonely – very lonely – interview-intensive month was an outstanding teacher on hands-retraction from tables as much as raised eyebrows. Keep your eyes on hers but stop the lip-biting. Unabridged silence will obligate Maeve to answer.

"Our family life really wasn't that melodramatic, I don't think. We kept our lives normal. For—"

No, Maeve. Studying me won't get me to back down because an award-winning psychotherapist raised me. "Yeah, but it couldn't have been easy."

"It seldom is."

I know that you know you owe me more than that.

"It's all in the past now. But the long and the short of it, I suppose, was that we were young, working hard in our careers, and as parents didn't have too much time to think outside the everyday."

"But at the time, your marriage *had* to be revolutionary. Oliver, in the RUC, yes? No? And your particular jobs hardly cocooned you."

"You know Oliver. I met a good-hearted lad who loved me. Even back then, love mattered more than any history, or family backgrounds, or norms."

She must know that Daniel isn't tight-mouthed about Ciaran and Oliver's dynamic.

"Aye, there were some tricky dynamics, of course … missed opportunities too … but time, I suppose, is the crucial factor in getting on. Here's me wittering on like a granny. You don't need me to be telling you clichés."

Maybe she doesn't know that Daniel gave up on me and not the other way around. With the barriers she broke, Maeve couldn't have issues with our relationship. Unless it was the threat of her only son moving away from here. Impossible: MIT was always in Massachusetts, long before my entrance. What you need from Maeve MacIntyre is a hint of whether a fighting chance is left with *your* love.

"Maeve, forgive me. I know it's pushy, but I really need to know. Were you, or Oliver, bothered by our relationship?" Oh, no, not another watch glance.

"Daniel is a big boy, Ella."

"I do miss him." Shit, was that audible?

"I have to get back. I'm very sorry. Good luck with your work."

Racing out faster than Usain Bolt. Faster than getting to add, 'and have a nice life.'

Among the many types of failures, this was a catastrophe. Now you'll never see her again, and Oliver learned, or is just about to find out, that you are a loser. The news should reach the extended Donnellys clan by tomorrow at the latest. Surely, they are getting together again in Cultra before Daniel departs on the flight your mother changed for you to avoid seeing him. The news would also be dissected on the lovely Broughshane patio in no time.

You fucked up any potential academic progress that a productive conversation with Maeve could have contributed. Now you'll never know whether the one child policy was the result of a stressful family dynamic, making Maeve decide 'never again.' Similarly, the train left the station on your chance to ask what the toughest decision was raising Daniel in a mixed marriage. What good did hours of playing this scene over and over in your head achieve when—

Unreal! How does Mom always know when to phone? No, you can't answer with so many tears in your eyes. You served her, all of the Goldins, enough drama for one summer.

Raining still? Why is there a police siren outside? Correlation may not mean causation, but it's spooky to ignore that you gambled on the wrong parent to help you get Daniel back.

Again? Sorry, Mom, I am still avoiding your call. Why? You know why, Mom: because I'll have to hear your usual 'we're living in a random universe.' And after a coffee sip and a head shake, you'll add, "No, Ella. I really don't think the police siren was a sign that you had to target Oliver instead."

And even if I managed to conceal from Mom that the woman I needed to connect with just deserted, what would you tell Mom anyway? That no one around gives a fuck about communal polarization? It'll take Mom two seconds to pull out, "Who are you to judge, Ella?" Yes, I don't need a reminder that the US isn't the promised land of integration, especially when we had quite the head start with *Brown v. Board of Education.*

No, Mom. These two middle-aged ladies enduring the wobbly corner table look nothing like you. Okay, maybe slightly something of Jemma Donahue across the street, maybe not. But one thing is certain: they are unready to stop talking about the sale in Marks and Spencer and explain sectarianism to an accented stranger.

Yes, Maeve, since you asked, this was, without a doubt, my most misspent day.

CHAPTER 15

FAILURE IS A NATURAL
PART OF LIFE

"Oh, hey, Ben."

You are yet to brush your hair, and he's already back from Nero.

"Dropping off a memento: your final *Irish News* in hard copy."

"The always thoughtful Ben. I'll cherish it, and miss our morning espressos more than you'll ever know."

"Any grand plan for your last day?"

"Beyond attaining a reason for depression? Don't look petrified. I'm kidding. It's nice to know you share the belief in the Peak-End Rule."

"What's that?"

"Ending on a high note would help me to, eventually, recall this trip as a nice experience ... No, not *that*, Ben. We tried that already, remember?"

"A refresher wouldn't hurt. Perhaps this time it'll be transformative? Are you sure?"

"I'd like to continue and remember our special relationship after the mutual awkwardness had faded, thankfully." Good, Ben caught the transatlantic reference. "I won't disappear without a proper goodbye. Scout's honor."

Maybe my original Belfast's To Do List has one last good idea. *Check out the on-the-brink-of-extinction Jewish community* – totally blanked on that one. Is it really worth the trouble of schlepping all the way to North Belfast in this rain? What would you find in common with an Orthodox rabbi beyond another Northern Irish male forbidden to your touch?

Of the entire Jewish spectrum, it's self-explanatory why Belfast could attract the Orthodox version, our version of worshipping in the oldest traditions of the past. But there is a touch of irony in that Protestants are Israel's enthusiasts when Jewish and Irish histories share so many parallels. The homeland-diasporic experience itself presents such a fascinating comparative study of these two nations. What portion of Irish Americans felt conflicted by the Troubles, the IRA? Does it correlate with the way Israel disappoints American Jews today? Unhelpful digressing when Rubinstein's office is seventy-two hours away.

If North Belfast is out, you shouldn't have rushed to dismiss Ben, the one local male who answered your questions without making you feel ignorant. Enough. Make this last day spaceless for melancholy. Retail therapy is a fine substitute for any grand plan immaterializing. You earned self-indulgence. You also need to find something for Natasha.

"Ella ... you're here ..."

What did you think a spontaneous ringing of the intermediary's front door could bring?

"Sorry, Michael. I didn't mean to crash your party—"

"No, not at all."

He doesn't believe you one bit. You are so stupid. How was it not foreseeable that Michael might throw a send-off party when Daniel is also flying out tomorrow? Where was your instinctive 'this can only end badly,' and when will you learn that every choice matters? Including wearing the bright pink blouse when your two armpits perspire more than the Northern Irish population combined. Now Michael knows the stinking you, in addition to noticing your ten extra pounds.

"Brilliant to see you again, Ella."

With a 'brilliant' as lit as a darkroom, someone is here with Daniel.

"Far from a party. Just drinks before heading into town. Don't be a stranger, come in and join the craic."

"I didn't plan on staying. Just came to drop off a small token of *merci beaucoup.*"

Well, at least he is appreciative of the whiskey and the Thorntons box. Long after you're gone, he can find the best time to graze the personally selected truffles.

Measuring sticks are inevitable, and a female duel wasn't the reason you came. A genuine, well-deserved thank you to Michael shouldn't need to last more than—

"Daniel, hi." Shit, he looks so good. A new shirt. Personal gift?

"You're looking well, Ella."

"I just stopped for a minute, to thank Michael—" Shit, not *her*! I thought she lived in London these days. Fuck. How could he? No, you cannot. You can't ask if she's his girlfriend when Hannah is ten feet away and hard at work pretending not to see you. YOU. SEXUALLY FULFILLED. SUPER. FUCKING. JERK.

"I'm staying around a bit longer."

No kidding.

"I'll text you in September. We'll catch up in Harvard Square, yeah? First drink on me."

Walk away, slowly. Slower. Everyone is looking. Yes, you can suppress your sniffling for another six short feet to the door. Daniel can pretend that he forgot how to read my face, but shifting to the 'appreciate what was' attitude regarding him isn't happening, ever. Friends, huh? Unintelligent was the one thing Daniel MacIntyre never struck me as being.

"Hey, stranger." Oh, God, Ben too. "Need company?"

A heart of gold, whispering his question so as not to offend the asshole deserving every possible insult.

"I need to pack, but thanks."

"We could order Chinese or something."

"No, stay. Stay special, long after I leave."

Shit. How would obsessing about your ex's 3am wild sex help you fall back asleep? Give yourself the gift of a reality check. With Daniel's speed, the only thing Hannah's overdone face is enjoying right now is his sleepy-warm neck. While the only thing he would be enjoying is a barrister unable to locate a stupid channel to teach her about make-up. This ruminating over something that isn't happening has got to stop. Why insist on torture?

There is no way to spin this. If Daniel is still post-ejaculation hard right this minute, he is also as naked as the truth. You are replaceable, and it didn't require a Cinderella – more like one of her ugly (okay, not that ugly) sisters. It's not like you needed further proof that Rational Choice Theory is a fucking fable. But you aren't the only one nor will you be the last to have to get through a breakup. It's over. You accomplished at Michael's what you could in the worst way possible: presenting an ex with the perfect display of vulnerability. Get some sleep because you know you won't get any on the flight.

The single regret? Well, Cambridge was out of your control, but not scheduling a London weekend in the span of five weeks …

"Miss, it's such a lovely day. Will we take the scenic route over the mountains? Takes the same amount of time, and from Hannahstown you can near see the whole Northern Ireland. No place more beautiful when the sun's out."

"Whatever you think is best, as long as I make the flight."

"No fear of that."

Well, I wouldn't be so sure with Hannah in the Road's name, but you're the expert.

No point in candor-spraying a cheerful taxi driver when he's responsible for your life. You must also remember how grateful you should be to many of his colleagues. Some of your best interviews. Still, you could wonder about the weight of history in the breakup. Dad tried to warn you in his clumsy way that there could be uneasiness. But Daniel ridiculing Northern Ireland for being stuck in the past, proud that he was sheltered from it all; then, transpiring as another scarred soul of the conflict – that was unpredictable.

Why can't this place move on?

Okay, this was never destined to be the vacation of a lifetime. But the Goldin in you is well-coached to take pride in molding excruciation into benefits. Yes, research would have brought me here regardless of our random bar encounter. And it would be dismally juvenile to deny that coming with Daniel simplified, however grief-stricken, some aspects of the visit. The uninformed you was committed to falling for this place from the get-go. Had you stayed back in Medford, these Islanders would all still remain exotically Irish at the end of the summer. Instead, you leave joyless, but with a 4D sonogram of persisting post-conflict animosities.

It's the right time to leave because the Northern Irish peace games had turned irritating. Belfast feels claustrophobic. Need another reason why it's the exact time to depart? The whole Northern Ireland is in front of you in a panorama, and the single thing this beauty brings to your mind is Belfast's iconic yellow cranes. Why name the city's symbols Samson and Goliath? Two giants destroyed in humiliating ways. See: there's always a silver lining, at least according to Susan Goldin. At least you'd make Mom proud for locating a silver lining.

"Ella!"

That cannot be him! It can't be Daniel. Mom changed the flight, the airport, and your destination from Boston to Newark to spare you this encounter.

"Ella! It is Ella, isn't it? Bumping into you here of all places."

Definitely not Daniel. What a relief. Definitely seen this guy before.

"Aaron, from your first night in Belfast?"

"Aaron, right." The Cathedral Quarter, when all seemed so promising. No doubt Aaron is well-informed why Daniel isn't here with me.

"This is Jennifer, my girlfriend. Just arrived from New Jersey."

It's nice to know that in a world of scarce resources, you are leaving Belfast to an excited fellow Tri-State resident. And more of an expert in the mechanics of choice, for sure. Aaron not only welcomed Jennifer with a dozen irises but thoughtfully ignores your own progressive decay.

For a Departures line, it isn't half bad. Sufficient time to spend the last remaining cash pounds in Duty-Free. I have already contributed financially to this region. Well, less so than the British Exchequer, but at least your modest contribution was genuine, while that country's might be prompted by fear of violence. Oh, well. One more question you haven't asked that Queen's professor at the time: why hadn't Britain jettisoned Northern Ireland already, Professor Campbell? She did it so many times elsewhere throughout the globe, and it would save billions of taxpayers' money currently maintaining this polarized society?

"On behalf of Captain Burns and myself, thank you for trusting us with your flight to Newark. We have been cleared for take-off."

I will take your word on that, Captain. Flying this iron bird against the wind, please keep in mind that your passenger in 32C has trembled quite a bit already.

Have *I* also taken off? Endless summertime teas and coffees, fifty-five interviews ranging between ten minutes and two hours, sixteen videos, 378 photos, and one unfixable relationship. Measured against the extent of the damage, the captains could certify your resilience. Turning the seatbelt sign off – maybe they are free to chat? Maybe they'd be interested to hear that they are flying you into the future, not back into the familiar. It's instructive to know the plane's current height and speed, but the captains may also be willing to share methods on leveling a plane during overwhelming circumstances. Hopefully, they'll omit the cheesy 'behind every storm there is a shining sun.' You'll have to do your best to steer them toward actionable advice: my captains, I'd love to know how you keep your planes from heading straight into the rocks? In my experience, it's really exhausting.

"Anything to drink, Miss?"

I followed your directions on where to find my oxygen mask, Stewardess Tara. Thankfully, my breathing is automatic. These days, I appreciate the rare break from hard chores. But you are so efficient. There is so much agency in your cabin-based performance. What would be your top tip for an emotionally demanding state of being, Tara?

You are probably right, Stewardess Tara. Yes, I *have* put too much time into this rarely-going-according-to-plan dissertation to be running out of fuel now. You're right again; my dissertation committee expects me to demonstrate that selective experience didn't navigate my research. They are social scientists, though; they don't need me to teach them that biases affect data collection. The Northern Irish had their own prejudices toward me too. American, female, Jewish, Israel. Rubinstein will remember meeting Daniel at the end of the year party. She won't be heartless, and she'll be discreet about your Northern Irish heart-butchering episode. But only if you do your part to convince her that your work surpasses realistic fiction.

BOOK THREE

CHAPTER 16

COMEBACK

EVER SINCE HE WAS BORN, Daniel possessed my special empathy. Yes, of course, it stems from seeing so much of myself in him. One difference defines us: he wasn't the child of warring parents. Maeve and Oliver never fought over his custody. His success was their joint goal, and my cushioned middle-class Belfast was their strategy. That said, Daniel's choices in his life as an adult, including where to make his home, still lay ahead.

As part of my post-ceasefire generation, Daniel grew up shielded from binary tribalism. Yet, the past is an unfinished business everyone needs to come to terms with one way or another. Secrets and guilt can be quite the hefty baggage to sort through. Even without Ella and her historical curiosity, returning to Belfast in January carried booby traps that an otherwise calculating Daniel didn't properly consider.

I am still not entirely sure why Daniel undertook his final thesis term in absentia from MIT and within my compressed borders. Boston's stunning autumn welcoming him back in September succumbed early to a harsh winter. With advanced entry and a near-perfect GPA, he accelerated the completion of degree requirements and aspired to an early practical experience start. Fond summer memories of working, studying, and researching at Cambridge University may have entered the decision to return home.

Never fully warming to the sourness of American competition certainly did. Ella didn't come back into the picture, and neither did a new American relationship. Perhaps it was this collection of reasons that ignited Daniel's urgency to continue his professional growth here in Belfast. I think he also hoped that the conversion rate of sterling to dollars would expedite repaying the bogeyman of student debt.

However, as history often told in her books, brashness is a proud parent of countless crises, and Daniel was overconfident about the re-entry process. Wrongly, he expected to compensate for a shortage of local professional contacts with his now-foreseeable prestigious master's degree and his middle-class, inter-communal background. The market here is small, as are the budgets. The growing neo-liberal world taught me to resentfully accept my inability to supply a spectrum of fulfilment paths leading my youth to seek futures elsewhere.

Yet, Daniel wasn't accounting for my compactness, nor for the fear of or threat posed by people like him coming from outside with new ideas. A humbling string of electronic rejections and, worse still, no replies welcomed his enthusiastic inquiries. But his professional hunger didn't wane, nor his peculiar ambition. He banked on physical interviews as the best way to line up a post-graduation job, and potentially sooner with a paid apprenticeship.

An unexpected cheerleader emerged – his academic advisor. With Walsh as a surname, the professor always hoped to explore his Irish roots. As an accomplished academic, he needed to self-justify the trip with a professional reason. Because my Queen's and Dublin's Trinity offered fresh lecture and contacts opportunities, he enthusiastically signed Daniel's departmental proposal to complete his thesis from afar.

Ecstatic succinctly captured Oliver's reaction when he saw his darling boy exiting my International Airport.

"Homecoming to redesign Belfast, hey?"

"Aye. One building at a time, Dad."

Placing Daniel's large dark blue duffel bag and backpack in the boot of his vehicle, Oliver inquired, "What's your career ambition for this place, son?"

"The chance to build something that others won't ignore I suppose."

"Sure I know you'll do us all proud."

His father appeared different to Daniel. Greyer, gaunter, shrinking. A contrast to the contemporary extension their South Belfast detached home now possessed. With two secured public sector jobs and one adult child, Oliver and Maeve could invest in trendy furniture. That's why Daniel couldn't believe that his grandparents' French-style chaise longue had made its way from Antrim.

"The decorator loved it. Mismatching and maximalism are things right now."

His euphoric mother had been giddy ever since her eyes and arms met her returnee.

"Test it out. We won't be eating the stew for a while yet." Father and son recognised Maeve's cooking wouldn't win a Michelin Star anytime soon.

"Believe it or not, we are even thinking about getting a wee pet." A happy Oliver contributed his own perspective on the slow-motion emancipation of previously held taboos.

Is retirement on the horizon?

Post-food, the reunited MacIntyres opted for a relaxed evening at home. No big discussions, just a chat about this and that.

The time when I missed long walks with Daniel is over, Maeve thought while nostalgic Oliver selected on their new TV the family favourite *The Godfather* to snooze to. Daniel reclined on the white velvet of the gold-edged chaise longue with the *Belfast Telegraph: A Fresh Beginning … New Programme for Government Reform … Cross-Communal Initiatives …*

*Same old Northern Ireland, independent of how long or far
I stay away,* Daniel concluded before surrendering to his own
deep sleep.

The next day, he met for a late lunch with his old mate Michael, now holding a steady Equality Commission job, seeing a
good career ladder ahead. At the city centre bistro (name omitted to conceal endorsement), Daniel complimented his friend's
swapping jeans and hoodie for a smart tweed jacket and khaki
chinos.

"Surprised they even let you in looking that scruffy."

"My new American accent opens doors." Daniel's unshaven
face and dark blue sweatshirt betrayed their old sameness.

Lately, Michael had started dating a rising-star accountant,
the daughter of someone high up in the civil service. This liaison
endowed a standing visibility amongst the 'great and the good.'
He invited Daniel to tag along for that night's function at the
MAC.

"C'mon, mate, put in a wee appearance."

Meeting Daniel's exaggerated yawn, Michael swiftly added,
with a smile, "You couldn't already forget that the relationship
between connections and job security is legislated into the Good
Friday Agreement."

Of course, Michael was only correct about that rule's unwrit-
ten cross-communal entrenchment.

"I'm underdressed for the occasion."

"I keep an emergency jacket and tie in my office. But it should
be pretty laid back. Artsy people. *And* you'll meet Jane."

Over a shared giant bowl of mussels, followed by seafood pasta with scallops, Daniel slagged Michael for getting hooked and
leaving most of his texts unanswered over the last few weeks.

"Speaking of love, what about yer one, Hannah now she's
living in Belfast again?"

Their espressos arrived, and while Michael was mixing two brown sugar sachets into his double shot, Daniel explained they'd kept in touch, and he was heading to Hannah's flat next. "But not before another of these outstanding brews. Nothing to touch it back in America."

"The yanks didn't take the lead on coffee after they had the balls to toss all that British tea into Boston Harbour?"

As the two friends laughed, Michael added, "Bring Hannah along tonight, yeah?"

"Depends on how well the reunion goes."

The bistro's atmosphere engrossed their conference for another hour, steadying conversation into the pace of enduring bonds, requiring a few sentences in between comfortable silences. Until Hannah texted that she was en route home. Then Daniel rushed towards the Cathedral Quarter, with a quick stop at the Queen's Arcade florist on the way.

Hannah dived straight into the centre of his open arms, and his chest didn't miss the anticipating firmness of her breasts.

"All ready, already? That's a record time even for you." Hannah laughed, finger-brushing his damp hair from the top and then from the bottom.

"I missed you. I missed your gorgeous twins."

Midway into the event at the MAC gallery, a delighted Michael noticed his mate entering with Hannah snuggled under his right arm (if I haven't mentioned yet, Daniel is a proud leftie). While Daniel changed in the gents, Hannah and Michael's Jane recognised each other from Girl Guides at a Church of Ireland hall in their distant past. Hardly a work of magic in my inextricable subcultures, but an equally pleasing relationship springboard for both lads and lasses alike.

Even in an art event, the real art for the upwardly mobile is networking. With a glass of complimentary prosecco in their hand, all four ventured into an independent blending journey. Daniel climbed up through the MAC's human-paced storeys like an alum at a reunion. Easygoing, heart-lifting exchanges crystallised a future bubbling with opportunities.

Reaching the MAC's top floor, Daniel spotted Belfast's leading architect leaning against the nearest window. While another attendee enveloped her in animated speech, Daniel prepared his opening line. Anyone observing him there would be minded of a lad ascending a library ladder to locate a dusty old tome. In recognising the architect, he looked as though he had tracked down that book's sought-after quote.

So, I was missing the one Earth location where seeing the same people all the time is what matters most. The good old is the grand new.

CHAPTER 17

REINTEGRATION

"Son, it's natural for Hannah to wish for a serious relationship at this stage in her life. In case you haven't noticed, we share the girl's concerns."

"Ma, please. None of this is useful."

The forward movement of ten weeks retreated Daniel straight into the past. Maeve didn't need Daniel's reminder of his abhorrence of her micro-managing his life. Yet, sharing the same roof since Daniel's January arrival was wearing thin. Not only had the professional mingling not reaped results, but setbacks kept coming, and Daniel wasn't earning money to get his own place. Hannah made the offer that he could move in with her. It was clear that was a step too soon and unfair on her flatmate. Therefore, neither Maeve nor Oliver missed their son's internal turbulence as he negotiated his sense of self.

Convinced that my own Belfast should be Daniel's forever home turned Maeve into Hannah's biggest fan. Whether or not Hannah was Daniel's rebound relationship did not matter; the girl represented the predictable, comfortable, conventional. Counter to his parental tendency to push Daniel out of his comfort zone, Oliver had also become satisfied that Hannah was his son's future. Thus, Daniel's difficulties in securing a post-graduate job justifiably flagged crisis to his adoring parents.

Hannah was reared as an Ulster Protestant, starving Maeve from any community-based leads over Hannah's roots. Levering information from Daniel was out of the question. That might present him with opportunities to quiz her about doors she didn't want to be opened in return. Untrusting of Oliver's background check, Maeve tried to remain moderately comforted that anything acute wasn't evident.

"You swear on our son's life of no UVF nor UDA skeletons in her family closet?" Maeve made a point to interrogate Oliver immediately following their lovemaking, counting on his confirmation under these circumstances as her best disclosure bet.

"Wind your neck in. The Troubles are long over. And the girl is a barrister with QC aspirations."

These days, I am proud to say, law is a huge industry in my capital. Thus, both parents had faith in the contribution of Hannah's professional ambitions to keeping Daniel locally. Lawyering everywhere demands complex specialisation and licensing. It isn't an easily transportable career. At worst, Hannah's profession would take them as far as England, Maeve hypothesised, while gift-giver Oliver got ahead of himself when he suggested they buy Hannah a hand-made barrister's wig.

"Absolutely not. That's for *her* parents to do, and Daniel would crucify us."

The wrapped-in-uniform Oliver gushing over Hannah's career aspirations is self-explanatory. But Maeve's delight plausibly invites further elucidation. Indeed, dropping the mandatory allegiance to the Crown in the Barrister's Oath back in the 1990s helped erase images of wigged prosecutors jailing my Catholics. But Maeve, the zealous 'moving forward' advocate, also appreciated the traditionalism woven into Hannah's respectable profession. The rigour and attention to detail required of the barristerial craft reinforced her approval of the (still Protestant) girl.

Following the precedent set by Oliver for the Donnelly family's penetration, Hannah was a welcome visitor in Cultra. Not that strategic Maeve would have left anything to chance. She actively pursued an affinity between her brother Ciaran and Hannah. Initially, Ciaran complied out of a sense of duty. With age had come remorse about how the actions of his youth had muddied family waters, especially where Maeve's life was concerned. If it weren't for Margot and his dear departed mother, they might still be on unspeaking terms. He also felt a little responsible for Daniel's bust-up with Ella. Yes, he only met Ella once, sufficient to impress him as intelligent and bold. He didn't mind American outspokenness. Indeed, when Margot inquired the next day what he thought of Ella, he remembered answering "pathfinder."

Progressively, Ciaran came to enjoy his professional debates with Hannah. He ran into her professionally on a few occasions, but these were brief non-substantive encounters. When she joined Daniel's visits, Ciaran found himself inviting Hannah to his study. There, the two engaged in long-standing disagreements about the role of law in society. Sitting across from his custom-made gold-framed 1916 Proclamation, they argued why and when people should disobey laws they disagree with. They enjoyed investigating if law is a mechanism to coordinate social activity or, rather, a vehicle for oppression, especially within deeply divided societies.

But, for all the joint Donnelly-MacIntyre nurturing of the relationship, Daniel's enthusiasm towards Hannah met a disappointing equilibrium.

During their next South Belfast cocktail bar rendezvous, over a second Manhattan, Daniel poured his doubts into Michael's ears: "I adore Hannah when we're together, but I feel I don't care as much as I should when we're apart."

As an avid follower of TV courtroom drama, Michael took the bait.

"Permission to approach the witness?"

Daniel's best interest was his part-time occupation since childhood.

"It isn't that I'm a bad boyfriend, or unkind or neglectful, or that we row even. I'm just … insufficiently dazzled."

"Go on then, describe your ideal woman."

"I reckon you know, mate."

"Well, other than the 'taking the edge off' kind."

"You *are* serious about the age-old preference question." Daniel laughed. "How long do I have to think it through?"

Daniel's response surprised Michael. Usually, his friend wasn't the hesitating type. "Tell me, whatever happened with your great American love affair? Did you never see Ella back in Boston?"

Daniel hesitated with a reply, but his body straightened up, provoking Michael to proceed. "Don't mind me. I've become a soppy big romantic these days."

But the memory part of Daniel's brain heard 'Action!'

"You know, Ella's most amazing quality was that she could see the person I could, ideally, become."

Recalling all too well Daniel's summer attitude and deeds, Michael opted for silence, presenting Daniel's mind with a further opportunity to rationalise.

"Hannah lets me feel appreciated, even satisfied, but in an undemanding way."

The only thing Michael could think was what a conundrum desire was. But unable to avoid Daniel's anticipating gaze, he uttered flatly, "I don't get your difficulty, then."

"I won't deny she's nurturing, but something about it anaesthetises my ambitions."

Daniel wasn't insensible to Michael's growing frustration, but his interpretation of it took an independent route. "Look, mate. I'm aware that the past is always tinged with nostalgia. But I think the key issue with Ella was timing."

Throughout his uni days, Michael justified every opportunity to skip psychology-oriented lectures with 'utter bollocks.' He felt infuriated yet fascinated by Daniel's selective memory.

"You were never the type to forget that absence makes the heart grow fonder." Michael tried to hide under his neutral tone that he was experiencing the curiosity of a cat.

"Be honest. You remember it the same way."

Dazed by how Daniel was editing his memories, Michael thought he should read a book or two about cognition, or better yet, listen to a podcast. But all he could say was a bland, "Chances are Ella moved on too. It's been a while."

"Aye. No doubt."

Michael cherished his old friend even for his transgressions. To steer the conversation to safer territories, he diverted Daniel into chatting about American football. It was an easy sell. Yet, once Michael headed to the gents, Daniel's re-immersed himself in pondering the wisdom of casting his die on Hannah.

I was as surprised as Michael by that development. While in the US, Daniel seemed to me to be much more at ease with himself. I was sure Ella was his chance to escape the two tribes inside him. A taxing observation, if I am honest. My younger generation increasingly detests the historical dichotomy, and I am apprehensive about other lands allowing them what I struggle with. But then came summer, the split, and the many days since.

Attempting to retrieve his last exchanges with Ella received no real assistance from his mobile. Of the few items Daniel had found in a public search of social media, nothing led him to suspect an alternative lover's arrival. Though Ella's visible virtual footprint did speak loudly of the distance walked from their shared history. Daniel didn't recognise any of the people next to her in the photos, and the backgrounds seemed unfamiliar too. Daniel grimaced, trying to fathom it out, but only momentarily, thanks to an incoming text from Hannah.

Near Sakura. Anything other than sushi 4 tonight?

On his way back to their table, Michael stopped to greet an acquaintance. This delay led Daniel back to the paradox of choice.
Aye, Ella had driven him a bit bonkers owning exploration as
he felt drained and bored by the lack of any discoveries relating
to her.

You aren't in a position to do a U-turn, he told himself. But
that reasoning neglected to convince his heart. Did he choose
rationally between the two women? Was he convincing himself
that everything was better with Ella when everything had been,
in fact, quite worse?

These love comparisons weren't healthy, to say the least. Indeed, contemplating preferences, Daniel managed to capture
all the standard self-interests, life-objectives, pleasure-inducers,
and unavoidable social constraints. But weighing most heavily
on Daniel's meaning-making process was the constant nagging
sense that he had wronged Ella. It was a growing certainty that
disturbed his sleep and depressed his appetite. He tried to raise
the issue again with Michael, but his otherwise excellent friend
was shrewd enough to avoid that trap.

"What's done and dusted cannot be undone."

Perhaps it was Michael's uncharacteristic seriousness leading
Daniel to conclude that his and Ella's was the defunct relationship. The one that, in the end, ran out of steam.

On Saturday evening, as part of the 'pushing Daniel towards
Hannah but not too hard' campaign, Hannah joined Maeve and
Daniel at *The History of the Troubles (Accordin' to my Da)*.
For obvious reasons, Oliver skipped the play. As a former RUC
officer, and the current Deputy Chief Constable, a comedy trip
down the Troubles' memory lane was the least of his interests.
Privately, he said to Maeve that he wasn't ready to find him-

self sitting next to someone he may have investigated back in the day. But at Maeve's request, he pleaded with Daniel to keep his mother company. She needed to be there as part of a work benefit, and Oliver had his own professional engagement that evening.

"In that hackneyed play? It's been on the go for decades. Weird choice for the Human Rights Commission."

"Some small p politics going on. But don't ask Mum about it."

Hannah was standing nearby, so Oliver refrained from saying, "ideal opportunity for your long-desired conversation with your mum about the meaning of being half Donnelly."

"How bad can it be, Daniel? Good chance to learn some history."

Daniel couldn't believe Hannah was agreeing to see that play. "They call that humour?" was Daniel's verdict as the three of them exited the Grand Opera House.

"Not even the line about the street barricade described as 'Belfast's greatest architectural triumph'?"

Daniel's dissatisfaction was the minority view amongst the high-spirited audience flowing out alongside them. Hannah's equanimity throughout the unsparing barbs against Unionism bothered Daniel.

Okay, Hannah wants to please Mum, but how could they stick this lads' banter? Especially as feminists.

Daniel's worry wasn't that he was experiencing a culture shock in his native land. Of course, he wasn't. He understood every comic reference. Yet, half a dozen minutes into the play and he was bored. *Why is the lack of political progress the subject of jokes?* A burst of uproarious laughter over a pun his wandering mind had missed cut short that profound thought. Looking at the two women engrossed in conversation next to him saddened Daniel. It was evident that the same force pulling them together kept him apart.

How much of this cheap ridicule was responsible for shaping our history? Why aren't people prompted to seriously discuss what they honestly think but instead use the guise of humour for everything they feel uncomfortable saying?

His own parents, having made things work despite opposing backgrounds, weren't immune from the general aversion to progress.

Is it really such a wonder that things don't move ahead in this village of a town? What, then, are the benefits of peace if we aren't truly post-conflict? Could this humour of resentment be our authentic cross-communal culture, then?

"You've gone quiet on us, Daniel. What is it that's turned you into a gloomy Rodin's *Thinker*, son?" Maeve startled Daniel out of his thoughts.

Your cotton wool overprotectiveness is suffocating me. But Daniel answered only, "I'm starting to have serious doubts about laughter being the best medicine."

CHAPTER 18

ADVANTAGEOUS HARDSHIPS

Every one of us consists of different versions, but the one I see of Daniel these days is like facing a mirror: he is unresolved. Spring spiralled him downwards. He is increasingly antagonised by life. It's distressing to see people getting sick of him turning up at parties empty-handed to drink excessively. Thank goodness he's young enough not to haunt wakes. The winter vitality he originally arrived with evaporated. His ambition too, except to hit the bottle. Daniel no longer searches for a real excuse to overdo it with the gargle, but most nights, he needs someone's steady hand to get him home.

Of course, my disquiet isn't just my own. His teetotal father, no longer recalling neither the taste nor sense of alcohol, was conscious the imbibing was a coping method and raised the issue with him. With Hannah in London, post-Friday dinner, Daniel walked into the lounge holding a cup of (hopefully only) tea, encountering an awaiting Oliver.

"I am a drinker, not a drunk, Dad."

Tolstoy's 1890 essay *Why Then Do Men Stupefy Themselves?* offering compelling concerns over intoxication, shot into Oliver's mind. "How does one differentiate?"

"For one, I am functioning."

"But wouldn't your possibilities broaden outside the blur of whiskey?"

Grapefruit – in name, colour, and physique – their recently adopted sociable Persian cat was next to enter the lounge, jumping straight into Oliver's lap. Perhaps that spurred Daniel's reply. "You shouldn't rely on my word alone. Herodotus' formula for Persian decision-making supports what I'm trying to say."

"Never heard of it."

"Neither had I until the leadership workshop last semester. Did you know Persians deliberated important decisions twice? Once sober and once when they were drunk."

As a principle, the MacIntyre residence was alcohol-free (Daniel's room – self-governed). Oliver suspected his son might be on his way to the second part of the professed decision-making process. With some attention still intact, Oliver gambled on Daniel's intellectual sense. He shared his challenge of trying to grasp why anyone whose profession rests on the stability of structures intentionally opts for a state of instability. Unfortunately, the final part of Oliver's thoughtful reflection was only to sweet, wide-eyed Grapefruit. Daniel slipped out of the lounge, and by the door's sound, hastily out into the street, and away.

A discouraged Oliver gently stroked the silky fur-ball twice over and placed him on the floor. Liberated, Oliver walked over to his bookcase cataloguing a representative sample of his print treasury. He pulled out *At Swim-Two-Birds* in search of his now nearly three-decades-old abstention motto. For Oliver, Flann O'Brien's observations on the mercilessness of alcohol and the imbecility of the drinker were truth itself. It made Oliver equally bothered by the double tragedy: O'Brien's death by alcoholism and the masterpiece's release too close to Joyce's final, *Finnegans Wake*. No author, regardless of objective talent, deserves such an unlucky book launch.

Having loaded the dishwasher, Maeve was the fourth to walk into the lounge that evening, gripping a pair of steaming teacups. Not that bickering between couples is necessarily bad, but seventy-two hours earlier, Oliver and Maeve were at each other's throats. Oliver offered to send Daniel back to the US and pay his rent while he completed his thesis. That sent the lad right back to another night of bingeing.

Daniel had grown up under an umbrella of minimal commentary on the Troubles' family legacy. Maeve attributed silence to being a big part of the family's ability to put the past behind them.

"Don't forget what silence did for our good relations with Ciaran," Maeve periodically reminded Oliver.

Much of Ciaran's reformation was due to Margot, who realised early on that the Armalite was losing to the ballot box.

"Stop being a hothead and express your political activism through the law." Margot's perpetual nagging had managed to coax Ciaran to try for a place in Queen's just in time for the ceasefire (and, to everyone's surprise, winning a place).

Quite the mastermind, Oliver remembered. Not only assuring his place as the Shinners' Consigliere until the lure of bigger money from property drew him away from politics; but Margot also had the wit to get into the tanning beds business just at the right time.

Naturally, Daniel's dual nature involved a fair share of navigation and delicate balances for his parents. Here and there were small-t traumas, always with the best intentions, but overall his parents had succeeded in sparing him living in one or the other's identities. Oliver was the academic nudger, breeding occasional arguments. Most recently, Maeve had blamed him for Daniel's choice to study abroad. But all these were now memories thickening the MacIntyres' parental arteries.

However, the present rapid descent of their dear son caused disequilibrium and brought a rocky patch to Maeve and Oliver's marital powerhouse.

"Don't start, Oliver. It's far too late to lecture me on how to parent."

"Be fair on the lad. He needs to know. Can't you tell he is begging for your answers on the past?"

Their exchange became heated; an unyielding Maeve was all that Oliver needed to persist.

"How long are you planning to injure him with this farce of a normal family background? Keeping omertà until he's a full-blown alcoholic?" Oliver couldn't understand why, if she wanted to keep Daniel in Belfast, Maeve was handling the situation with blinkers on. Uncomfortable and unexplained truths tormented Daniel.

Bitterness and the lasting conflict's fallout aren't the sole after-effects in communities. Decades after a peace deal, the impacts often reverberate nonverbally through families.

"Can't you see he is self-medicating?"

"Everybody has a relationship with their past, Oliver. Not every stone needs lifted."

A radio programme Oliver heard on the silence culture in families of Holocaust survivors wasn't leaving him. Discussing the grandchildren and great-grandchildren, experts explained how withholding information was an effective trauma transmitter across the generations.

Making sense of his life would move him away from drink. His mother needs to give our boy a coherent narrative.

Given his professional brushes linking drug and alcohol abuse to conflict trauma, Oliver's heart was inevitably heavy. Normally an early-to-bed, early-to-rise advocate, he spent long nights reading about walls of family silence, impatiently awaiting Daniel's stumbling 2am entrances.

As soon as Maeve does her bit, Oliver will be free to tell him about his Granny Eileen, mother of two Provies, gradually melting her steely heart towards an RUC man. Maeve's life with him shattered many dreams for Lorcan, who remained haunted by his grandson's integrated upbringing. Oliver never doubted that the IRA didn't enlist Malachy or Colm; they lacked the personality profile. And once Declan left the land of the living, he no longer cared about his IRA credentials. One detail Oliver still hoped to confirm as fact was who radicalised whom: Ciaran – Patrick, or vice versa?

If Maeve won't, time, or perhaps an archive somewhere, will. New information is always emerging.

Ultimately, intimate clemency delivered the final joint match point between the MacIntyres. They accepted that the real fight was their own against the bottle. To avoid another bust-up in the lounge, Oliver endeavoured to appear to Maeve calm and empathetic.

Dwindling monetary resources are now a challenge for Daniel's intoxication routine. The decent wage he earned as a sought-after teaching assistant in MIT's School of Architecture + Planning can only take one's excess so far. He sponges off Hannah, who isn't ready to undertake difficult choices. The poor girl loves him too much to want to probe the extent of his drinking patterns. However, Michael has cut off funding because his Jane has already established boundaries with respect to his mate. Daniel is as yet unbothered by any potential changes, perhaps because he finds companionships amongst others with a weakness to the drink.

In the interest of clarity, Daniel's practices aren't pathological in my thriving licensed vintners' sector. Actually, aside from periodical shameful side effects, alcohol served Daniel one unequivocal advantage. Sure, he vanishes into the bottle to blot out his untenable state: stuttering career, confused identity, messed-up love life, lost opportunities, troubling secrets, and uncertainty over where to live – here or back in the US? But while under the influence, Daniel attributes to the clear spirits the power to wash away the unimportant noise and futile elements of thought.

What is it now, over ten, twelve weeks since I have done a single sketch or plan? Whatever it was, it feels longer.

Job hunting goes nowhere. Not even in the direction of an unpaid summer opportunity. His original overconfidence about his ability and qualifications – in tatters. In the rare occurrences when Daniel reached the interview stage, the always saturated waiting rooms made him more appreciative of an insight often attributed to Albert Einstein:

He's dead right. Insanity is doing the same thing over and over, expecting different results.

"Daniel, Daniel MacIntyre. Who'd have guessed! Didn't you clear off to America? MIT, was it? What possessed you to come back to *this* place?"

Someone always recognised him. From school, uni, South Belfast, an acquaintance's younger sibling. And they always knew each other too; many studied together at Queen's. Welcoming as he endeavoured to appear, his feelings of superiority never melted.

"Back for a bit," Daniel faked modesty unconvincingly. "Aye, testing the waters with a local placement as part of my masters. My plan is to cover more bases; get transportable experience and qualifications in a globalised world. You know how it is."

Daniel always felt the rebellious glory of making it beyond local qualification options. His ambition never focused solely on the UK, Ireland or Europe, Brexit or not. Nobody denied his training wasn't the best. Yet, by the time Daniel walked from the waiting area into the interview, the repetitive format deflated every last molecule of his self-esteem. After a few moments glancing through his portfolio, the prospective employer was always more eager to share details of a recent visit to the US.

"Look, lad, your work is promising, and interesting," then followed by, "but possibly not applicable over here. We'll keep you in mind, but we won't have any more openings before September, placements or otherwise. You'll have your thesis by then, won't you?"

Daniel's stalled creativity wasn't a question of space. Maeve and Oliver set the scene for his Belfast return with an adjustable drawing station in one of the spare bedrooms with a padded stool and table with blueprint-sized drawers. They also added an Anglepoise desk lamp and a paper trimmer. The wheeled drafting chair arrived when Daniel mentioned that he needed seating that could move.

After the first couple of morning beers in lieu of a coffee break, work felt possible for him. Further consumption road-blocked most of his motivation.

On tonight's moonless night, the nearest open bar proved too noisy for Daniel's pounding headache. He proceeded to a cosier one closer to town. A trio of double brandies amplified the boisterous scene for Daniel, urging him to choose an early exit. Lurching unsteadily towards what he assumed was his home's direction, an oversized butterfly perched on a caterpillar caught his eye.

Oh, fuck! Will a pink elephant come next?

He tilted forward and squinted, surprised by the urgency of a slightly hidden-by-bushes bronze with fibreglass sculpture to tell him something.

"The damn booze is distorting my miiind!" Seated with his thoughts on the low brick wall surrounding what is Belfast's *Regeneration* sculpture, concentration built inside Daniel.

Professor Walsh is due here next week. I don't have a single sketch for my thesis, let alone an idea to discuss. Not even experimental efforts or stabs at concepts. I'm screwed!

He was turning into one of the horror stories Professor Walsh would tell his colleagues over lunches at the Faculty Club.

"Look, Daniel. I am your advisor, not your therapist. I think you are extremely promising, but you'll need to decide if this field is for you." Walsh wouldn't even waste an ultimatum. He'd drop him faster than a pencil stub.

A feeble attempt at standing proved utterly premature. The only thing that could continue to race was Daniel's imagination.

Time isn't on my side. I need to think, to focus. Guilt and shame over his creative inactivity terrified him. *What happened to my all-consuming passion for architecture? The single thing I always wanted to do was build; reshape relationships between a city and its residents.*

Typically, this phase in his thought process would lead Daniel straight back into the pub, rationalising it as needing the drink for clarity to emerge. But on this occasion, he just couldn't let go of the motivational pressure, in fact, sheer panic, to do something about it. Or as we'd say here, the lad was bricking it.

"Hop in, fella. You're a bit the worse for wear. We'll run you to your bed." A police vehicle stopped next to Daniel.

"Cheers, officers, but I'm grand where I am." His pitch was still drunken-high, but the speech far less stammering. "Still steamin' though. I'll sober up here. It's a nice night and I've not far to walk. Just having a wee wallow in self-pity. That's no crime, is it?"

Daniel's lack of aggression reassured the officers enough to leave him to his own devices. If the rat-arsed numpty wanted to get robbed or beaten up, they couldn't do anything more about it.

Once Daniel steadied up his head, he looked directly into the empty night, permitting time's movement to nurture his creative thought processes. It was the first time since his return that he felt an alerting thrill of insight.

"Of course!" he exclaimed. "How can people find their way in streets where the buildings themselves are gazing at each other in purposeful contempt?"

His inner conversation bloomed as he walked. Thankfully, no one was too close as parts were spoken aloud, though not in any form decipherable to the human ear.

Why was Belfast's pattern non-visionary? Waterfalls of peace money poured into incohesive regeneration. Post-conflict rebuilding without an overarching coherent plan to dismantle boundaries. Housing developments that must bore themselves with similarities. That's how we arrived at this. All over the place: a messy mosaic of community centres, housing estates, half-empty office buildings, a couple of new sports stadia and a Titanic Museum. A city divided between two communities outperformed mathematical axioms – slicing its two halves into seven (not four) quarters while keeping all ghettos intact. Is it any wonder that a half-baked place inspires her people to perpetually look back?

By then, Daniel's hands were trembling, but no longer from the drink. For a moment, as he looked around and saw exactly where he was, Ella shot through his brain.

Last time I was around here Mum was collecting the pair of us.

Not only did he break Ella's heart, he demolished her optimistic approach towards his homeland. Late-night revellers packed the nearby pizza place, but a couple had just walked out of the kebab shop. So he walked inside, extracted the crumpled papers permanently inhabiting his jeans' right pocket and walked to the counter asking the drained waitress for a pencil. She brought back a pen and Turkish coffee.

Placing his right elbow on the tabletop and a hand on his cheek, Daniel stared at the smoothed-out sheets, pen twirling in his left hand. Surrounding noise dissolved out of his mind quicker than the sugar dropped in his coffee as he began a furious re-sketching of the Shankill and Falls. He felt his thighs rupturing as though they were the physical peace walls he was cracking apart on paper.

Daniel failed to notice the other customers were long gone, and the waitress was performing the final pre-closing tasks.

"Excuse me sir. Our closing time was half an hour ago," she said.

But he didn't hear. The congestion – in his body and the re-imagined space – disappeared. His paper featured an innovative design for urban culture to emerge anew. For an area resisting connectivity, he offered an integrative alternative: a tunnel for traffic flow in addition to a bike route towards a sprawling park. In a city where green spaces often act as emerald borders, he compelled linkages through a well-organised web of paths. He situated buildings in ways that prevented them from serving as buffers, and their entrances were intentionally designed to prevent the emergence of sub-communities. New elevations puzzled together workspaces, stores, and cafés framed by terraces intended to showcase indie music and art. Lights added illumination while projecting flair. Marks of blue ink decorated his numbed fingers.

Sipping the end of his now-cold coffee, Daniel tasted the coarsely ground particles. His nostrils filled with pleasure, thinking about the analogy of good brewing to designing a flavoursome, aromatic, energised city.

Walsh likes to quote Churchill: The way we shape our buildings will subsequently shape us.

Not only does he have the beginnings of something to show Walsh, now he also has a research question to discuss with his advisor next week. In Northern Ireland, dismantling the old in favour of the new doesn't bring people together. Is there a causal relationship between architecture and peace? Does architecture have solutions to move a boundary-obsessed post-conflict society into a reconciled future?

Yes, I want to be an architect. The sober type.

He took a deep breath and added at the bottom of the sketch: *Daniel MacIntyre, Choice Architect.*[4]

BOOK FOUR

CHAPTER 19

REALITY RECALCULATED

It's Gideon. Stuck in traffic. There is a coffee stand right after Customs. Wait there.

Logical for my first incoming text in Israel to be Tamir's dad.

Found coffeeshop 😁 No rush.

Excellent: that mom-child duo is also just sitting here purchase-less. Coffee is the last thing your nausea needs. Should I get some cash shekels? Well, the airport fits the 'modern and international' categories. Everything was faster than Newark on a lousy day. Though, it helped that the foreigners' line was shorter than the one greeting Israeli citizens. You don't want to get stuck with extra cash for a two-week trip. When he gets here, I'll ask Gideon whether a credit card or phone app suffices inside the Holy Land.

David Ben-Gurion won't be disappointed by his airport. Even if he wanted something different, or bigger, he'd appreciate this re-enactment of the *Love Actually* final movie scene for every arriving passenger. Have they all been away from each other that long? Unfortunately, it's 5:30am in DC, because only Natasha would appreciate that Mom's rebuking voice is stronger than the airport announcer's: "Surprised, Ella? It's time to abandon the expectation of Israel being less than modern and less than welcoming."

No biggie. Natasha won't have patience for your impressions because she'd want to pick up where we left off at Logan.

"You *are* going through with it. Honestly, I thought you'd bail last minute."

No way! Was she sitting by the phone waiting for my plane to land?

"Missing out on family drama keeps me awake."

That's her post-morning run voice.

"Yes, fresh air helped me figure out your sudden motivation, I think. It was the combination of the two: invisible Daniel, and Emily and Climber's apartment takeover – it was getting too much."

With such darting accuracy, how unfortunate that Natasha chose tennis over archery.

"You're forgetting Tamir."

"Of course. The new son our parents never had. You're right. I should have guessed the six months' supply of six-packs and sympathy throughout your 'where does my future lie?' phase would make a difference."

"I won't qualify for someone you don't know."

Oops. I didn't ask Tamir for a photo of his father. Will Gideon come with a sign? Hopefully he knows I can't read Hebrew.

"The final detail to complete your nearly perfect description – there was the penning of a 'Dear Daniel' series."

"You didn't send them. Oh, shit, Ella! Tell me you didn't."

Only because it turned out to be such a disappointing literary result: *Daniel, I miss us so much, blah ... blah ... blah ...*

"Before bossing me about everything I need to do in Israel, did you know that Freud diagnosed the Irish as impervious to psychoanalysis?"

"Don't tell me that Mom's practice has gone global."

The entire busy terminal can hear her snickering enjoyment, though she's the only one that knows the shitty lows of my love life.

"I am not laughing at you, only at what you endured as part of Mom's 'perspective-shifting.' After that, harsh Middle East realities should be a piece of cake for you. Hold on; I need to answer a moronic email that just popped up."

Mom made a good point about the direct approach being the standard in Israel, unlike Ireland. The reserved Grandpa Edward and Granny Rosemary may not be as prepared as they think for the over-expressiveness and the queue-jumping in this café. True, the Irish Catholics were more extroverted, more jokey, but did they show their true feelings? Like you would ever be the expert anyone calls upon to decipher what an Irish person, especially one inhabiting multiple identities, really thinks.

Did you make Daniel more special than he was? Did you mythologize, idealize and project all your aspirations onto him? Can something like this ever be measured? Any such evidentiary consideration dips, no, drowns in hindsight and confirmation biases. The fact that your outsider status could have offered him the easier choice doesn't mean it was. Mom's explanation of the breakup makes sense. Yes, potentially Boston, along with our relationship, offered Daniel a path to avoid choosing between his tribes. But not everybody grows up inside the Goldin's 'meaning-making' aquarium. Why, after a lifelong overload of rejecting Northern Ireland's Us and Them codes, opt to season his life's soup with the difficulties that you bring?

"The world of intermarriage doesn't melt away struggles percolating through the generations." Mom more than hinted at all these explanations when you were in Belfast. Not only did Daniel not falsify her point, what little he shared about his lineage supports her contention. And maybe the fact that he refused to share his feelings was your unequivocal evidence? A path of least resistance could be the identity monster Daniel is already familiar with instead of taking on my new baggage. There could be multiple ways to hypothesize about our breakup.

"Where were we, Ella?"

"You were helping untie my Gordian knot known as Daniel MacIntyre."

Interesting. Natasha didn't pick up on the inaccurate trope. Obviously, our relationship is the Gordian knot and Daniel – Alexander. No, Natasha picked it up all right. She keeps quiet because Daniel disappointed her too by turning out the opposite of Great. "Are you already sitting down in your padded ergonomic chair?"

"Almost. Just putting in a load of laundry."

"Well, I am not waiting. Want to know what originally convinced me Daniel was the real deal? He quoted *The Fountainhead* on our first date."

"No way! No wonder you never told me that."

Natasha earned the shock. I agree that neither the repulsive nor the irresistible of *Howard Roark* was ever detectable in Daniel.

"All the more reason for high hopes on finding your pot's lid there, in the Jewish homeland."

"It's good to hear you laugh, even when it comes with Grandma's love advice as your inspiration. Would you say you guys are over the hill of the last couple of months?"

"We're getting there, bit by bit. Mark's still hit hard, and Mom and Dad too, still touch on the miscarriage in every conversation. Oh, I forgot, texting you right now the link to that book I wanted you to read."

Shit. My book must be in the plane's overhead bin. When will you cease to be the Santa Claus for cleaning crews? But this is convenient: a bookstore right across from the coffee shop. "Surprised again, Ella? Don't forget you're in the land of the People of the Book." Natasha is right – Mom has overtaken my brain.

"Excuse me. Do you have an English section?"

"Of course. It's an airport. In the back." Russian accent, maybe explaining the blunt reply?

Let's see ... *Dear Zealots: Letters from a Divided Land.* That's an alluring book title, and sweetly short too. Amos Oz – a name I heard before. And he seems to think there is a way to cure fanatics. A promising opening.

"Hi, Gideon. Hello?"

"Where are you, Ella?"

"In the bookstore. Across from the coffee shop."

Unmistakable older and balding version of Tamir, same adoration of relaxed jeans and oversized T-shirts. "Yes. Lime sweatshirt, that's me. Yes, waving."

"Welcome, welcome to Israel, Ella. You look just like family! Horrendous traffic, you'll see on our way back to Tel Aviv. Don't worry; we'll break it midway with great hummus."

CHAPTER 20

"I'LL TEACH YOU

DIFFERENCES"[5]

GIDEON *IS* A PROPHET in his own land. Wi-Fi isn't great, but Tel Aviv grasped that coastal tourism comes with family-friendly marina cafés. Now you see what Mom meant by 'Israel's child-oriented mentality.' You are the lone table for one and the single customer yet to order. Funny: all three adjacent tables have three hyperactive kids and two parents sharing creamy mushroom pasta, Neapolitan pizza, and chicken nuggets with extra ketchup. Well, it's post-lunch, the portions sizes justify division, and unlike you, they didn't wait for the waitress to notice them.

Where did you hear that cities mimic their dwellers? Tamir inherited Gideon's maple eyes, hopefully for him, not the balding gene. But his 'sunny with a dash of danger' is all Tamir's mom Tsippi. No, it's Tzippi. No, Zzippi, as in pizza. The least you could do for your gracious hosts is pronounce their names correctly. It's Day Four of their constant optimism-injection into your life, and extra laundry is the way you reciprocate. That's inaccurate. They loved the apple strudel, and Zzippi said she'll try to make your ginger tofu for this *Shabbat* dinner with her sister's family.

Their savviness could tutor Professor Rubinstein. She'd endorse with open arms their advice on securing a local conference presentation. Pure brilliance to highlight domestic demand for English editorial services as a boundless resource you could dip into. As non-academics, they sounded more authentic than that dean from your college days. "Far-reaching benefits to mingling with crowds other than your own" was his mantra, but Gideon and Zzippi got you to listen. Especially Zzippi's supersonic brevity.

"You're two centimeters from being Dr Goldin. Go for it. Research sightseeing – best thing in academia. No money, but you'll see the world." Zzippi has it all figured out.

At some point, you do need to wean yourself off the family dependency plan. True, this time, parental rescue was the last ship to this shore after all travel application deadlines flew by. Poor Mom and Dad are still stumbling through undergraduate payments, when you no longer recall what those four years were about. Exaggerating once more: the Junior Tutorial on Talking Points facilitated this single choice destination as 'sponsorable.'

Your unbroken 'Discovering Zion' dismissal record – who could envision that such autobiographical detail would make a helpful comeback? Rejecting every proposed Christmas in Israel for fifteen years in a row; evading all study abroad programs Mom and Dad forwarded; systematically missing the Hillel's campus excursions' deadlines; and ethically objecting to the Birthright trip, even though it could have gotten you ten free days in Israel. Any judge, anywhere, would reject insincerity of travel purpose.

"What can I get you? English? Sorry you had to wait. The espresso machine was acting out. Want an English menu?" Dark dreadlocks framing husky eyes, but her olive skin shouts Middle Eastern.

"A large cappuccino and one of those sugary donuts on the counter, please."

"You mean the *sufganiyah*?"

"Sorry, what did you call it?"

"Suf-ga-ni-yah. You know, Hanukkah. Ring no Jewish bells? Well, it's like, it's like your American jelly donut, only better."

"But it's almost May."

"Mmhm. As you see, popular demand keeps them year-round. Except for Passover. That week they are vegan style, with almond flour."

"Is the vegan version still better than the American?"

"Naturally." Was it Adler pointing out that expressing superiority is a defense mechanism against the inferiority complex? "But, full disclosure, I am vegan."

Of course she is. The V-neck emerald cotton dress and yellow rubber sandals are perfect for showing it.

Vegan Waitress could probably make some extra shekels as a licensed honesty coach.

'Israel is sparking my academic curiosity' as a reason for this pilgrimage bordered unprincipled – if not fibbing – even for you. For all their overall support of my 'injustice in Palestine' perspective, Mom and Dad were always hesitant about tiptoeing toward that academic swamp. Time and time again, they insisted my leafy suburb privileges warrant delaying all criticism until Israel buried its dead in terrorist attacks.

In Dad's case, the clever comparison to Northern Ireland tipped the scales. You *were* much more critical of Unionists until the summer visit contributed complexity.

'Embracing the existence of nuances' is straight out of Dad's life-lessons inventory. He couldn't resist your proposition to similarly engage the circumstances of our Israeli-based clan. Mom's gravitation to counter logic competed with her love of U-turns. But the 'Irish Nationalism had better PR in a shared war' analogy to Palestinians sealed her excitement over her personal crusader in the Holy Land.

And Tamir, a genius in his own right, advocating to Mom

and Dad on your behalf with the cost-effective approach. "Look at how many days I have been lodging with you. Ella's accommodations, her kids, and grandkids – all fully covered in my parents' apartment in Tel Aviv. From there, anywhere in Israel is a day trip."

Cupid, too, must be the image of *Smiley Face*, now that Emily and Climber can finally enjoy some private love life. Covering my share of the rent in Medford was the natural step for them and the most calculated step for me. Israel's popular unpopularity – another winning card. Mexico would have been the obvious choice for an aimless break. Southern Europe for the ancestry-tracing trip. But the way you deployed Tradition is worthy of a new verse in *Fiddler on the Roof*.

A success story. Okay, there was some past monetary waste regarding the Jewish cultivation enterprises throughout your early life. Your Bat-Mitzvah went down in memory as the fanciest backyard Bat-Mitzvah Scarsdale ever saw. They needed a truck to donate the toys and accessories dedicated to making being Jewish fun for us. Mom would spend it all again as means to counteract her doomsday prophecies over your neglectful Jewishness, but it's a rebuttal to Jews being good with money.

You need to be more honest, at least with yourself. It's hard to miss the irony of your sole non-Jewish partner seeding yearning for our Promised Land. And Mom picked it up from the first moment you suggested this Israel getaway. Of course, she did. Mom wasn't trying to hide that funding your trip was an opportunity to jump-start your love life. Huh. All these self-focused years on meaning and purpose, yet, ultimately, my marital age was her engine.

Hands down, the jewel of the convincing dance belongs to winning over your formidable dissertation advisor.

"The academic comparison to Palestine and Israel is cluttered with scholarship. Your time is better spent sticking just to

Northern Ireland."

"I am not switching hypothesis, Professor Rubinstein."

Good thing you kept the next thought to yourself. *It isn't like I am doing a clinical drug experiment that will kill people if I get it wrong.* That would have turned the meeting into an argument. Confining it to "It's only to think through the single-case study versus a comparative method for the dissertation," couched it in cognitive elasticity.

Skeptical, Rubinstein still appreciated my next argument: "Interest energizes research. That's what you always say is the way to choose what to work on."

"Differences in comparisons matter a lot. I remain hesitant about this, Ella."

"By going to Israel, I will prove to you that self-fulfilling prophecies are exaggerated."

"And what if you don't?"

What's important is that you are here basking in the Tel Avivian sun. I wouldn't be surprised if the potential to chase passions beyond the academic ones were obvious to lukewarm Rubinstein too. My decreasing self-esteem is a universal worry. She is Jewish too. And mother to an unmarried girl around my age.

Why not experience the straight-talk type of guys? *Dugri* – I think that's what Tamir called how they talk around here. For all you know, these tad-too-hairy dudes, who have no issue stripping sweaty bellies on the beach wearing Speedos, might prove refreshing. Some are sporting briefs, but they don't dress their beach look with college merchandise. Military symbols are trendy. You may end up hating each one of these Casanova wannabes, but if not, at least you'll know true love exists.

"One large cappuccino, one *sufganiyah*, and two wipes to rescue you from the sticky red jam about to attack you from the middle. Enjoy."

Gotta give it to Vegan Waitress. This sufgi bake, or whatever she called it, tastes less processed than Dunkin's, though over-blown as a permanent menu item. Yesterday's coffee in the pro-fessor's office at Haifa University gives this pretentious cappuc-cino a run for its money. Kudos to Professor Ali from the School of Political Sciences for brewing up pods-based aromas without a bean of an annoying wait. But a slam dunk on your part too to gulp his book during the fifty-two-minute train ride to Haifa University. Even wiser of you to tape the conversation.

Okay, with self-love now sufficiently fulfilled, onward to to-day's agenda: annotating Professor Ali's voice of wisdom.

"The minor distasteful aspect to my pleasurable time in Northern Ireland was the endless procession of teacups. That's why I make a point to bring only coffee to my office … and outlaw milk. A visitor once spilled it and, counter to common perception, I did cry a river over that reeking disaster."

Fortunately, your hyena's cackle didn't terrify Professor Ali. You really should smile more and guffaw less, during interviews for sure, and in life generally.

"Trust me, Ella, nothing helped. I informed my wonderful col-leagues that an Arab, even with an Israeli passport, a prize-win-ning PhD, and tenure at Haifa University is, and always will be, an Arab. Coffee brewing is our first vocation. Their insipid teas kept gushing like a spring.

"Now, to your question. Yes, the Israeli flags in Protestant neighborhoods caught me off guard. Yet my Palestinian flags flying high on the Irish Catholic side of their peace walls filled me with pride. But because you asked me to describe my exact feelings, I should say it was borderline infuriated. I distinctly remember feeling at the time: you guys think the British are dif-ficult? Try living with the Israelis.

"But that was then. I grew honest since. A young person such as yourself should know that looking in the mirror becomes more challenging the older you get. So people seek reflections in other ways. Here is where academics, with introspection as our life pursuit, have an early start. Northern Ireland taught me the lesson I shared in this last book you say you enjoyed. I realized that *Anna Karenina*'s spectacular literary opening was empirically inaccurate. If unhappy families are, metaphorically speaking, divided societies, they aren't as distinguishable as the brilliant Tolstoy described. They share plenty in common."

His accidental pushing of that Pisa Tower of papers off his desk is imminent.

"Oops. Let me help you, Professor."

"It's fine; leave it on the floor. Clumsiness is the story of my life. What I was saying was, that picturesque island elucidated my understanding of nearly all the ancient problems we, Palestinian and Jewish Israelis, are facing here. Contestation over land, identity complexes, perpetual disagreements over what happened in the past, political violence. These are commonality boosters of divided lands all over the globe."

"My apologies, Professor Ali, but I feel I am not exactly following."

"Well, you wouldn't be the first. That's an everyday state-of-mind reported by most visitors to the Middle East. So, let's make some order, shall we, Ella? Firstly, call me Mahmoud. You are now in a region enslaved by informalities as much as divisions. Now, what would you like me to clarify, Ella?"

"I just finished reading Amos Oz's *Dear Zealots*. A persuasive argument that the only pragmatic solution for the conflict is the two-state solution."

"I am listening."

"Wasn't the Belfast/Good Friday Agreement effectively the Northern Irish delivery of that solution?"

Funny. I didn't hear the bird chirping when he gave me that cat ate the canary smile.

"Please don't take it the wrong way. You are joining a proud section of every library dedicated to probing an Anglo-Irish relevance to Palestine and Israel. And that is why my book is on the yet-to-be designated shelf. Don't look so puzzled. I am about to explain the correct comparison between us here, and Northern Ireland over there. The comparable conflict is between Palestinians like me and the Jewish majority, who are all citizens of this Zionist State. Most others likened the larger, take your pick, bi-lateral, Middle East, or global Israeli-Palestinian problems with Northern Ireland's."

"But isn't it slightly artificial to dissect a conflict into smaller parts?"

"As a Palestinian-Arab, I see megalomaniac Israel doing everything in its hefty power to bypass peace with the Palestinians. But as an academic, I seek scholarly parallels. It's the comparison of internal Israel to Northern Ireland that multiplies those similarities. The Brits played havoc with us too, you know. Now, wouldn't that be a familiar narrative for a Catholic in Northern Ireland?"

"Yes, but for Catholics, Northern Ireland was always 'the North.'"

"But the Troubles erupted over discrimination. So, this is your vital takeaway. Conquerors don't give rights out of the goodness of their hearts. Blood and war were these rights' platter. And we Arabs who live inside Israel as unequal citizens have eyes. What's more, our love of coffee – and hookahs for that matter – nurture our best trait: patience."

"So, you disagree with Amos Oz that the future is a two-state solution?"

"Amos Oz was a gifted writer, and his daughter, by the way, is a university colleague. But the two-state solution wasn't something he could even take to his own grave because it died of irrelevance before him."

Professor Ali made sense. The last Gaza campaign almost

unleashed a civil war inside Israel. There is the demographic assumption a border poll will bring about a United Ireland, but no
one knows that for a fact. Social identities are shifting too. Yes,
you cannot rule out that those telling you they were Northern
Irish did so as a social etiquette, or to strategically disguise their
identity. But you cannot rule out the counterargument either.
Economic opportunities and wellbeing help recategorization.
What is Israel waiting for? The Iron Dome is only protecting
from above. If they don't make Arab citizens equal citizens, this
country could expire by rockets from below.

"Look at the time, Ella. That's my Office Hours crowd you
hear behind the door. Unfortunately, I must leave your enjoyable
company. A final new thought, then: you appear to be an informed liberal. Don't you find yourself betrayed by your Jewish
homeland? I mean, isn't power-hungry, ethnic-cleansing Israel
the complete reversal of anything American Jews cared about
all these ..."

Oh, friendly Vegan Waitress intends more than just clearing
the table.

"So, the *sufganiyah* conquered you too. Another one?"

"As soon as I locate a boot camp to work off the first one."

"Now you know why the café is next to a gym. Right over
there, see the two shirtless guys next to that palm tree? Pretty
intense cycling classes. But don't let them rip you off when you
sign up. Negotiate."

Israelis' appearance is formless and irregular, except for the
single common trait of unsolicited advice. Was it fair of Professor Ali to claim that Israel manipulates the world into believing
it can't make real peace with the Palestinians? Too bad there
wasn't more time to develop that point with him. You should
have pressed a little harder. Politics has yet to meet rivals who
don't claim it's the other side that's cheating. How would any
politician get votes if they don't dodge responsibility and blame

everything on rivals?

But even if you asked him directly, which you should have, because directness is a virtue here, Mahmoud wasn't sending vibes of interest. He sure looked as though he'd answered your arsenal of questions many times before. He never tried to argue over facts either. But one thing he definitely did was to choose his words carefully. The recording proves it. Mahmoud intentionally enunciated when asking what Israel meant to you as a Jew.

I am on to you, Professor Ali. It was only the cheapest professorial trick to adapt my thinking process. Hmm. So, he aimed for something. What was it? There was something Professor Ali wanted the novice in me to embrace. Hmmm. Why did he play the Jewish-American card as the final point in a conversation about Northern Ireland and Israel? Clearly, the theme was comparisons, and not the ones I had in mind. Not the ones we were discussing. Did he want me to equate the German-Jewish trauma and the Israeli-Palestinian one? Huh. That might be it. Yes, completely. Holocaust = Palestinian injustice.

Interesting. But wait. Digest this. Slowly and carefully. Is this a comparison that sharpens understanding or sharpens a mirage? It isn't clear-cut. Can anyone really equate suffering? This is one conversation I could take up with Mom. Hold on. Don't jump to call her. Consider this a little more. There might be a comparative angle here, after all, and not the one suggested by the professor. If you hadn't reminisced with Mahmood over Northern Ireland back in Haifa, resemblances might never come to light in time for this Tel Aviv sunset.

Okay, here goes. Britain saw Northern Ireland as a security problem, while for Irish Catholics/Nationalists, the North was always a political issue. Israeli Jews keep thinking of people like Professor Ali as *their* security problem. Could one persuade them otherwise?

One must! Otherwise, this place will become late 1960s Northern Ireland when the Troubles exploded. This peaceful beachside will see a tsunami of violence if Israel continues treating its Arab citizens unequally. Nominal citizenship for Israeli-Palestinians like Mahmoud is one ticking bomb this proud security empire refuses to hear.

Rubinstein will be ready for you with the rope at Medford's center over this research direction change. Unless she is sustainably convinced that I can bring this fresh-start comparative dissertation to a close. Overworked hardly grasps what you need to become ASAP. From now on, only books – no, preferably journal abstracts or short book reviews about the *internal* Israeli-Arab tensions. When you jog or cook, podcasts. You should have all the rest more or less covered in what you've handed Rubinstein already. The only other literature that would require close reading is conflict theories on divided societies.

Geez, you are addicted to eureka moments. Finally, a dissertation that you love: drawing on Northern Ireland to deliver for Israelis – Jews and Palestinians – new ways to see each other's perspective. It will offer new knowledge on conflict management, and it will be brilliant – the dissertation you always dreamed of.

Delivery requires a daily writing goal. No coffee refills before a thirty-minute non-stop writing sprint. Starting now.

CHAPTER 21

THE PURPOSE OF MEMORY

"Hold that thought, Zzippi; Mom is texting."

When will I hear about Independence Day?

"She wants to know about *Yom HaAtzma'ut*."

"Yarkon Park awaits you. It'll get scorching hot before you know it. I'll call Susan while you jog."

"Promise we'll pick up this conversation? I need your perspective on this national switch from Remembrance Day grief to Independence Day parties. Still can't get over the abruptness. How can you take it every year?"

After Zzippi, you'll ask Mom about this last couple of days' events. Inhuman flipping from bereavement to fireworks. So instant. Even in Mom's 'Israel is different' dictionary, this mourning-celebration linkage can't be a normal ask.

"Coming from America where Memorial Day is just about the biggest shopping day of the year, I wouldn't rush to judge other countries."

Zzippi and Gideon – always ready to help you with cultural pitfalls.

"We are a traumatized nation. When you hear the Remembrance Day sirens, stop whatever you are doing and stand erect. Someone could lash out at you if you don't. It's very sensitive. Don't panic, though. In a rocket attack, the siren is ascending and descending. In that case, you need to run to the nearest shelter. But you won't confuse the two. The Remembrance Day siren makes a continuous sound."

You knew it wasn't a rocket attack because Mark made you download the Red Alert: Israel app to your phone, warning of any launched rockets.

"Yes, why wouldn't there be an app for that, Ella? Northern Ireland may have a proxy culture war, but Israel could flare up any moment."

Zzippi's siren instructions were accurate, yet insufficient to encapsulate the mind-blowing sensation of those moments. A whole nation coming to a standstill twice in one day to listen to the unified scream out of silent graveyards: "Before you celebrate the birth of this nation, remember my sacrifice."

Gideon's "Of course it's deliberate!" logic clarified why a major city park would house a fallen soldiers' memorial garden. "That's our collective pledge to families who paid the ultimate price. We'll endure your pain long after you are gone."

It took the three of us fifteen, maybe twenty minutes at most, to walk from their apartment for Tuesday's commemoration ceremony. The Garden for the Casualties of War should be coming up on the left, right about now.

There it is. Kudos on your excellent memory. Zzippi and Gideon versed you with every detail of the Remembrance Day evening ceremony. It was good advice on the part of Gideon to come here in the daytime and take a closer look at the Memorial's design.

One, two, three … forty-one black pillars, thousands of grey lines with Hebrew letters. Each line is two or three words, so each must immortalize a fallen soldier. Building something of this magnitude had to involve competition over the type of structure. What made Tel Aviv choose this design for its Memorial? Everything in this park will die one day, but these granite pillars will forever remember the sacrifice.

If ancient cultures considered the sun's path across the sky, the pillars' location couldn't have been random for a contemporary Israeli architect. Even if geography isn't your subject, accessibility should dictate the design. You paused your afternoon jog to take a photo and walk around. And that woman over there has stopped her busy city day to bring a flower to a name. Bereavement at fingertips, saving a trip to the actual grave. Yet, the dearest and greatest sacrifice to the family is distilled into a single line in a combined memory for many wars. And what if a family hates what the city decided to build? Satisfying everybody on such a sensitive matter would be challenging. Impossible?

Black granite, but it's very American of you to intuitively look to Iwo Jima as an inspiration. It's nothing like it. They have enough wars here to be original in memorializing. The Second Commandment might have stood in the way of the human figures that we have in Arlington, Virginia. If they were able to set aside a special beach for religious Jews, enough people in Tel Aviv could have demanded a modest Memorial. It must have been a pressure cooker trying to design a patriotic past.

No, the inability to read Hebrew shouldn't stand in your way on this one. None of the ideology and politics on how and what to memorialize would be written here.

This structure isn't new. What about the names of those who died since? You could safely assume that Professor Ali wouldn't be happy about the pillars' broken tops.

"The Jews grab our land and sanctify it with memorials. Would you contemplate a peace agreement over territories for which so many died? Memorials don't commemorate past sacrifices. They ensure present and future ones."

For any of your inconvenient winces, Professor Ali would have immediately pulled out the decision to place Remembrance Day right before Independence Day. By never thinking of asking him, you saved yourself the need to argue. Anyway, there was no way around the look Gideon gave you for suggesting we all attend the alternative Jewish-Palestinian memorial service.

"With full respect to my dear son and his brilliant ideas, this is your first visit to Israel. You need the real context of the Israeli experience. You need to feel what *Yom HaZikaron really* means to most of us."

Gideon as the Israeli equivalent of Margaret Mead.

It was important to adapt to their thinking even for the functional reason that, unlike in Northern Ireland, you needed Gideon's translation. The special remembrance prayer *Yizkor*; the reading aloud of the soldier's journal, but most of all, the words of *HaTikvah*, the National Anthem. Gideon was right to insist on coming here to an official memorial along with them.

Mom would know whether this collective hug helps the families' unending pain. Can lives embark on recovery after such a sacrifice? She'll pull a Viktor Frankl. Finding a meaning in suffering.

"Hey, Mom."

"Yes, it's a very taxing season for Israelis. You missed their Holocaust Memorial Day by a thread."

Right, I forgot about that one. April must have quite the mental impact on Israelis.

"And you must remember that Passover was just before it too. And that people on this side are counting on your delivery of *this year* in Jerusalem."

"Yeah. No. With everything I still want to get done in my last week, Tamir recommended to skip it."

Also, being in love with their hipness could be a documented Tel Aviv syndrome Mom doesn't know about.

"Too bad. I was counting on you to check out Jerusalem Syndrome for me. First-time visitors losing their minds, imagining themselves as biblical figures."

"Another reason to skip it then?"

"Or for your mom to join you there."

"It's already way too hot here for your comfort level."

It's also very post-barbecue filthy, now that the human masses have finished banging their independence on each other's heads with inflatable blue and white hammers. That urgency on Independence Night to spray each other with fake foam was just as weird. Even during celebrations, Israelis enjoy an altercation. Ella, you are an intolerable elitist.

Yes, America infatuates Israelis, but that doesn't automatically mean *Yom HaAtzma'ut* should be an imitation of The Fourth of July. Shoving everything into a pita was so much tastier than our hamburger bun. *A Mizrahi* adaptation to the Goldin barbecue would be refreshing. Though nothing should replace the corn from Ramsey's Farm stand or their tomato salad. But the keto-okay falafel and tahini will be an instant hit. Mark will love you even more if you incorporate the amazing spring chicken skewers. You'll need to find the kosher brand, so the salt makes them as juicy as they were here.

"Since when did you turn BBQ *MasterChef*, Ella?" Natasha will ask, and you will have your answer ready.

"Since I interviewed the chief *mangal* guy – that's Israeli for barbecuing. Reduced cooking time too." That will stun her.

Oh, a working water fountain. It's safe to drink now that you're almost back in the apartment and the bathroom is within reach.

When most Israelis live in apartments, they need their parks to barbecue. Going with Gideon and Zzippi to their private Independence Day party deprived you of the authentic Israeli park version. Tamir told you his parents consider themselves an elite enclave. If you weren't in the car with them, they'd never buy that Israeli flag for the car. It was so clear they did it for you. On his own, Gideon would never have opened the window to that flag-selling guy at the red light. Zzippi made him do it, all for you. Even after they bought it, the flag never made it to the car's window. Now, what would the Northern Irish flag-wavers say about this reluctance for nationalist displays?

Social status and self-image aside, Zzippi and Gideon still live in a Tel Aviv apartment. They still needed their Herzliya friends' pool for a fancy gas barbecue instead of the park's low-tech charcoal options.

If I get Mom some of the Yemenite *schug* spice in the market, would they let me through Customs in Boston? It would be a nice substitute for the standard oregano and olive oil.

Stop with this food obsession right now. But how can I not pig out when the food is so delicious? Don't forget that it took you longer to shed Northern Ireland's extra pounds than to stop weeping over Daniel. And there, you only ate to survive, enjoying nothing. Run a little faster and take the stairs to their seventh-floor if you want a taste of Zzippi's couscous tonight.

CHAPTER 22

SOCRATIC DIALOGUES

"GOOD MORNING, ELLA. You are in sync with the coffee machine."

Gideon and his 'at your service' life-motto is hosting someone who is 'in Israel's service.'

"This is my childhood friend, Oren."

Did he also leave the *kibbutz*? This could be Gideon's plan to get you a place to stay near the Sea of Galilee. He already introduced you to a quarter of this country and Zzippi to a further half. Silver-fox Oren likes hair shorter than our Marines.

"His military insignia shouldn't alarm you. A lamb is more combative than Oren." Gideon asks for a big imagination leap. Half of the coffee table is decorated by his red beret, aviator sunglasses, and a phone flashing faster than a lighthouse. Barely any space for Zzippi's fabulous babka loaf, which Oren seems to be relishing as much as you did last night.

"All I've been hearing for the last two weeks is Gideon raving about his American cousin."

How often do these two speak to each other?

"My raving isn't over. Ella has returned from yet another fact-finding mission. Her doctorate on divided societies will include a quote from every milk-and-honey citizen."

So, Gideon's complaints that I overdress by local standards

but my underdressing on the history of this country are only for my ears then.

"Are we living up to your divided society standards?"

How best to answer this quizzical combatant who is taking a call on one phone while his second one is buzzing on the coffee table. Yes, you are clueless about what Oren's Hebrew is selling or what guides his oval pacing between the living room and balcony. All this shouldn't undermine your intuition. Staying alive requires a dialogue, not a debate with this high-ranking officer. 'At ease' to your debate trophies standing to attention on the middle shelf back home.

"So, we were in 'are we as divided as you expected,' yes?"

He remembers his pre-two-phone-calls-ago question.

"Divided or not, self-definition is an Israeli consensus."

Laughing dents Oren's battle-focused demeanor. If Gideon weren't being the picture of a fussing host overeager not to disappoint his visitor, you'd be able to enjoy your first morning coffee. Despite taking a third slice of babka, and despite his middle age, Oren is fit enough to beat you in a race, easily in a wrestling match. But both men await your meaningful response.

"Well, I suppose I did have a couple of insightful conversations with—"

"Wait. Let me guess. One or two Arab academics up in Haifa, a few café-sitting intellectuals here in Tel Aviv, and a group of anti-government demonstrators in Jerusalem. On target, Ella? Thought so. Walk me through your bottom lines, then."

What are the chances of getting this soldier to think critically about the government for which he risks his life? Without the Israeli army, he might be out of a job. Why would a soldier be sick of war?

"Silence is unlike you, Ella. A serious peacebuilder needs courage. Folks like Oren are the people you'll need to convince."

How did Gideon end up a space engineer when there's no universe in which this ends well? Oren doesn't stop moving; that sweet babka is an energy bomb.

"I am all ears, just searching for an outlet."

Israeli males aren't as short as I anticipated. Shorter than the Dutch but who isn't? But very much in the vicinity of Americans as well as the Irish.

"Ella, I meant what I said earlier. This is a priceless opportunity to challenge a true *sabra*, you know, a real Israeli, like Oren. An infrequent opportunity, but it's very handy for your research. A good life skill too."

"One of my primary takeaways is that Jewish and democratic Israel might just be an oxymoron."

Is that a third phone, or is Oren reaching for a handgun in his leg pocket?

Oren is too confident to repeat his last statement, and Gideon's anticipation will wait out my silence. Yes, Oren was confrontational. Yes, he wants to get under your skin. But the question he posed is a valid question: why did *you* come *here* of all potential destinations? As he said, there are other divided societies I could focus on.

"It's a fair point, Oren. My Jewishness is likely the reason I came."

"Finally, we agree on something. You see, Gideon, progress after all."

You need to give him some logic to think about your criticism of Israel. It mistreats its Arab population; it unlawfully rules the Palestinians. A soldier should recognize a time bomb. Take some inspiration from the Georgia O'Keefe flowers on the wall behind him. Didn't she paint them intentionally large for urban New Yorkers to notice nature?

"As I was saying, Ella, of course Zionism was a diasporic invention. But unlike the graveyards of Jewish ideas overseas, Zionism fulfilled its promise over here, affirmative?"

Okay. This is a line of thought I can work with. Zionism was a response to antisemitism, which imparts responsibility on modern Israel not to misbehave with others.

"That would be tangible if you further agree with me that Jewish real estate claims conflict with that of the Palestinians. Tel Aviv and Jaffa, much of the Galilee, and many examples split right in the middle – Jerusalem, Haifa, Akka."

His silence is far from mesmerized by my geographical grasp. Maybe Oren is from Gideon's *kibbutz* after all and hates that I used the Galilee example?

"All I keep seeing over here is how much opinions mirror each other without—"

"Except the Holocaust. Some mirrors are too reflective to be covered with smoke."

Jesus. Neither side lets that elephant out of the room. Not for a moment. The Palestinians claim they live it right now. For Israel, it is never history.

Gideon doesn't mind Oren's phone interruptions one bit. But this third one *is* a charm because it gives you the space to prepare an argument that should make military headway.

"Last summer, I was in Northern Ireland—"

"Nice place."

So he's been there.

"Enlighten me, how could Christian denominations who fought over a *real* island over there be relevant to the only democratic island in the Middle East?"

Not every point Oren makes must be malicious. Israelis do take directness to the next level. If he insists on head-nodding, and Gideon smiles at every one of his syllables, the uptight posture might just be a military habit.

"It wasn't long ago that Northern Ireland experienced terrible—"

"Aren't you overstretching analogies, Ella?"

Okay. He didn't let go of Israel as an exception just yet.

"But—"

"No, wait. I don't want to lose you again. The Middle East is *nothing* like the Irish problem."

"But Northern Ireland was – is – also a product of a sour partition and war."

"Only to spur Christian mini-struggles in a conflict entitled the Troubles, affirmative?"

Oren isn't wholly ignorant, but not an expert either if he's only answering for the latest decades of that conflict.

"Whatever your thesis may be, it needs to infer from the starting point of *our* conflict, far into ancient history."

"But the number of centuries doesn't necessarily negate likeness." You may have finally conquered this soldier's interest. "If you compare the native-settler dynamic, the siege mentality. Sure, circumstances are different, but the conflict perceptions here and there are similar—"

Those phones again!

"Sorry. Duty calls."

Like I could ever tell if that's true.

"Definitely with blood-thirsty terrorists—"

"The IRA and Loyalists were real terrorists."

"Okay, Ella. I only have ten seconds to give you corrective feedback."

Arms folded across uniformed chest, and not the slightest effort to hide that he'll be mansplaining a security mindset to a naïve woman.

"My British uniformed buddies all taught me the same lesson about *their* conflict. Peace chants came *after* the IRA was brought to its knees. Your comparisons should never lose the global sight. Yes, Britain certainly showed all of us how to neutralize a terrorist group incapable of countrywide destruction. But Hamas, Hezbollah, Jihad, ISIS, Iran, that's a partial list of those who will slaughter you and, of course, me without batting an eye."

His mind and ego already exited the door he's opening.

"It's always a thrill to meet young idealists."

Gideon is still here with me, so a last effort isn't hopeless.

"The perils of Israeli mistreatment shouldn't go unseen by a soldier, Gideon."

"Perhaps the single thing that *Tsahal*, the Israeli army, or any of our security agencies could never be accused of is unrealistic expectations about annihilation."

Gideon appreciates your scholarly motivation, but it's important to proceed with caution. It's one thing to crash and burn with a professional patriot and a whole other matter to sacrifice family balance. You can't forget that he won't accept the comparison between Jewish pioneers in Palestine and imperialism. Zzippi doesn't either.

"Gideon, I am not trying to minimize differences. But Israel is replicating the Catholic experience of pre-Troubles Northern Ireland."

Uncrossing his arms and legs is a good sign.

"Gerry Adams, Martin McGuinness, the Provisional IRA were British nationals during the Troubles."

Escaping to the kitchen? Gideon did say, "I am still with you, Ella," and it won't sit well with their brutally honest reputation if he stopped listening to me now.

"It's Conflict Theory 101 that violence will ensue when exclusion and discrimination aren't addressed."

"More coffee?"

"Oren is a war expert, so he knows that conflicts between neighbors and fellow countrymen are the bloodiest. I am worrying about the situation because I am putting one and one together."

"Look, Ella. Zzippi and I gave our word to your parents that we'd look after you. If you only run around Arab towns all the time, I don't think Adam and Susan would endorse future returns to Israel. Something to eat?"

What more could I reason to make Gideon understand?

"Every Middle East attaché, along with problem-solving, makes a point to enjoy Israel. That way, there is always *some* return on their trips. You too, Ella, should incorporate more fun into your busy schedule."

"It would be fun to solve some of Israel's problems."

A faintly smiling Gideon is still a small step.

"Everything is reversible except death, isn't it?"

"Here's an idea. Why don't you direct your convincing to Oren's son instead?"

Un-fucking believable. A secular Jew matchmaking in the age of Tinder. No longer a doubt that he's related to your mother.

"Shai is hard Left, which is, by the way, very tough on Oren. Think how many election cycles are ahead for his contemporaries? Your sphere of influence could be far more dramatic."

"I'm leaving in three and a half days, Gideon. My industrious dissertation advisor barely replies to my emails anymore."

"Let's not strap the horses in front of the carriage, shall we?"

That must be Hebrew's 'put the cart before the horses.'

"What have you got to lose? A success could help with the problems you are worried about." Touché to Gideon. "Worst come to worst, you will have transport to one more peace demonstration."

Why are all of them refusing to engage with my reasoning?

"Shai is a materials science major. He said once that political science is more like science fiction, so meeting him should be a blast."

This has advanced planning written all over it. Did Oren come here to check me out for his son?

"Zzippi is worried a young person like you is not seeing

enough of the famous Tel Aviv nightlife." Aha: Zzippi is written all over it. "Ask Tamir if you don't believe me. He thinks the world of Shai."

Poor Gideon looks downcast at the prospect of disappointing his wife.

"Okay. A farewell Tel Aviv-by-night with you and Zzippi tomorrow or Wednesday sounds like fun."

"Is that even a question in an Irish pub? I'd lose my licence serving you fake Guinness."

So much for your savvy globalism. It wasn't as though the four-leafed clover inked under her pixie cut or the Harp-brand glass didn't speak volumes of mass-market authenticity.

"Here we go. As good as in Ireland, the best you'll get in Florentin."

Exactly eighty hours left. You can do it, Ella. Your best analysis absorbed motivation from Belfast pubs. Schlepping here was to demonstrate that the outdoor street art and indoor Irish atmosphere reinvigorate the comparisons of your daily grind. Put in your headphones, stop procrastinating and start typing.

The 'brutal villains' category can't be easy for Israelis. Yet, the country confidently tunnel walks toward alienating its Arab minority. Protestant Northern Ireland was once as unconcerned about Catholics' conditions, an example lucidly demonstrating the causal connection between a minority's marginalization and the emergence of Bi-Nationalism.

Why is Israel shutting its eyes to the jeopardy of controlling future outcomes? The writing is on every wall segregating this tiny piece of land. Northern Irish violence brought the demise of Unionist-dominated Northern Ireland, ushering in external players to interject their own preferences. Bloodshed consolidated Anglo-Irish cooperation, activated America and Europe to intervene, and sealed the final power-sharing outcome.

To remain a Jewish state, Israel urgently needs to readjust its majority-oriented path. Otherwise, she is opening the Pandora's box of outsiders deciding on her future. The window of opportunity for an inclusive democracy with Jewish identity is threatened by the gusting winds of conflict.

Telepathic Rubinstein won't need more than a quick read to bring up every one of Oren's earlier points. If you read four British Intelligence memoirs on how the IRA became hollower than Swiss cheese, there is no way Rubinstein doesn't know about the Dirty War. She'll know it was taking place, and of course, she'll push you on whether it was making the difference.

And in the small chance that she doesn't, Fletcher's own Kissinger, Professor Becker won't be opting for the subtle critique. Gideon was right – Oren's blitz simplified the process of raising alternatives. If force did win the war for Britain, can anything wrestle with the Israeli infatuation with its mighty Israel Defense Force?

"Ready for more of the *authentic* black stuff?"

"I apologize for doubting your beer before. It's delicious. A stressful day, you know how it is."

"Stressful in Israel? That's a first. Did the beer help? You look like you are on a furious search for an epiphany."

"What I should look like is very lost."

"What are bartenders for, if not reliable advice? Try me."

Why not? Her ping-pong-style conversation is intriguing. Your therapist would be the first to accept that financial relationships don't necessarily negate good counseling.

"I am trying to look at Israel's Jewish-Arab relations rationally."

"Here you go. For that, you need help from the top shelf. Whiskey. On the house."

"Israel has such promise to show the world that a country can be both Jewish and liberal—"

"Says who?"

"Your Declaration of Independence."

"Wouldn't make my list of Declarations that Changed the World."

"How about the Golden Rule then? Jews and Arabs have so many shared bonds, shared destinies. Where else should neighborly love resonate more?"

"You must be aware of our indigenous caste system, yes? We love enacting laws to protect this place as a Jewish state. And we don't miss out on any chance of showing it too. If you were an Arab, would you be excited about the flag of your country?"

"Agreed. But I'm a proud American, and a liberal. I refuse to think of that as an unrealistic combination."

"Well, that may be a doomed comparison. In America, you don't suffer 'the sucker' complex."

"I keep being tutored on how not to be a *freier*. But no one likes being a sucker."

"Here, it's a phobia, so *letachmen*, you know, cheating the system, is a reflex."

How has a country pioneered by the *kibbutz*, all programmed for solidarity, turned into this anti-suckerhood shrine? Surely, they must be exaggerating this phenomenon.

"Oops, the regulars just walked in. Sorry to leave you, but we don't want *them* to feel like the *freiers* on duty."

Shit. Relationship between society and individuals is so fucking hard.

CHAPTER 23

DISTANCE AS A CURE

You'll miss my parents faster than you realize 😨 .
I miss you, Tamir.
FaceTime?
Y not?

"Tamir, why didn't you warn me? This airport is packed. Check-in line is so long!"

"It's Israel, Ella. Security questioning first, then check-in. Still don't get why you're rushing back."

He FaceTimed you almost daily. He cared about every detail on your trip. Tamir is the last to deserve your unedited vent on Rubinstein. What could Tamir do anyway about her "Ella, this new direction isn't working out" blow to the draft you emailed her?

"Told you: the more Israel broadened my mind, the more it squelched my advisor's interest. I didn't tell you yet; she called my research academically ineffective."

"Harsh."

"Fortunately, your wonderful parents turned out to be almost as good a support group as yourself. Zzippi organized a girls' spa day, and your dad kept comforting me with Hebrew idioms."

"Did 'Rabbi Gideon' recite his favorite 'capturing too much captures nothing'?"

"You know your dad. Rubinstein's favorite is 'this needs to get past being a dissertation in slow motion.' So, I am surrendering to Northern Ireland. Theoretically, not actually. Wait, are you in Brookline?"

"It's your fault. If you hadn't stopped at Nordau Falafel on your way to the airport, I wouldn't be starving. The Massachusetts version remains a close second to the one you enjoyed."

No kidding, he drove forty-five minutes for a falafel?

"It's my turn to order, I'll call you right back. *Ken, Ivrit—*"

Well, at least you picked up these two Hebrew words, but instead of *Ken*, you would have answered *Lo*, no Hebrew. Did Gideon also update Tamir that your final Israeli falafel wasn't to his liking because you bombarded him about food appropriation in the conflict? Insensitive, but pointing it out was irresistible when both sides ignore their mutual mass consumption of hummus, falafel, or shawarma as a vehicle for peacebuilding. Arabs and Israelis love it so much; why not harness commonalities to advance coexistence?

Oh, crap. My unwelcome remarks didn't build any peace between Gideon and Zzippi. She's probably still arguing my side now on their drive back to Tel Aviv. The easiest scenario to imagine:

"Israel has Bar-Ilan University, with a built-in yeshiva inside it. When will this country offer an Arab equivalent?"

"As soon as the Council for Higher Education develops its Terrorism Curriculum, Zzippi."

Line is moving. Bon Appetit.
Text flight number. I'll pick you up at Logan tomorrow.

My turn, finally. "Hi ... no, sorry. Only English ... Yeah, I am an American citizen ... Yes, first time here."

"May I see your passport? I work for Ben-Gurion Security.

I need to ask you a few questions. Ella Goldin, yes? My name is Daniel, by the way."

It's never possible for me to say farewell only to the country, is it?

"What was the purpose of your trip?"

"... Yes, wonderful, thanks for asking ... Yes, luggage was with me the entire time ... Tel Aviv with day trips ... Stayed with family the entire time."

This trip must be the longest stretch yet where Daniel Mac-Intyre was absent from my thoughts.

"Don't forget your passport, Ella. Check-in line is to my right; safe flight, thank you."

Thank *you*, Security Daniel, for the radical realization: a different Daniel could be redefined as irrelevant.

OMG. Security is pulling this family aside. If profiling necessitates emptying a Colgate toothpaste tube, good luck to the dad's laptop. Smart move keeping the keffiyeh on to mask the detection of any justifiably fearful sweat. Whatever Rubinstein might choose to think, I do bring back new knowledge. An American Goldin walks to check-in with a smile from a security officer; Israeli-born Palestinians better arrive at the airport three days early to make their flight.

Ben-Gurion's oversized bronze head back at the entrance might like to differ. But would he be content with the way his country currently balances his original 'Jewish' and 'Democratic' promise?

This endless queue will give you plenty of time to think through the veneer of 'Israel has the best of everything' new mantra you'd adopted. Yes, it's great that a country exists that would take you in, no matter what. Noisy, pushy, demanding, and crowded were all predictable. But don't deny that the constant eye contact with strangers and the lack of interpersonal space carried some freaky appeal.

But what was the impact of self-confidence in understanding

cultural cues, unlike the smoke and mirrors you felt back in Northern Ireland? Assess how you came across in either place. As a Jewish New Yorker, you are on the Israeli end of the expressive spectrum; at the same time, a terrifying personality for the reticent Irish.

What about the power of food? You are the last to underestimate that. Five weeks in Northern Ireland produced one St. George's Market Ulster fry, and that was only to see if it beats the praised Granny Rosemary's. How many falafels did you hungrily swallow over two weeks? More than you care to remember, but at least three were in the cool Carmel Market and two in Jaffa's Flea Market.

It's juvenile to forget that expectations always play into plans. A summer of homesickness to develop your relationship with Northern Ireland cannot compare to the breather you experienced over here. Family warmth did wonders for your Israeli integration. You never once left Maslow's 'self-actualization' pyramid tier.

So, you are mad at Rubinstein for forbidding the comparison of the conflicts. Good for you! But she has a point. You can't stand more than five minutes in the check-in line without instinctively making a Northern Ireland connection. A PSNI officer would never be as relentless as these Israeli agents with that poor Arab family. Patten was huge in transforming policing. See: you can name the Independent Commission on Policing for Northern Ireland but haven't a clue on the literal meaning of *Mossad* or *Shabak*. And you don't even have the motivation to Google it to find out.

You weren't ordained for a comparative dissertation, so what? There was zero way around Rubinstein on this one: "Doctoral education done incorrectly risks your success in what is an intense job market, Ella."

There are still modest reasons to reassure Mom and Dad this

trip was fiscally responsible. The post-doctoral phase is down the road. Seeds could already be planted in this dissertation's 'Recommendation for Future Research' section. The way Israel treats its Palestinian citizens – decades of work are cut out for you. And that's a lesson you couldn't appreciate without your research in Northern Ireland. Post-conflict for more than two decades and still so divided. Israel hasn't even left the 'live' phase of the conflict.

Yet, if you managed to get over Daniel MacIntyre, there is hope for anything. Not only for a peaceful Middle East, but also for revisiting Israel as Oren's future daughter-in-law.

'Peace takes time' was your first Northern Irish lesson. Martin McGuinness and Gerry Adams were younger than you when secret negotiations were taking place with the British Government as war raged on.

Most importantly, Rubinstein turned her own corner, from demoralizing to active consolation.

"This trip gave you a useful lesson in the best of academia's spirit. Research is arduous, entangled with disruptions, and redemption comes from forgetting disappointments."

Okay, Ella Goldin, you won't be the one letting down either your single case study or your professors with sluggishness.

"Yes, I am next. Hi. *Shalom*. El Al, the direct flight to Boston."

BOOK FIVE

CHAPTER 24

BURNING DESIRES

THE FIRST THING YOUR DISSERTATION committee is going to look at is whether you understood the people you studied. Not touching July 12th in a peacebuilding dissertation on Northern Ireland smells more than amateurish. One of the three will undoubtedly bring up the Marching Season as an impediment to peace and expect local perspectives. And July has come around again to give you a second chance for such first-hand experience.

Rubinstein, as your committee's chair, will actively support heading back to Belfast for that flashpoint.

"It isn't enough to read what their culture means to them. Identity evolves over time. Your observations should build on any primordial answer written in some textbook."

Meanwhile, conflict-smitten Professor Becker seems to have lost scientific interest in the project since the first literature review draft you submitted. Contemporary visuals of barriers might be his only incentive to find your work passable. It was a war crime letting that jock head up Fletcher's Security Program. His vision of the world won't contemplate anything remotely implying collusion between state and paramilitary forces.

Fresh images of Northern Ireland should prove restorative too for Professor Ford. Mostly enjoying reading his own writing, a picture or twelve could kindle the conclusion that he is saving himself a thousand of your dissertation words to edit. He looked more bored than a driver in a traffic jam during your sampling presentation last week. The original mistake of joining these two frenemies in your dissertation committee might end up saving your skin. If Ford realizes you're powerless against Becker's militant criticism, he might get momentarily merciful, awarding your PhD to get you out of his life.

For an extended Belfast weekend, this round-trip flight isn't a bad deal. Nope, I won't be paying extra for luggage, thank you for the suggestion, airline.

'*Success! Your flight is now booked.*'

A seventy-two hours' mission-focused trip can't accommodate an extended heart-to-heart with Ben. You'll get much more done if nobody knows you are coming. Except Derek, the East Belfast bandsman.

"Our boney is a cracker! Best in Belfast. Must be near four storeys high, or more. For real. If you want to know about our culture, come along. Bring your mates. Show the world. The atmosphere is mental!"

Well-positioned in his community organizing role, he went on and on until he moved you into action.

Last July exhausted the Holylands. Best to avoid the city center as well, which would be on the marching route. The Botanic area is residential enough and within walking distance to the parade. An inexpensive Bed & Breakfast instead of Airbnb, why not? The perk of breakfast and some form of on-site staff presence during the July Twelfth shenanigans is a good idea. It's only for three nights, and tourist-loving Belfast will embrace the opportunity to thrill me in minor style. God knows, she's seen me at my worst.

Derek wasn't joking about his sequoia-size bonfire in the lower Newtownards Road. Given this clear Eleventh Night, Derek's towering inferno must be visible from the International Space Station. It must have taken them months of work to collect this number of wooden pallets and tires and then stack them so precisely into four stories. How many flames does one Protestant estate really need?

No way! The Irish Tricolour will go up in flames once the fire reaches the top. On its way up the structure, it won't miss burning Sinn Féin's election posters. Is it freedom of expression or incitement? Offensive to Irish Nationalists, for sure, but whether it is or isn't inflammatory depends on who is watching.

The Nolan Show's recording should still be available when you get back to the B&B. Maybe that will clarify more about this community's tradition, explain what the Northern Ireland Tourism brochures don't. Not under 'Must See,' not under 'History & Heritage,' nothing in 'Explore More.' Why would a country's promotional literature omit an experience of thousands of residents gathering around huge bonfires? Controversial is still an interesting tourist attraction. I could see the Tourist Board's concerns over a crowd all fired up with drink. A single, random twist of wind could ditch you into a mass grave with 100+ mesmerized spectators.

Geographically, it's the working-class neighborhoods that are all festooned in red, white and blue; curbstones, bunting, red hand of Ulster and Union Jacks, and freshly painted Loyalist murals. Those who don't wear the Union Jacks sport Rangers tops. Ladies are dressed head to toe in the correct colors. Whoa. The Star of David necklace on that guy is larger than any decorations you saw in Tel Aviv.

Why are they choosing fire as the medium to compete over? If each housing estate aims to construct the biggest and baddest bonfire, they must be expressing more than a 1690 battle. Anthropologists would cite the bond between existential threat and firepower. Taming fire protected homo erectus all the way to Disney's *Jungle Book*. There could very well be a hidden Protestant lesson for Catholics: be careful trivializing us because we are as dangerous and unpredictable as fire.

Collective self-defense or not, burning with communal passion or not, Protestants must, on some level, be aware of their image problem. Not the issue to raise with Derek, not when he is so busy and surrounded by his buddies, all wearing paramilitary gear. Not your responsibility to point out the potential tragedy of kids circling way too close to the flames.

The only thing to do is thank him for the ideal photoshoot to illustrate why 'paramilitaries' was the chosen term for the Troubles' combatants. Indeed, if the UDA and UVF looked anything like these chaps, Professor Becker might finally accept the RUC's interest in intelligence leaks and occasional help from paramilitaries.

Are you in any position to judge a flame-adoring tradition? There may very well be a place in this world displaying 30-foot-tall Hanukkah candles. One more helpful question that should have but never did come up back in Haifa with Professor Ali. Oh well, it wasn't like he rushed to answer most of what you did ask. But Tamir would know where to search in fervent West Bank settlements. Maybe you just need to take Derek at his word that this is indeed the *Numero Uno* bonfire.

"Cracker, isn't it? This here is the one thing in the whole friggin' year that's ours, that marks our people out. Our pride in our traditions will never die and nobody is going to stop us from expressing our culture. Amn't I right lads?"

Sure, you could think of a climate-oriented explanation – seeking intense heat in a Northern Irish summer. Still relevant in the age of global warming. As an academic, you should strive to raise alternative explanations to any of your assumptions.

"Hey Kirk! My Man! 'Bout ye!"

"Stickin' out!"

"Nice one on the boney. It's class this year. Ella, allow me to introduce my bestie, Kirk. Chief architect of this particular bonfire, and probably top man in Belfast. He oversaw every detail of the construction. No pay, just dedication to his art."

"Och it was wee buns."

"Congratulations on the impressive display."

"Welcome to the best party in town. Yeoooo! There's no better place to be in Belfast tonight. Beer? Vodka? Buckie?"

Why not? Medicated, you may be able to get your negativity under control and enable this friendly and lavishly inked Loyalist to educate you.

"Kirk is a very busy man, so he is. Not just the boney, but practising with the boys most nights for the march tomorrow. He's been in the local band since he could walk. You'll be there?"

"Thank you for the invitation. Where will you be marching?"

"There's parades all over tomorrow. We're in the biggest. Marching down the Lisburn Road, so if you dander that way, it's the best place to catch us. Do you know it?"

Daniel never mentioned he lived just off the parade's route.

"But get there early, and we'll look out for you."

"Rain or shine?"

"Ha-hah, this one's a geg. You know how many years the Glorious Twelfth has been on the go? Only World War Three or a global pandemic would keep us off the Queen's highway. Bucketin' or blizzarding, we'll be there."

"May I toss something into your fire?"

"Fire away as long as it's not petrol, hah-ha!"

No, it's my last year's journal, not that it makes the same difference to you.

"Leather-bound stuff takes a wee bit longer to get going. Something to do with the taigs? You know, fenian shite?"

Kirk is getting too interested.

"Uh ... a gift from someone half-Irish."

"Do rightly!"

If jolly Derek or Kirk knew about the other half.

Do I love her? Could intense feelings truly ever materialize to-ward a city other than the formative one? I've gotten acquainted with many of its streets and some of her people but lack any trace of Irishness or Britishness. So, what could fuel my love of Belfast?

Perhaps the Jewish roots explain an adoration for a place torn by walls, or might it be the shared sentiment between diasporic nations?

Sounds forced at best and immodest at worse, but Mastercard could vouch as a character witness for the perennial July choice. Still, why would a New Yorker be drawn to a city without ur-ban bustle, a segregation junkie, where summertime is the least attractive season—

"Anything else to eat, love? Another drop of tea?"

"Your porridge is excellent, but I'm stuffed, thanks. It's Break-fast that should come first in your B&B sign."

"Aw, that's kind of you. Now, not to rush you, but you asked me about the handiest place from here to view the parade? I sug-gest by the BBC building. From here it's a fifteen-minute walk, so you'll need to get your skates on."

Derek and Kirk must have greeted this partly sunny day with unblemished delight. Oh, people in patriotic gear have set up stalls for the big day out, so this must be the start of the parade route. Wow, so many roads are blocked along the Lisburn Road. The crowds and drunks can't be fun for those living in the area.

Should I check to verify Daniel's version that the MacIntyres aren't around in July? I get why Maeve wouldn't want to be in Belfast for the Twelfth, Daniel's birthday. Oliver's position might dictate otherwise.

Cut. It. Out. Right. Now.

It's not the time to speculate why Daniel was damaged, Maeve far too secretive, Oliver overly unruffled, or whether Margot was neurotic, if good at hiding it. The fact that everyone around is consumed by the weight of the past isn't a recipe for reciprocity.

Ah, these are the stands where fans stock up on regalia. Your jeans and black sweater stand out in the throng. Bowler hats, sashes, cute mini flags, but no, you won't be buying a red hand flag or Union Jack glasses as your mementos; it's not inclusive. Okay, maybe a clacker, if they have one other than red, white and blue. Huh. A centennial hat. Northern Ireland *is* really one hundred.

Shit. Fairer weather doesn't help with the uncertainty. Why shouldn't Derek, Kirk, or anyone else around here not think of you as an outsider 'noseying around'? Why should they have any interest in your inferences? Why should they think anything you propose is credible? Be minimally honest with yourself: if it were the other way around, an Irish person plunging into your culture, would you take her advice seriously? Wouldn't the first thing you'd do be to comb every one of her words for errors, so you won't need to listen? Why on earth would you trust anything she'd diagnose? Not even Daniel, with whom I had an advantage, stayed impressed. Yet, here you are again, insistently infatuated by their issues. Can I really be telling *them* why they can't get their act together?

As an outsider, you shouldn't, you cannot! The best you can do, if best is anything to claim with a straight face, is to suggest very modest ideas. Maybe I should frame this entire project as friendly feedback. If I ever wish to motivate anybody around here, phrases like 'thinking outside the box' are the first out of the laptop's window.

The B&B owner was absolutely right. You should have left earlier. The parade – on its drums and piping flutes – is already well underway; everyone is too absorbed to be talking to an oddball like you now. Interesting: each band has its colors and banner, with their uniforms and drums matching the banners. Hello to the Shankill Protestant Boys, Sandy Row District, Pride of Ardoyne, Sons of Ulster. Glasgow Young Defenders apparently got the ferry over too.

Gotta give it to these little guys – mastering complex, high-flying baton throws from a young age. But it's very hard to be unmindful of the gender imbalance in these bands. Token women marchers at best, none of them with the Masters' Orange Sashes nor as flag bearers.

Dialing down the militaristic style wouldn't hurt either. If marking a 330-year-old battle is so exciting to them, it might thrill Professor Becker, so snap away as many photos as you can. A video too, in case he'd be interested in the repertoire.

Hey, that's the banner Kirk showed you last night. And that's the man himself! Yep, Derek's description of his dinosauric Lambeg Drum was precise. I'd give a lot to look as self-assured as he does walloping that beast.

He is really focused; it shouldn't surprise you that he didn't catch your wave. No, you don't have to read it as one more sign of your dissertation's future impact. Choose optimism and be thankful for Derek and Kirk's hospitality. Sharing with them that their murals, gardens of remembrance, tours, flutes, and military atmosphere reminds you of similar trappings on the Republican side wouldn't amount to gratitude.

Your submission deadline is two very long weeks ahead. That is just an FYI, Northern Ireland, in case you are also keeping track.

CHAPTER 25

SUBMISSIONS

WHATEVER TRANSPIRES, IT'S EIGHT HOURS to the expiration of your extended dissertation deadline. Even the Medford crickets have concluded their night chirping. Without exception, this will be your final skim. Seven is a lucky number, and only the opening sections were amended on the sixth reread, so that's the single part demanding word-for-word inspection.

How ought peace and reconciliation be promoted for divided societies? had been this dissertation's original quest. Early in my research, Henry Fielding's wise observation came true.[6] Indeed, a cook could have gone through all food types before I had exhausted the subject. Thus, my modest attempt to turn theory into actionable advice for peacemakers will focus on Northern Ireland, the historical example of a transformed intractable conflict. Given the region's undeniable status as one of the most heavily studied, I didn't attempt the possibly impossible. My modest endeavor consists of generalizing from Northern Ireland's continuing identity battles a forward-looking guidance for peacebuilding.

Failure to disclose full truth about one's journey, especially the personally heartbreaking parts, was never in Fletcher's dissertation submission guidelines. You're doing fine.

The pages to come call upon my fellow peace practitioners to actively take a closer introspection into the techniques underlying our work. Our attempt to incentivize polarized societies to leap into the post-conflict unknown isn't providing the legroom for our prescribed steps. Instead, we supply peacebuilding devices geared toward negating violence in tandem with the blockading of healing.

Writing up peace agreements with orderly elections and functioning institutions, we engineer the sharing of power between adversaries instead of the reconciliation of enemies. Crafting legal works of art for quarreling societies, we build equality-obsessed countries left with a vacuum on ways to coexist. Paraphrasing the Northern Irish Nobel Laureate John Hume (1937–2020), our task as peacemakers is 'to unite people,' albeit we are entirely consumed in 'uniting territories.'[7] Why, then, are we repeatedly surprised when conflict re-escalates? The constitutions we leave behind crystalize warring identities while the goal of a shared future rots with neglect.

Alliances for mutual benefits are as ancient as civilization itself: Abraham with the Canaanites, Jacob with Laban. As peacebuilders, we ought to be honest and admit that our wholesale efforts have persisted in that spirit. Our preferred power-sharing arrangements ask little of rivals beyond parity of esteem.

A realist perspective finds our proposed social structures adequate, so long as they keep stability, give, or take. Pragmatists would justify power-sharing as the most, if not the only political option for competing groups in societies with antithetical identities. But strategic cooperation is by no means reconciliation, and without it, enemies they remain. Unprepared to deal with inherent tensions, opponents are predisposed to the re-inflammation of old grievances. Persisting to hope that power-sharing would eventually melt into a collective identity isn't realistic. Thus, crusading the world as peace salespersons with insufficient solutions for intractable conflicts is an outcome we – as peace designers – must reckon with.

While the bloody conflict of Northern Ireland was part of the 20th-century chapter, its 21st-century polarization presents a convex lens for the effectiveness of peacebuilding. It has become a site at which to look closely for lessons so that mistakes won't be repeated. Examining the paradigmatic story of Northern Ireland's creative truce, this dissertation challenges its portrait of relatively peaceful streets as the sole criterion of sustainable peace. Instead, it will argue that remaining shackled to the past turns a peaceful future into an uphill battle.

An honest approach recognizes that whatever comes naturally to us as peacebuilders yields a social landscape that is light years away from reconciliation. Once peacemakers depart, a dysfunctional society is left to its own devices, engulfed in profound distrust, and prone to an imminent re-escalation of the conflict.

Face your time guillotine already – another revision at 5:40am won't produce a masterpiece. What you have is good enough to suggest some novelty. Because it's far more critical now, make damn sure Acknowledgements omits nothing and nobody.

A debt of gratitude to my singular dissertation committee: This dissertation would have never been constructed without the support of Professor Martin Becker and Professor John Ford. Professor Joanna Rubinstein served as chair and my imperishable guiding light. Her mentorship – in both assistance and critique – nurtured this project from its start and brought it to the finish line … without my patient family's encouragement …

Good, all interviewees are also listed. The journals with the earlier chapters are all here too. *I am indebted to the patient Ginn Librarians and the Fletcher School's academic staff …*

Resist the urge, resist. Yeah, like you'd ever. *Finally, the political is (eternally?) delivered through the personal. Rousseau taught us to begin with the human heart.[8] Last but not least, I dedicate my dissertation to (formerly) my Daniel. Your increasingly dwindling love defined my insight into this conflict, tormented my stay in its land, but always sharpened my conclusions. You are, even now, my everything.*

Okay. With formal proof that you are pathetic, now highlight these last lines, and – click, yes, all deleted. This is how it should be.

Battery: 11%. My poor, dear, food-stained laptop – you earned your sleep mode fair and square. Sure, I'll connect you to the outlet, and you won't die mid-sending the document to the dissertation committee.

Is that the doorbell? It's too early for it to ring.

Again? Really?

Who in their right mind, unshowered and wearing the same PJs for the third day in a row, opens the door when it is barely dawning? Well, an apartment without a peephole doesn't leave many alternatives to choose from. At least turn on the entrance light before reaching for the doorknob.

That's weird: a package on the doorstep. Hmm. I don't remember ordering anything. Amazon's competition has revolutionized, steroidized, in fact, the US Postal Service. It is addressed to you, not Emily or Climber. A hefty, spiral-bound report of some sort. Let's see:

A National Museum for the Troubles in Belfast, Northern Ireland. Submitted for a Master's Degree by Daniel MacIntyre, School of Architecture + Planning, Massachusetts Institute of Technology.

No way!

We share the same submission deadline!

This isn't a race. Comprehending anything with your shaking hands and vibrating heart requires a slow read of *Biographical Note and Dedication.*

I was born and reared in Belfast, Northern Ireland. These are responsibility-inflicting roots for an architecture student because my discipline allows me to shape, re-envision and re-configure spaces delineated by struggle and fear. Northern Ireland attained her centennial with a nearly equal number of peace walls still caging Us and Them perspectives.

Upon commencing thesis prep, I was asked by my advisor, Professor Andrew Walsh, what I could design to counter my birthplace's stubborn segregation. The proposed outline in this thesis aims to answer that challenge. Whilst architecture cannot change the past, it can enhance interaction.

The Northern Irish peace agreement ended violence, laid down shared politics and mandated the diversity of views. Its post-Troubles architecture and engineering were endowed with reconciling aims. Shared spaces were erected in the form of tunnels, parks, leisure centres, bridges, housing, but divided memories overpowered bricks, mortar and vegetation. Abandoned parks, unwanted living units, siloed communities – our regenerated built environment endures communal stains. Our shared future remains hostage to a divided past.

We continue to disagree on the Troubles, our common heritage. We dispute our conflict's causes and interpretations, articulate our preferred truths, and preserve our culture war. The result is little, if any dialogue around the past. Artistic endeavours resurrecting a shared memory of the Troubles have begun but remain embryonic. Suggestions on how to mutually retell our history enjoy insignificant implementation. Northern Ireland persists in tinkering around the edges of our fused suffering. This stubborn unwillingness to come together around our shared past leaves us powerless to enter a shared future.

Visiting Belfast's peace walls in search of a site for my thesis project suggested the consequences of zoo enclosures. Physical barriers keep warring species alive but bring with them abnormality and welfare problems. Social scientists have criticised Northern Ireland's peace boundaries as accentuating and perpetuating segregation. Well-entrenched social and government infrastructure including churches, the GAA, Orange Order, Department of Education and the Housing Executive supports our physical, social and legal segregation.

In recent years, local voices have recommended that a national museum for our Troubles history could open the required conversation to chart us forward. Though architecture won't dismantle socio-political structures, it can construct a home for our history to live together.

This thesis explicates and illustrates my proposed museum for the recent conflict. Its overarching goal is to invite the negotiation of shared memories over a painful past.

The design's proposed properties don't burden established curatorial practices except for one: staging exhibitions with competing visions. Ceilings, floors, walls and windows will all be constructed to avoid the potential of mirror-imaging the Troubles. Instead, my model impels collective remembrance.

Similarly, the project's dimensions are the result of envisioning the Troubles as a shared experience. For example, the grand entrance's scale was dictated by the space necessary to inscribe the names of all the conflict's victims. By the same logic, local industries and resources dictated the proposed building materials, tools, and techniques.

For every project, location is everything. Potentially, placing a national museum alongside one of our iconic peace walls would incorporate such an artefact into the museum structure. Alternatively, using the open spaces in the Titanic Quarter could reimagine the historical yellow cranes as currently lifting Northern Ireland into its future.

But visualising a national museum in a segregated city demands architecture's edifying function. Therefore, my proposed site for the national Troubles Museum is the Stormont Estate, the seat of Northern Ireland's government. Here the museum would directly engage in dialogue with Northern Ireland's legislators and decision-makers.

Under the terms of our peace accord, stakeholders must concur on everything placed inside this museum. Based on our history and track record on cross-community collaboration, this would leave a museum for the Troubles initially empty. A hollow giant, vivifying our stifled reality.

This striking emblem of their inability to move us forward will greet members of our Executive as they travel to their offices. At the same time, legions of daily visitors to the impressive Estate won't miss the visual irony in that location.

Yet Heraclitus of Ephesus noted that nothing is permanent but change. Antipathy included. Thus, once brimming, the building will truly reflect that overcoming an unshared past readies us for the challenges in a shared future.

Wow! It's an absolute stunner. No one draws like him.

The dedication.

Polarised societies need to reimagine coexistence. Peace needs architecture, and architects need inspiration. This thesis is dedicated to my inspiration, Ella R. Goldin. An indefatigable compass towards progress, Ella was also this project's map, implanting in my own mind the need for this museum.

Go on, do it! Force your eyes upward. It's simply a question of will. Like you can even help it anyway.

Yes, those are *his* hands extending from *his* slender (slenderer?) frame. That's the way he leans against the streetlight pole. Good for Medford to finally repair the streetlight. Same calmness. Though, something is different. A new haircut? Ah, he has glasses now. Perfecting that singularly shy smile ...

Four hours till Rubinstein said she'll be in her office. And you – never again doubt anybody claiming they revised an entire dissertation on submission night. But where will I ever find scholarly giants' shoulders for a whole new introductory chapter,

Mr Isaac Newton? Think, think! George Meade said that we are continuously reconstructing. He could be one. Anthony Giddens' similar version is already inside the literature review chapter. You'll use his theory too. No matter how polarized and immovable reality appears to be, individuals' actions can always move things forward.

Of course, that's possible! It's possible because the data on human agency stares at you. And not only as the sexiest data ever, as one making perfect sense.

Transformation will come from the people. People can surprise.

But would that be enough for the dissertation committee? Rubinstein's heart will grant another extension. With the right vocabulary, Becker's and Ford's are reachable too.

Your email extension request must make them smile.

I know. The one and only Marcel Proust is your literary lifesaver: the real voyage of discovery consists not in seeking new landscapes, but in having new eyes.

EPILOGUE

My Dear Reader,

Ever since my Prologue, I have been undecided over how to (or how Ella would) bring my novel to its apt end. Now, "Hallelujah!" encompasses all I ever wished to say.

ENDNOTES

1   Jeremiah, 1:14.

2   William Shakespeare, *Julius Caesar* (1599) Act III Scene II.

3   Charles Osborne, *W.H. Auden: The Life of a Poet* (New York: Harcourt, 1979) pp. 332.

4   The term appears in Richard H. Thaler and Cuss R. Sunstein, *Nudge: Improving Decisions About Health, Wealth and Happiness* (New Haven: Yale University Press, 2008).

5   William Shakespeare, *King Lear* (1603–6).

6   Henry Fielding, *The History of Tom Jones* Book I, para 4 (London: Andrew Millar, 1749).

7   Hume at SDLP Party Conference 11/6/99.

8   Jean-Jacques Rousseau, *Emile*, or *On Education*, ed. and trans. Allan Bloom (New York: Basic Books, [1762] 1979) pp. 236.

REFERENCES

Page 2 and 158 – Thackeray, William Makepeace. *The Irish Sketchbook of 1842*. Nonsuch Edition, 2005, pp. 318, 282.

Page 8 – *In the Name of the Father*. Universal Pictures, 1993.

Page 8 – *Game of Thrones*. HBO, 2011-19.

Page 10 – Longfellow, Henry Wadsworth. "The Theologian's Tale; Elizabeth." *Complete Poetical Works*. 1893. Online.

Page 10 and 246 – Rand, Ayn. *The Fountainhead*. Bobbs-Merill, 1943.

Page 15 – Heaney, Seamus. "Whatever You Say, Say Nothing." *North*. Faber and Faber, 1975.

Pages 19, 21 and 23 – Frost, Robert. *The Poetry of Robert Frost*. Henry Holt, 1979.

Page 25 – Pink Floyd. *Dark Side of the Moon*. Harvest records, 1973.

Page 26 – Rostand, Edmond. *Cyrano de Bergerac*. French, 1897.

Page 26 – White, Barry. *The Right Night*. A&M, 1987.

Page 52 – Whicher, Stephen E., ed. *Selections from Ralph Waldo Emerson: An Organic Anthology*. Houghton, 1957, pp. 334.

Page 55 – Weber, Max. *The Protestant Ethic and the Spirit of Capitalism*. German, 1905.

Page 59 – Lévi-Strauss, Claude. *Tristes Tropiques*. French, 1955.

Page 67 – Genesis 49:4.

Page 71 – Romans 14:19.

Page 76 – Napoleon Quote in Lathrop, Charles E. *The Literary Spy*. Yale University Press, 2004, pp. 135.

Page 85 – Graves, Robert. *I, Claudius*. Harrison Smith and Robert Haas, 1934.

Page 87 – Smith, Adam. *The Theory of Moral Sentiments*. A. Millar, 1759.

Page 88 – Hardy, Thomas. *Far from the Madding Crowd*. Harpers and Brothers Publishers, 1874, pp. 232.

Page 90 – Hawthorn, Nathaniel. *The Scarlet Letter*. Ticknor, Reed and Fields, 1850.

Page 98 – Daniel 6.

Page 103 – Dickens, Charles. *Letter to William Charles Macready* (Letter 9), 22 March 1842. Online.

Page 134 – *Hair*. United Artists, 1979.

Page 167 – Bentham, Jeremy. *An Introduction to the Principles of Morals and Legislation*. T. Payne, and Son, 1789.

Page 170 – Morrison, Van. *Days Like This*. Windmill Lane Recording, 1995.

Page 217 – *The Godfather*. Paramount Pictures, 1972.

Page 226 – Lynch, Martin et al. *The History of the Troubles (Accordin' to my Da)*, 2016-.

Page 229 – Tolstoy, Leo. *Why Then Do Men Stupefy Themselves?* 1890. *New England Review* Vol. 19(1) 1998 pp. 142.

Page 230 – O'Brien, Flann. *At Swim-Two-Birds*. Longman Green & Co, 1939.

Page 230 – Joyce, James. *Finnegans Wake*. Faber and Faber, 1939.

Page 238 – Churchill, Winston. House of Commons Speech. *"We shape our buildings and afterwards our building shape us,"* Hansard, HC Deb 28 October 1943 Vol. 393 cc403-73.

Page 243 – *Love Actually*. Universal Pictures, 2003.

Pages 247 and 255 – Oz, Amos. *Dear Zealots: Letters from a Divided Land*. Mariner Books, 2018.

Page 252 – *Fiddler on the Roof*. United Artists, 1971.

Page 255 – Tolstoy, Leo. *Anna Karenina*. Russian, 1878.

Page 264 – Frankl, Viktor. *Man's Search for Meaning*. German, 1946.

Page 265 – *MasterChef*. Banijay, 1990-.

Page 280 – Maslow, Abraham, H. "A Theory of Human Motivation." *Psychological Review,* Vol. 50(4) 1943, pp. 370–396.

Page 288 – *The Jungle Book*. Disney, 1967.

Page 300 – Newton, Isaac. *Letter to Robert Hooke*, 1675. Online.

Page 300 – Meade, George. *Mind, Self, and Society from the Standpoint of a Social Behaviorist*, ed. Charles W. Morris, The University of Chicago Press, [1934] 1967, pp. 386.

Page 300 – Giddens, Anthony. *The Constitution of Society*. University of California Press, 1984.

Page 300 – Proust, Marcel. *In Search of Lost Time* Vol. 5 Chapter 2. French, 1923.

ACKNOWLEDGMENTS

Behind this novel was my family for whom gratitude is beyond expressible. My singular in countless ways husband, Avi Loeb; our daughters, *our* works of art, Klil Liviatan Loeb, and Lotem Liviatan Loeb; my mother, Yael Liviatan, who redefines the possible daily; my beloved baby brother and senior counselor, Omri Liviatan; and my sister-in-law and in-heart, Osnat Tsipper.

An incomputable number of people guided my fascination with and understanding of the Emerald Isle, and I am indebted to each of them. Among them were several champions. This novel would never have happened without my dear friend and colleague Dr. Robert (Bob) Mauro. It wouldn't have been completed without the matchless Eva Grosman. Lord John Alderdice, Sir Jeffrey Donaldson, Conor Houston, and Emma Little Pengelly have all inspired me in more ways than I could describe. Joe McHugh took time to read an awfully rough (!) version of the manuscript. Jonathan Kearney's generosity and patience endured a blitz of questions. All errors and inaccuracies are my own.

The writing process benefited from a family of friends: Caroline Friedman Levy, Nina Frusztajer, Hanni Lifshitz, Tsafi Nathans, Rachael Perkins Arenstein, Noya Rimalt, and Tamah Rosker – each with her wisdom helped me in this rollercoaster.

I won the editing lottery with the most graceful, thorough, and exceptionally dedicated Siobhan Dignan. Thank you, Jason Anscomb for the perfect cover, Susie Ryder for your masterful editorial eye, and Victoria Nelson for invaluable Northern Irish polishing. Massive thanks to the kindest Daniel Andrews and Ike Williams for your help in the publishing process.

Finally, Ido (my Dorinin), it's probably impossible to reciprocate your contributions to anything I do. But I am the luckiest you were the next Liviatan to sprout, so I could keep trying.

Ingram Content Group UK Ltd.
Milton Keynes UK
UKHW040636190323
418778UK00002B/17